1K

B

*By the same author*

THE HOUSE
THE MADRIGAL
THE BATH DETECTIVE

# THE KILLING OF SALLY KEEMER

A Bath Detective Mystery

## CHRISTOPHER LEE

VICTOR GOLLANCZ

LONDON

First published in Great Britain 1997
by Victor Gollancz
An imprint of the Cassell Group
Wellington House, 125 Strand, London WC2R 0BB

© Christopher Lee 1997

The right of Christopher Lee to be identified as author of
this work has been asserted by him in accordance with
the Copyright, Designs and Patents Act, 1988.

A catalogue record for this book is
available from the British Library

ISBN 0 575 06346 7

Typeset by CentraCet, Saffron Walden, Essex
Printed in Great Britain by St Edmundsbury Press Ltd
Bury St Edmunds, Suffolk

97 98 99    5 4 3 2 1

# SATURDAY

## One

The matron with the pink lipstick was sure they were film stars.
They certainly looked like film stars. This was rather exciting.
She'd never actually seen any. Not in the flesh. But these two
had to be. Just look at them. Had to be. Yes. Definitely film stars.
They stood, almost entwined yet without touching. Staring up
at the black departure board. Hair-lines, cheekbones, fleshless
jaws and gleaming, even teeth all in ideal and parallel angle. The
dream of some revolutionary artist. In another land and another
age, they'd have worn overalls and would have clasped huge
spanners upon which the sun's rays shone. But neither had ever
donned bib and brace. These were children of Armani, not Gum.
Capitalism not Collectivism. He tall, dark. Cream, soft, closely
cut trousers. Nice bottom. Very nice bottom, she thought. Had
to be foreign. Not an English bottom. Too much gold. The ring
obvious. The necklet not nearly masculine enough. Perhaps he
wasn't. One really never knew nowadays. She thought the small
handbag most odd. But he had the style to get away with both.
The pony-tail was short. Not at all effeminate. Yes. Definitely
foreign. After all, look at the way he was carrying just one rather
ordinary plastic bag when the poor girl had so many. Now she
was interesting. The matron knew her, of course. Sure she'd seen
her before. Seen her in something. Maybe theatre? No. Definitely screen. A model? Very likely. But somewhere.

Very long legs. Skinny, really. But she'd never have swollen ankles after a day's spending. Very brown legs. Everything else went with them. The silkiest, skimpiest dark blue shift. The smoothest expensively cut Titian hair. Yes, definitely well known. How annoying. Couldn't quite place them. But she was sure she'd seen them in the social pages she read and reread every day and, of course, in the magazines.

The matron shifted on the steel seat perforated for cleanliness, not stout comfort. Thought some more about them. They were the only really interesting couple she'd spotted during all the time she'd been sitting there. And that was an hour or more. Waiting. She quite liked waiting. She was of an age when it took longer to catch her breath. She was exhausted from her shopping day in London, but not tired of putting her signature to charge card slips. Her late husband had left more than she could ever spend, but Melissa Hanbury-Collings was doing her best.

According to the very cheerful voice of the girl announcer, the late arrival of the incoming train meant a further delay. How could she? How dare she? One would have thought that cheerfulness was most inappropriate in the circumstances. Some of them were foreign, of course. Often blacks. But this one didn't sound it. Nevertheless, it really was too bad. Mind you, it didn't really matter. Matrons were rarely idle waiters. As a breed they watched while they waited. Certainly this one did. Paddington Station did not have that same excitement as Heathrow, but she enjoyed people-gazing. Guessing where they'd come from. Where they might be going. Who they were. What they did. What they were worth. Sitting on quite a lot, indeed all of the mesh metal seat, Mrs Hanbury-Collings was quite content to watch. She was now into her second hot cheese and spinach croissant. She stopped chewing and dabbed at her mouth with a greasy, lipsticked tissue. She looked. Nonchalantly – or so she thought. The matron gawped instinctively. Now she gawped with no inhibition. She followed their search of the broad black departure board but didn't miss the

6

casual way he brushed his fingers across the front of the silk dress, nor the mischief in the girl's movement as she stretched to whisper and then kiss his ear.

And then the stage shifted. Now this was interesting. The half-chewed croissant was suspended between paper bag and thickly sticked lips. Now *them* she hadn't seen before. Must have come from the taxi rank. He was sturdy. Thick, black, tufty hair. Strong black leather shoes. Big toecaps. Dubbing dull, not buffed for a barrack room inspection as her late and darling husband's had always been. And the kilt. Very smart. Intriguing. Blues and greens with all the yellow symmetry of an intelligence test. The woman was disappointing. Maybe predictable. Very ordinary. Cuddly. The fresh primrose summer frock loose and cottony. One day, the fuller figure madam. But not this day. Not yet. The hair red and curly. Legs full of calf, but not thick of ankle. Two suitcases. Brown. Square cornered. Leather. Old. Not affected. Perhaps parents who once travelled in great liners.

All these matters Mrs Hanbury-Collings observed with some certainty as she took the last mouthful of spinach and cheese, dabbed once more at her smudged lips, brushed pastry flakes from her blue pleated skirt and wondered what to do with the tissue. She looked about her. Waste bins on mainline stations were things of a past when terrorists were unlikely to drop timed bombs among the debris. She screwed the tissue between her podgy fingers and thought of dropping it to the glistening cream concourse. The approaching electric sweeper cart put her off. Instead she popped it into one of her five Harrods carriers.

The cleaner was approaching. So was another figure. The man who walked with such perfect timing in front of the cart was odd. Or so she thought. Here it was in strawberries and cream summer, and there he was in tweeds. Dark green. Not prickly, but certainly tweedy, with waistcoat and brown shoes. No. Boots. Mrs Hanbury-Collings called that very odd. He was tall, slim. Gingery curly hair. Metal-rimmed spectacles and a slight stoop. Or was it a stoop? No. It wasn't. This one was a leaner. Leaned into a nonexistent wind. Probably a poet. Certainly he dressed like a poet, although Mrs Hanbury-Collings had only met one poet. That had been at the Bath Literature Festival and the poet had been very drunk. But as he was a poet, and Irish, she rather expected him to be. Now this one? Well, he'd gone. Straight under the departure board and on to Platform four where an unannounced train waited. She wondered if the train might be her train. Then it would be the poet's. Poets did go to Bath, so perhaps she was right. But how did he know that train would go there? Some people were good at trains. They knew which platforms before the official announcement. They knew where each carriage would stop at any station in the country. They knew where to stand. Mrs Hanbury-Collings never understood how they could possibly know. And these people annoyed Mrs Hanbury-Collings. She disliked people who knew such things. Smug, she thought. No. She had decided. He could not be a poet. Poets were vague. That was the whole point of being a poet. A poet would never work out station platforms. In the distance, she saw he was boarding the first carriage. That would be first class. Couldn't be a poet.

The film stars had drifted to the other end of the waiting area. He was now talking into a mobile telephone and she was searching the innards of an array of carrier bags nearly as great as those collected by the Bath matron herself. The girl was bending from the waist and hardly a male head was left unturned. Mac-kilt tried not to look. But he did, and the tightly-curled redhead at his side lowered her eyebrows, tugged at his arm and pointed to the departure board. Vertical rows of westward destinations flipped over until times and platforms matched. And there it was. 18.30. Platform four. Bristol Temple Meads. First stop Reading, then Didcot Parkway, then Swindon, then Chippenham, then Bath Spa. The Bath Spa matron, with a single sweep that would have won applause at any congress of nannies, gathered her bags and parcels and headed

8

for her much delayed train. It was already twenty minutes to eight.


# Two


At seven-forty, the small white Renault pulled into the furthest parking bay. For a moment, the driver sat in the silenced car, eyes closed as if remembering a dream. A stout Bavarian blipped the alarmed Mercedes in the next bay and took his time looking at the girl. Very pretty. He liked the profile. He liked noses that turned up and short black hair. He hoped she was staying at the hotel. He wanted to see the rest. The slam of his door and the Mercedes ignition brought the girl back to the evening sunshine. She climbed out without trying to pull down the hem of the little black dress. The Mercedes was reluctantly driven away.

She liked the garden. Seen it many times. Well tended. Something reassuring about it. Proper hoes for the borders. Proper edging tools. Pruned when it should be pruned. Trees thoughtfully planted for coming decades. Very English. Very colonial. The first of the few scented roses were just out. She bent to smell. Didn't know the name. Her father would have known. It was the sort of thing archdeacons always knew. She walked on in the evening sunlight. A swinging walk from high, loose hips. Free and easy. Unhindered by the slim, alligator skin briefcase in her right hand. A porter held the door for her and she smiled her thanks and made his evening. The other girl was waiting in the lobby. She was as blonde as the other was dark. Taller. Healthy. Probably hunted in the winter. Flat-bottomed in her tight, fawn-coloured straight dress. They didn't greet each other. Knew each other though. The dark one handed the younger girl her briefcase and asked at the desk for Mr Firmani and was told to go right up. Room 212. The windowless corridor was evening warm from the soft wall lights and thick dark blue carpet. She tapped with her fingertips on the cream panelled door and waited no more than fifteen seconds.

He was almost paunchy, well barbered, in his late fifties and his white bath-robe complete with hotel monogram.

'Mr Firmani? Hi, I'm Jane. This is Nikki.'

His teeth were very white. His eyes flicked over her slim figure from ankle to urchin-cut hair. He got as far as the blonde's bust. He liked what he saw. His teeth, then his eyes, said so.

'Please come in. Come in. Thank you, yes. Please come in.'

'Thank you.'

Jane let him close the door for her and tried not to twitch against the heavy aftershave. The blonde put down the briefcase where she wouldn't forget it. He moved quickly, perhaps too quickly, to where an ice bucket stood by the bedside.

'I ordered champagne. Yes?'

'That would be nice.'

'You bet. Dom Perignon. Only the best.'

Krug? Never mind. The accent. New York? Jane didn't really know. Nikki hadn't thought about it. Firmani was hardly a spurs and Stetson name. The bathrobe was open to the belly. Grey, tight, curly chest hairs. Not subtle, but then the way he was struggling with the champagne suggested he wasn't. Maybe nervous. They both liked that.

He poured with no style, but a lot of enthusiasm. They each got half a glass and he had to top them up. That was good. It made them laugh. Made it easier. He raised his glass and spilt some.

'Here's to a great conference and, especially, a great evening. Cheers.'

'And you, Mr Firmani. And to you. Welcome back to Bath.'

The second glass came quickly. He looked at his watch.

'I guess we can eat downstairs. That okay by you, eh . . .'

'Jane.'

'Jane. That right?'

'It is.'

'Okay. Okay. I like that. Jane. Hey, you Jane . . .'

Wait for it, she thought.

'You Jane, me Tarzan.'

She'd heard it done with better timing. But she did her best to produce a first-time smile.

'Okay, Tarzan. Whatever you say. Now, Nikki will be looking after you tonight. I'll be back with you in the morning.'

Mr Firmani's little boy look wasn't that good.

'You mean you can't *both* stay?'

''Fraid not. 'Fraid not. Busy busy. You know how it is. But I can promise you with Nikki here, you'll not notice I've gone.'

Mr Firmani looked at the blonde. She really did have a nice smile. Nice eyes. Nice figure.

''Course, I was only joking.'

'Now you're telling me I'm not wanted.'

More laughing. More champagne.

'Now, first thing in the morning, Nikki will see you for a breakfast meeting. I'll try to join you, but I'm hoping to fix something special for you. But the rest, Nikki will explain. Okay?'

She was backing away as she spoke. Heading for the door. She gave the blonde a smile and soft wink. Before Mr Firmani realized what had happened, she'd gone. He turned from the closed door and raised his glass to the other girl.

'Nikki, right? That short for something?'

'Absolutely. Nicola. But everyone calls me, well, Nikki.'

'Right. Nikki. Right. Here, you're falling behind.'

More champagne.

'I got them to fix a table for eight–fifteen. You like that?'

'Absolutely. Really nice. Really.'

He looked at her face, but not into the eyes. Then at the quilted bed.

'I guess we could . . .'

11

His voice tailed away. He seemed nervous. They often were. She smiled. Tried to help him. Them both. She looked at the bedside clock. It was coming up to eight.

'Absolutely. That would be nice as well. Why don't we say eight-fifteen for eight-thirty?'

They both laughed again and then she reached behind and unzipped the little fawn dress and let it fall to her feet. He stopped laughing. He stared. Put down his glass. This was better than anything they'd told him.

## Three

James Boswell Hodge Leonard was deep into his book. He didn't expect to have the carriage to himself. He was sitting with his back to the engine not so that he could observe who came aboard, but because he preferred to travel that way. He found it easier to watch the countryside passing than coming. Now he looked up and kept looking. She was rounded and he was in a kilt. Leonard wondered if they were going to a party or had been. She looked a little flushed. They'd been. He pushed two leather cases into the luggage compartment and swung two overnight bags on to the overhead rack. Two? Leonard instinctively looked to her left hand. Ah. An engagement ring. But no wedding band. So they lived separately. 'Couples' tended to share one case. Or did they? He was no longer sure about these matters. He lost interest and settled back to Belloc. He didn't get very far. The matron wasn't noisy but she puffed and her carriers crackled. She couldn't decide whether to squeeze into the double seat and leave her bags on the square table, or put her bags on the other seats. After all, it was a Saturday evening, this was first class, it wasn't likely to be crowded. The Scot offered to help put her carriers on the shelf. She said that was very kind, but there were what she called 'breakables' in them. But she thanked him again and watched from the corner of her eye the neat way in which he slipped back into his seat across the aisle without disturbing the dignity of his kilt. She busied herself arranging her bags. There should be no doubt in everyone's mind that she'd shopped at Harrods. She caught sight of the poet. No. She'd decided he wasn't a poet, hadn't she. What then? Professor or whatever they called them? She couldn't see what he was reading. But it was a book not a magazine. Yes, probably university. Bath or Bristol.

Leonard, three seats down-train from all this, flicked back a page but never caught up with his place in the cruise of the Nona. The figure in the doorway had all the style of a woman who could balance on any catwalk, even when clutching handfuls of designer parcels. The man close behind was tall and stooped instinctively as they entered the compartment. They piled her bags on to the first table, took no notice of anyone else in the carriage and returned to the platform as quickly as they'd arrived. The man was considerably taller than the girl. She stretched high to kiss him goodbye. So did the hem of the pretty silk dress. The kilted Scot, perhaps an expert in skirt lengths, gulped. His fiancée said something about the train times to divert his attention. Didn't succeed. Mrs Hanbury-Collings, who was facing the wrong way, missed all this. But she heard their return from the platform. They were very noisy indeed. She supposed show business people were. Not that nice Alec Guinness, of course. But then her pigtail fancy was hardly a theatrical knight. His voice not at all thespian boom.

'Okay then, darlin'. Call me when you get home. Just so's I know. Okay?'

How dreadfully disappointing, thought the Bath matron. How dreadfully disappointing. How London. Slightly American. No, London. Mrs Hanbury-Collings, with more puffing, squeezed out of her seat and plonked into the one opposite. That was better. A proper view of what was going on. The girl was giggling. Far too young for her age, thought Mrs Hanbury-Collings. Giggling was for girls half her age.

13

'Don't worry. Now off you go. You'll be late.'

That was better. Not at all his London.

'They can wait.'

He put a bronzed arm about her waist, pulled her close. Up went the skirt. Up went Mrs Hanbury-Collings' eyebrows. Up went Belloc in front of Leonard's face. Up went the temperature in the third seat along the aisle. The girl giggled again. Made a mock effort to escape.

'Rick. Stop it. Not here.'

Rick laughed. He glanced casually along the carriage. Boring old lot. Give them a thrill. He put his hand on the girl's bottom. This time she was serious. She started to pull away. There was a commotion behind them. Leonard looked up. Four youths. Roughly dressed. Dirty. Not just casual. T-shirts. Baggy trousers. Beer cans. Barging. The man turned quickly. He was very big. The first youth was stony-faced.

'Sorry, mate. Looking for a seat.'

The next one was cocky. He looked about the soft furnishings.

'Not really the sort of thing we had in mind. Know what I mean?'

The man was smart enough not to say anything. Instead he was standing between the boys and the girl. They squeezed past. One of the carrier bags was knocked to the carriage floor. The third youth, the skinniest and youngest by the look of him, quickly ducked and handed it to the girl.

'Sorry about that.'

The fourth boy was big. Lumpy. Wet lipped.

'Bleedin' clumsy he is. Ain't you, Pepper?'

He shoved Pepper in the small of his back, and he and the girl nearly collided. She sat down with a bump. Her boyfriend had had enough.

'Right. On your way. Had your fun. Okay?'

But they were half-way down the compartment, throwing comments at each other.

'Cor. You clock it?'

'Gotta be a star. Yeah?'

'Gotta be.'

'This first class?'

'P'raps we should sit here. It's for everyone, isn't it?'

'Right.'

Then with a statutory punching of the carriage bulkhead and the tossing of a half-full beer can over the end seat, they were gone. Heading through the next first class carriage, then the buffet car, and beyond. Their passing had spoiled the boy-friend's playtime.

'Okay?'

She nodded and the hair bobbed.

'Sure. Don't worry. Just being silly.'

He looked down the aisle. There was no sign of the youths.

'They won't come back. Made their point.'

'Sure.'

She rubbed her hand over his chest. Smiled a too little girl smile up at his face. And he pecked her on the nose.

'Okay, luv. You got everything?'

'Sure. Now go on. I'll call the minute I get in.'

'Promise?'

'Promise.'

He bent down and kissed her quickly on the lips. Turned. And was gone. The girl looked out of the window and waved. More stretching. More narrowing of the fiancée's eyes. And then there was calm. Mrs Hanbury-Collings took out a copy of *The Lady*. The Scottish couple scanned a Great Western timetable. Leonard returned to Belloc. As the train pulled out of the platform, he glanced up at the sound of a double metallic click to see the girl taking something from an expensive-looking slim briefcase. Alligator skin, he thought. Wrong, but enviable. A greetings card? Looked like it from where he was. Then the gold fountain pen. He watched for a while. This was no happy birthday card. A small life-story. She wrote, paused, thought, wrote again. He watched her hand. Expensive watch. Small writing, he thought. Didn't sweep across the paper.

15

Didn't look the personality for tiny writing. Finishing school script. Straight up and down. Straight along the bottom. Nice cheekbones. A thinking face, intelligent as well as beautiful. He wondered why he should think the two were unlikely together. And that was that, or should have been. The senior conductor passed among them, franked their tickets, guessed which would travel first if there weren't weekend concessions and then moved on, leaving the carriage in good order.

It takes about thirty minutes for the Bath train to get from Paddington to Reading. So it must have been about half-way when the girl started scrabbling among her parcels and bags. The next moment she was on her knees, peering beneath the seat and the table. Whatever she was looking for wasn't there. She stood. Stared at the scrum of bags and packages and then, as if she'd discovered a huge and hairy spider in her knickers drawer, let out a shriek.

'My bag! My bag! It's gone. It's gone. Where is it?'

Leonard ducked even further behind Belloc. The Bath matron, startled from an article about linen napkin makers, stared from the window and into the middle distance of, she supposed, Berkshire. The kilted laddie smiled inanely. The fiancée instinctively felt for her purse.

The girl looked about her. A wild look. Panic even. Leonard thought that odd. And read on.

'It's gone. Someone call the guard. The communication cord. That's it. We must pull it. Call the police.'

Leonard turned another page. Mrs Hanbury-Collings looked up and smiled. The highlander could no longer contain himself.

'Is there something wrong?'

Leonard thought it the most crass remark he'd heard that week. But then inwardly praised the lad. After all, he was the only one who'd reacted. But then he was not English.

'My bag. It's been stolen. It's gone. It's not here.'

The Scot was out of his seat, leaping the burn of social decorum as he rushed to the rescue of the most beautiful girl he had ever seen.

16

'You're sure, are you?'

The girl's beautiful face twisted in contempt.

'You fool! Of course I'm sure. It was here. Now it's gone.'

She was back among her parcels. Ignoring him. Knowing he wouldn't go away.

'Have you looked down the side of the seat?'

What else would she have been doing? But she stepped aside as he, with an excise man's thoroughness, rummaged the creases and nooks beneath the table. Nothing.

'What does it look like?'

Leonard, still behind Belloc, thought this equally idiotic. It was hardly likely there would be more than one hidden beneath the seat.

'White plastic. Like all bags. Says Europa on it.'

Bath matron nodded to herself. It would be.

'You sure you had it?'

She was about to damn his stupidity again, but didn't. The openness of his face. The real concern in the deep brown eyes. Deep breath.

'Perfectly.'

He wanted to suggest that he looked through her parcels and shopping bags. But he didn't. What might she have bought? The most intimate things. His fiancée came to his rescue.

'Seemingly, Dougie, the lady would know whether she had her bag or no.'

The girl tried a smile at this dumpy little creature. What a ghastly dress. And gloves. My God. Dougie nodded with the expression of a man whose heritage was one of inevitability.

'Can you no remember where you had it?'

The girl shut her eyes. Dougie imagined her face on a pillow. His pillow. He was in love. When she spoke, it was as if in a trance.

'At the ticket office. Gave the guy my Amex. Then . . .'

Leonard, still hidden, thought that odd. The girl was trying to get her thoughts to tumble into a sequence.

'Then, then, then . . . put the Amex and the ticket in my bag . . .'

'The one you've lost?'

'Of course not. My handbag, of course.'

'And?'

'Shush.'

She was thinking it through. Mrs Hanbury-Collings thought her quite rude. Clearly not a person of any substance after all.

'Then I think I had it then . . .'

'So you might not have?'

She opened her eyes. Stared at him as if contemplating whether or not she might have.

'No. No. Because I had it later.'

Mrs Hanbury-Collings had her eyes closed. Not bored. Not hiding. She was trying to remember the picture of the couple on the station. There was a handbag. Where? Where? Where? Of course. She twisted in her seat. It was quite an effort for her. And the seat.

'May I interfere, my dear?'

No one said anything. Simply stared. The Bath matron decided to stand for what she had to say. A committee member proposing a vote of thanks from the body of the village hall. Bizarre, thought Leonard who had already decided in his own mind exactly what had happened but was reluctant to become involved. The last weekend of his leave. Precious enough. Every moment thinking, willing it to be always like this. The Bath matron had cleared her throat. She stood. One hand on the headrest. My God, thought Leonard, the old bat's going to sing. It's a happening. An event. *Candid Camera*. But it was none of those things. Mrs Hanbury-Collings had a point and she was determined to make it.

'Did you not, my dear, give your bag to your, ahm, young man?'

The girl looked straight through the other woman. Not rude. Just remembering.

'Right. You're right. How did you know that?'

18

'I noticed you on the platform and, well, I must say, well, I must say, I thought it strange for you to be carrying so much when he had but the one. But, but then I thought, well, the young nowadays.'

'I did. I did.'

'Then he's got it. Mystery solved.'

The Scottish lad was beaming.

'Don't be silly.'

Dougie blushed.

'I was only . . .'

'He carried it. We made a joke of it. Then while he was phoning he gave it back to me and, and . . . and I don't remember. Yes I do. I was looking to make sure nothing had spilled.'

Dougie looked. They all looked. Spilled?

'Feta cheese salad and baklava. I bought some feta cheese salad and baklava. I love it. My supper, don't you see? Someone's stolen my supper. It's gone. Oh my God. This is crazy. Where?'

'Seemingly,' said Dougie's intended, 'it might be a good idea to call the guard.'

The woman nodded. Slowly at first. Then furiously.

'Right. Right. There's a thief on board. But where?'

Mrs Hanbury-Collings had not sat down. For the first time, she had seen the woman in close up. The eyes. She knew those eyes. The hair was different. But she knew her from somewhere. Something nagging. How annoying. She never forgot a face. *Hello* magazine? A weekend supplement? Something she'd read at the hairdresser? It would come. It would come. But now to the immediate problem. As secretary for many small but worthy causes in Bath, she was good at immediate problems. Everyone was watching. Waiting. The throat was once again cleared.

'I believe the way to do that is to go to the buffet bar. They will make an announcement.'

With that she turned to Leonard. He was wiping his steel-rimmed spectacles on a green silk handkerchief. They were calling the guard to hunt down a lost supper. And from the buffet bar. Bizarre. He looked up. She was there all right. Fuzzy. But she was there. He slipped the thin arms over his ears. Smiled a little and nodded.

Dougie was sent off to the buffet car. A minute later the voice that had earlier announced that a 'selection of teas, coffee, hot chocolate, wines, beers, spirits, fresh sandwiches and hot and cold snacks were now all available', and that there was 'no queuing at this time', now asked 'the senior conductor to come to the buffet bar'. In five minutes, Dougie returned with the short-sleeved official who had marked their tickets and cards at the start of the journey.

The man took it in his stride. He'd been there before. But it needed Leonard to prompt him into action.

'Excuse me, but just a thought.'

They all looked at him. Mrs Hanbury-Collings very suspiciously. Poet? Academic? Thief?

'Just before the train left, there were some youths, four of them. T-shirts. One of them with Hard Rock Café printed over the chest. Another with a blue baseball cap with NY in white. The smallest one was wearing a black rubber Casio watch but on the right, not the left wrist. He's the one who picked up your bag from the floor. Maybe while he was doing that, another of them took your food.'

Mrs Hanbury-Collings looked amazed. The girl peered at him as if she'd not heard it all. Dougie and the future Mrs Dougie looked at each other. The senior conductor looked impressed.

'That's very observant of you, sir.'

Leonard shrugged. Smiled, a little, shrugged.

'Just a thought.'

He returned to his book. The senior conductor asked for a list of objects in this missing bag. Cheese and a balaclava? No, not balaclava, baklava. A sort of gooey pastry. That was it? Yes, of course. The girl seemed adamant. The senior conductor said he would look into it and went off in the direction of the standard class carriages. The train was slowing. They were entering Reading. Leonard carried on with Belloc, considering what would follow as predictable. About ten minutes after leaving Reading, the conductor returned with a crumpled Europa bag.

'In one of the toilets. Doing it all the time, they are. Nick it. Strip it. Hop it. They probably got off at Reading. This gentleman was probably right.'

Leonard looked up. Briefly. Smiled. Briefly. He didn't want to get involved. The bag was empty. No cheese. No pastry. Leonard wanted to ask one question, but would never do so. The girl was agitated. She took the empty bag. Didn't look in. Felt it. Kept feeling it as if she expected there to be something, any something left.

'There was nothing else in it?'

The senior conductor, a short, sturdy Londoner with steely cropped hair looked puzzled. They all looked at the girl and then at him.

She shook her head. The expensively-cut hair swayed as the commercial said it should. Then stopped. One hand went to her mouth.

'Oh my God, yes. Oh yes.'

'Wallet or something, miss?'

She looked in her other bags.

'No. Well it wasn't so important. Just a small present for someone. My son. Being silly, that's all.'

But Leonard observed that she wasn't being silly. She was being very worried. Something in the eyes. The hands that kept pressing the once smart, now shabby, plastic bag. The senior conductor wasn't sure what to do next. After all, as he told his mate on the next run up to Paddington, 'Bit of cheese and a funny cake. Not exactly worth bombing Cairo for, is it now?'

But the girl wasn't finished.

'Where did you say you found this?'

21

'In the toilet, you know.'

'Will you show me?'

He looked surprised. But under the new rules, the passenger was now a customer. He'd show her the crown jewels if they had them in the guard's van.

'Sure. You like to follow me?'

She paused by Leonard as the train swung over points. For a brief moment a scent he had never before known wafted over him. Then gone. No one said anything while they were away, or if they did, Leonard didn't hear them. He was already feeling dozy. Missing a word, then a line. He stirred when they returned. That scent. What was it? As fresh as a summer sea wall. The girl was no less worried. But when the others asked if she was 'all right' she seemed to relax. Or was it resignation? Leonard wasn't sure. Still on leave.

The rest of the journey turned into a small party. The conductor played the sheriff. Called all sorts of people. Came back to say that the police had been informed. Dougie went off to the buffet and returned with what seemed to be the whole stock of freshly cut sandwiches and hot and cold snacks. And then from one of their bags he removed a shiny bottle. Dougie was none other than Dougie Gordon, son of the distiller of the finest single malt on the mainland. At this, Leonard's attention returned. But not for long. He managed to stay apart from the gathering. Closed his eyes and dozed. When the train jerked, so did his consciousness. In and out of consciousness. Ticking the muzzy conversations out of ten like some dreamy schoolmaster. A wedding in London. First visit to Bath. The fiancée contradicting him. Well yes, first visit together. Did he really want to marry a nag – even a Scottish one? Widowed for ten years last February. Of course we were in Rhodesia for most of our lives. Grand days those, didn't they know. Wouldn't have tolerated this sort of affair. Taken a whip to them or better still ... In packaging, didn't they know. Bet they didn't. Dreadful snob. But maybe lonely. Just a shopping trip. Long week next week. Few odds and ends. Not odds and ends carrier bags.

Boyfriend? No mention. No one ill-mannered enough to ask. Live in Bath but going through to Bristol. Son at boarding school. Divorced? But by the time the train had left Swindon, Leonard was fast asleep.

He woke, disturbed by the reaching for cases and bags, by the huffing of the Bath matron as the train ran along the gentle curve to reveal the panorama of Bath with its summer sandstone buildings, spires and hills. He was the last off, and as he unchained his bicycle from the platform rack, he glanced up to see the unblemished profile of the woman in the wonderfully thin blue dress. All alone in the first class compartment. She was really rather beautiful. Really nice. Once the panic had died down, good fun. As he wheeled his bicycle to the railing gate, the train pulled away and she gave a half-smile which later he wished he'd returned. As he scooted his bike down the slope to the archway and on to the main road, he thought about that. But not for long.

# SUNDAY

## *Four*

The matron had Sunday lunch with her son and grandson. Sunday was family Sunday. Ashley stayed. Was supposed to stay. He always did. But this time he didn't. Ever since the divorce, he'd brought Richard to Sunday lunch. He'd been just a toddler in those days. She hadn't seen him when he was born. Ashley was still looking after his father's interests in Rhodesia. Mrs Hanbury-Collings couldn't bring herself to speak of Zimbabwe. She'd been born in Rhodesia and that was that, although she, of course, regarded herself as English. That fickle wife of his had behaved disgracefully. Not surprising when one considered her background. If that's what it was called. Gone to South America with some, well, some dago. Good riddance. And well done Ashley. Kept Richard. Only right. Ashley had been a good father. Sometimes a little distant, but that was good for boys. Mrs Hanbury-Collings had been both mother and grandmother. Richard had warmed to her. Never mentioned his mother. Why should he? Didn't remember her. Had a nurse. His mother was never spoken of. Didn't exist in the family. Now Richard was eleven and looked forward to Sunday, especially in term time. He didn't like boarding. Never quite got used to it in the two years he'd been there. Most of all, he liked her cooking. It was the only meal she did cook.

When Hanbury-Collings died, she'd stayed on in the house,

but it eventually became too much. Finding people to clean and garden became harder. The ones who did come didn't stay. Some were gossips. She hated gossip. She heard about other ladies for whom the cleaners did. Of course she was always interested. But then it dawned if she were hearing about them, then they were hearing about her. So any sign of gossip, out they went. Gardeners, she decided, were lazy and ignorant. Didn't know how to prune. Always seemed to need something new for the lawnmower. Not like the old days in Rhodesia. That was proper living. No problems about servants. Plenty of them. Slightest sign of trouble, out. Yes indeed. Those were the days. Fought for what you had, fought to keep it. Then the whole blasted thing was thrown away. She missed her servants. Times had changed. Now so must she. One morning it dawned on Mrs Hanbury-Collings that it was time to give up the house and move further into the city. A nice tall house on three floors at a good address of course. Room for a live-in maid at the top of the house. Forget the agencies. Useless. Advertise in *The Lady*. One could always rely on *The Lady*. The maid-cum-housekeeper was from the north country. Although Mrs Hanbury-Collings did not care for her accent, she did care for the way in which the place was absolutely clean. After her husband's death, she became obsessed with dusting and smells. Her doctor said that was common enough in bereavement. Now she lived for her committees, bridge and Sunday lunch. It was the only meal cooked in the house. The building was tall and thin. Cooking meant smells got the better of it. Not like the last house, where the kitchen was miles away. And so, eventually, she stopped cooking. Wouldn't allow Mrs Much to cook. But Sundays were quite different. Roast beef, Yorkshire pudding and big, flat roast potatoes.

Today they'd brought another lad. Ian. Same dormitory. Nice enough boy. Well mannered. Which was more than could be said of Ashley. Forever looking at his watch. He was a lawyer. She supposed he charged by the hour and allocated her his attention in hourly blocks. But the boys made up for it.

This Sunday she told them about the lady on the train and the stolen bag. Richard thought it great fun. Ian was enthralled. Ashley outraged. Declared that 'something should be done about it'. She had thought her son above such meaningless statements. But he wasn't. Never had been. They'd hardly arrived when he excused himself. A client, he said. He couldn't lunch. Had to see them at one-thirty.

'On a Sunday, darling?'

'People do work on Sundays, you know.'

'If they're in trade, darling.'

'Don't be impossible. You know you don't believe that.'

She supposed that she did not.

'Important is it, darling?'

The boys had gone into the sitting room. They knew better than to bounce on the sofa, but she half-listened. Just in case. Ashley looked at the open door and lowered his voice.

'Actually, you'll have to know soon enough, Mother. I may, I just may be in a little bother.'

'If it's money, darling, you know you only have to . . .'

'No. No. No. Well . . . in a sort of manner of speaking it is. I may have to sign a rather large cheque.'

'Oh dear. How large?'

'Well actually, Mother, very large. I, um, got into something and, through no fault of mine, you understand . . .'

'Naturally, darling.'

'Quite. You know the usual thing. It seemed a good idea at the time, but now, well, it's pay-up time and well, I'm not sure I have the, um, the readies. So you see, I simply have to see this, um, this person and try to negotiate with, um, well try to negotiate.'

Ashley shrugged his rather fleshy shoulders. He really did look like his father. Hadn't his brains, mind you. His mother looked at the oven. This wasn't the time.

'Oh dear.'

'Mm. Oh dear indeed. Anyway, if they will see reason, all well and good.'

'Who is this man? Do I know him?'

'It's not exactly as simple as that.'

'What do the partners say?'

'My God, Mother, they don't know.'

'You still haven't answered me, Ashley. Who is this person?'

The children were calling. They wanted attention. That was Ashley's get-out clause. He pecked her on the cheek.

'Back about four.'

The boys didn't seem bothered. The almost too perfect Bath house with its carpets that were never dirty, the curtains always warm in winter and bright in the summer, the sitting room with deep down-filled white cushions and dining room with deep bowls of proper puddings and usually a chocolate or two was far better than any school regime designed to give a little learning and a great deal of character building. They were content to sprawl that Sunday afternoon. Mrs Hanbury-Collings half-listened to them and half-listened for her son. She knew her son. She knew his casual explanation was far from casual and most certainly not an explanation. Was he telling her the truth? The partners? He'd been in that sort of trouble before. He had the confidence, perhaps lawyer's arrogance, to get out of it. This time he was nervous. She didn't believe him. It was so much easier never to believe her son. He was such a rotten little liar.

John Smith spent Sunday morning in bed. He'd arrived from London at two in the morning. She was already there. Waiting. Smiling as she always smiled when she saw him as if it had been too long. Maybe a week was too long. She'd arrived just thirty minutes before him. Called him on his car phone while the taps ran steaming. When he'd got there she was still damp from her bath. Her short hair rubbed dry. They drank Irish whiskey as they always did and then made love in front of the fire she'd built from the summer-dry kindling and logs. Then they'd slept until even the embers had died and the chill from the draughty hall where the door never quite closed woke them. Upstairs, they'd huddled beneath the enormous duvet he'd brought back from his last trip to Boston and they'd made love again. In the morning she'd sneaked out and returned with eggs and bread, though from where he could not imagine. He'd woken to the smell of coffee and warming bread in the Aga. He'd wondered about getting up, but instead was content to lie there listening to her quiet humming from below and the gentle chink and rattle as she prepared the butler's tray. The tiny porcelain vase with its tender, blushing Albertine picked from the old trellis. The basket of toast hidden beneath the small blue cloth. The crisp cream napkins. Typically her. No half-washed mugs, shared plate and paper towels. They lolled in the snow-white pillows and bolsters, spilled fluffs of scrambled eggs and then giggled when they discovered crumbs as they made love.

They dozed and chatted and dozed until lunch time and he wished that they could drive over to the pub on the other side of the valley for roast beef and pints of beer. But they could not. She didn't exist. Not yet. Instead they drank more whiskey, spooned at the half Stilton from the cold larder and scoffed the rest of the bread and a bottle of burgundy that he'd saved for a special occasion. After lunch they had talked about the future and what had to be done and then made love again. Shortly after four o'clock, she had dressed, kissed him goodbye and slipped from the low-ceilinged bedroom. He heard the latch on the side door, then the distinctive sound of what he called her 'funny French box' as she drove away. He smiled at the memory of her, then, instead of sleeping, lay there, his face sombre as he wondered if he would have the courage.

Dougie Gordon stayed in bed until eight o'clock on Sunday morning and then went down for a big English breakfast, for which the hotel claimed to be famous. His fiancée remained in her room. She had been the worse for drink the night before. When Dougie's fiancée became under the influence, she spent a considerable amount of her remembering time explaining to others that she was perfectly all right. Once that remembering

29

time had gone, then she became quite bearable. Even amusing. She would, when she awoke, deny that she had danced an eightsome reel – by herself. By late morning, she would be angry at any suggestion that she had to be helped to her room and then to her bed. Now she slept. Now she would sleep until gone lunchtime and then complain that no one, that no one being Dougie, had bothered to wake her. But he loved her and he loved her petulance. It was, he thought, the little girl in her. Dougie had never considered the advice that if one wished to see one's wife in a generation from now, then look at her mother. Dougie couldn't stand his future mother-in-law. But that didn't much bother him. He got on very well with his future father-in-law and Dougie was much of the opinion, not unknown among his countrymen, that women knew their place and, if there were doubts, then they only had to ask because men knew where that place was. For the moment, the argument was with Dougie.

At eleven o'clock, he had listened at his fiancée's door. Heard nothing. The Do Not Disturb sign remained looped over the handle. He returned to his room, picked up the telephone, dialled 9 for an outside line, paused, thought about it, changed his mind, replaced the receiver and went downstairs. In the lobby, he waited for the public telephone to come free, and then made his call. Having done so, and still with a look of pleasant surprise, he extended their booking by a day and asked the receptionist to tell Herself that he had gone for a stroll and would be back for lunch. The receptionist, who had not been on duty during the night, had nevertheless heard of some of the 'goings on' as the night porter called them. She understood the absence of the lady in number 204. She also admired the clear-eyed look Dougie gave her and indeed gave the whole bright Sunday morning world, as he strode purposefully across the foyer and then, with a sharp hobnailed step made his way down the stone steps towards the city centre. In fact Dougie, sleeves rolled above the elbows of his strong arms, kilt still swinging, might have been heading for hills. He wasn't. He looked neither right nor left. Admired no monuments. Caught no eye. Dougie, as he usually did, knew where he was going. It took fifteen minutes' brisk walking. He stopped outside a dark green door and rang the bell. While he waited, he admired the damp hanging basket of small pink and primrose flowers, and thought the world smelled and looked very good indeed. The tall slim girl who answered the door smiled and looked very good indeed and as he brushed by her in the neat hallway, smelled as fresh as the basket of flowers. As she led him up to the first floor, Dougie was in one of his more light-headed moods.

It was now five minutes to six o'clock. Mrs Hanbury-Collings had sat down to read the Sunday paper and noticed the rum truffles. Ashley had given her them. That was the very least he could have done. Very sickly rum truffles. This was her fourth and she knew that she would finish the box. That meant another six. She knew also that she would feel sick later in the evening. A Gin and It at six o'clock would help. Ashley would mix it for her. She'd told him to come back after taking the boys into school. He'd said he was busy. She told him that was nonsense and she knew he'd come. Then he could mix her Gin and It. Not too much It, and it was, as her good friend Marjory remarked, a very clean taste.

Mrs Hanbury-Collings never drank before six o'clock, except lunchtime, of course. She wished Ashley would hurry. Usually such a thoughtful boy. Always had been. Like his father sometimes, but not often enough. Sometimes he whined. Was inclined to blame others. His father had never whined. Got on with it. Made a fortune from one business. Then another. Then another. Then died making a fourth. That was the way it should be. A man needed to keep busy otherwise he went to seed. The Bath matron took the fifth truffle and nibbled at it. She hoped he would sort this business of the poor investment. If that was what it was. No fuss. She wouldn't bail him again. Not another cheque. The last one had been excessive. It was

31

the way in which he asked for it. He'd get it all when she was gone, but she wasn't going yet. He'd have to wait. She was going to spend as much as possible before she did. But that didn't mean she wasn't worried. He'd be here shortly. She remembered the look on his face when she told him to come back. They'd had a spaniel when he was a child. It too would snap, but never bite. Good.

Ashley was afraid of his mother. Always had been. Not his father. Father was always enormously old. Kind. Not her. There were moments he hated her. There were moments when other pressures were too great and so he simply feared her. Tonight was one of them.

At the door, he'd thought about going away. Telephoning later. Making an excuse. A migraine. But he didn't. He let himself in, of course – it was six o'clock. She had told him to be there. He was. He washed his hands in the small cloakroom, sprayed his throat with Fresh Breath and rehearsed his smile in the gilt mirror before opening the sitting room door. She sat where she always sat, on the edge of her small sofa. She was eating chocolate. And he hated her for that. She was greedy and she looked greedy. She ate with her mouth slightly open and as he approached to kiss her cheek, he could see the brown mess of her tongue and gums. As he bent to kiss her, he could smell the foul truffles. She didn't get up. She was his mother. She didn't have to tell him to pour himself a whisky and prepare her cocktail. He'd been doing so all his adult life. He opened the Chinese lacquered doors, shuffled glasses, bottles and ice bucket and mixed what she called Gin and It and prepared himself for her comment that no one but Harry in the American Bar really knew how to mix a martini.

He hated it when . . . and when . . . and when again. When she talked of the old days. When Harare was Salisbury. When London could be had for two pounds a night. Dancing beyond midnight. When she talked about Going On to a show. Didn't matter what show. It was something to Go On to. A thousand

32

middle-class women on any one night in London's West End restaurants, repairing their lipstick between courses. Ashley shuddered. It was what he called the Gin and It generation and he hated it. Hated to be reminded that he was its offspring. And now he mixed the gin with the vermouth. Then the olive which she would suck with that horrid noise she surely never heard. He glanced in the mirror in the cocktail cabinet. Cocktail cabinet, for Godsake. She was sitting very upright. Electric blue and too much gold. God, he hated her. She would demand to know. And he couldn't tell. Daren't tell. And yet he knew that he would. He hadn't the courage to tell her. He hadn't the guts not to.

'Ashley, dear, do stop swizzling that thing. Bring it here before it evaporates.'

He handed her the long-stemmed glass. She didn't say thank you. He didn't expect her to. He sat with his whisky and waited.

'Now what's this all about? Who is it that you've involved yourself with?'

'Just some people, Mother. No one in particular.'

'Don't be silly, Ashley, we only know people who are in particular. Now who are they?'

'No one you know.'

'Does that matter?'

'Not really. I was simply making the point. Anyway, it's no longer important. I think we have come to a conclusion.'

'What sort of conclusion?'

'A way to settle the matter.'

'You mean another pay-off?'

He gulped at his whisky.

'I don't mean it actually like that.'

'Then you'd better tell me how you actually do mean it. Ashley, you are making me angry. I am not a fool. I advised your father on a number of important matters. He trusted my judgement. You would do well to remember that.'

33

He wanted to say how in hell's name could he ever forget it. Didn't. Hadn't the guts. Anyway, wouldn't be smart. Instead, he tried another story.

'It really is very simple, Mother. I've made this, um, this person, see reason.'

'I doubt that very much.'

She swigged the last of her cocktail and held out her glass. Arm, wrist and hand quite steady. So was her gaze.

'How much?'

He got up. Took the glass and prepared the drink without any hurry. Time was important. No point in saying he didn't need money. Not any more. She wouldn't believe him. Best tell her what she would expect to hear. He could then avoid the truth.

'Just a few thousand.'

'Ashley, there is no such thing as just a few thousand. A thousand is not a few of anything. Even one thousand is one thousand of something. Now, again, how much?'

He put her glass on the small table by her knee. He would make one more attempt. Looked at his wrist-watch. Then her mantel clock.

'Now, darling, I really must go.'

'Sit down.'

The command was just that. Uncompromising. The two words cut like a stick to a cur. He let himself fall back on to the sofa.

'You really mustn't concern yourself, Mother. Really.'

Now she was smiling. This was her motherly smile. The one where she used her mouth quite a lot. The aged mouth had few muscles that remembered the routine, and the smile was closer to being a smudged leer, even a snarl. The eyes, caught up in the overindulged cheeks, were tiny. Piggy.

'I *am* concerned, my darling. I'm your mother. Now tell me what has happened.'

'There is no need, Mother. Absolutely no need.'

'Shouldn't I be the judge?'

34

'Certainly not. It is my affair. You must allow me to cope with it.'

'Just as you've coped with everything else in your life?'

He sat head down. Head into his chest. Hands in his trouser pockets. Fists bunched. God, she was detestable. But she was so because she was right and she reminded him that she was right. She had always been right, even back to his first memories. That business in his first term at school. Of course he hadn't stolen anything. He didn't have the nerve to steal. But he was the new boy. Joining so late because he'd been poorly. Because She had said he was too ill to go to school. Not allowed to board. A day boy. An outcast. Picked on. Easy meat for nine-year-olds. Accused. Innocent, but made to say sorry. All to do with his illness. Then sent back to England. Boarding. He hated it. But it was better than being at home. And then that stupid bloody summer. Really, really stupid. What was her name? Rose? It really was. Rose. The silly little girl. Should have known better. It had cost his father money, but he never knew. She had taken care of it. She had said there was no need to tell his father. And when he said it couldn't have been him, She told him to take his punishment like a man. She bought off the girl, her family and then him.

There were others, and then there was Sonia. She was amazingly lovely. They'd met on a flight back from New York. Advertising. He'd proposed inside a month. He looked rich. She'd said yes. They were married that summer. Biggest wedding in Bath. She had seen to that. And then Bath was boring. Too slow for Sonia. He talked about his career. She about parties. Then openly about other men. First the racing driver. Then the pilot. Then, oh God, who knows what was then. She'd got to the point when she laughed at him. Then one night she told him she was going out and not to wait up. She'd be gone the whole weekend. He'd said she wasn't to go. She'd laughed. He'd snapped. He'd hit her. Pretty damn hard. Went on hitting her. It meant a doctor. Should have been a hospital. But She had rescued him. Again. A private doctor.

35

They'd arranged for him to go to Harare. That end of the business needed someone. He'd do. Sonia went with him. But within a month of parties she'd discovered her Argentinian. The rest was a disaster. And now this.

Ashley stared at his feet. She was still talking. Tried not to listen.

'You see, Ashley, I will not have you treating me this way. You will tell me and you will tell me the truth. I, I am your mother.'

As he told her, he hated her for making him tell. When he'd finished telling, he hated her for knowing what he'd told her. And he hated her so much that it much pleased him to see the agony in her eyes. And as he told her, she remembered where before she had seen the girl on the train.

At five fifty-five, John Smith locked the side door and, out of habit, ran his eye over the upstairs windows to make sure all was secure as he walked over to the barn. He opened the boot of the white BMW and placed three bags in the centre of the large upholstered well. He'd not be back. As he drove out of the yard and over the cattle grid on to the dusty lane a tractor pulled to one side to let him through. It was a tight squeeze and the farmhand wasn't best pleased. But John Smith hardly noticed. Not even a wave of thanks. He was wondering about the house, the place, the future. The now half-empty wardrobes. The few things he hadn't bothered with. He remembered little of the drive. Took little notice of the warm peaceful evening. The last of the weekenders making their ways to their cities. Then the comfort of the motorway. No thinking. No silly bends. Trailers and caravans in their proper places. He slipped Sinatra into the CD player and accelerated into the fast lane.

Sixty-five minutes later, John Smith was driving down the hill into the eastern end of Bath. A woman, who did, didn't, did and then thankfully didn't dash into the road after her child's ball, went entirely unnoticed. He found himself flexing his hands on the steering wheel. Impatient. He snapped off 'Come Fly With Me' on its third time round. Rotated his neck, trying to free knotted muscles. Rubbing the side of his jaw. Needing a shave seemed important. Made him irritable. He punched at the radio. A phone-in. Broadcasting on the cheap. A lonely old man who called every station who'd have him. A disinterested female presenter, working on getting into television where her thin, interesting face and large breasts would compensate for the nasal whine she thought was a come-hither broadcasting voice. He started to curse her and missed the turning on the roundabout at the top of Walcott. He hit the steering wheel with one hand. Angry at the voice. Too tense. Switched off. Concentrated on what he was about to do.

It meant going right down the hill, by the least wonder of the architectural world called the Hilton and a u-turn along and up the narrowing Broad Street. At the lights on the slope he watched the street ahead. It would be easy to fork right instead of going straight on. Easy to find the motorway and head for the safety of London. A sharp blast from a pompous Volvo driver behind brought him back and he squeezed over the lights. Straight ahead. Then two turnings on the left. Down and into the perfect form of The Circus. Students on the grass beneath the huge tree. What sort of tree? He didn't know. He didn't know about trees. What a ridiculous moment to wonder. Across and into Brock Street. Slowly now. Waiting for a Rover to come through the narrow gap left by a huge yellow rubbish skip. And then behind the trough of broken panes, snapped lathes and torn papers, a parking spot. Right outside. He went by, stopped, reversed into the space and switched off. He leant over to the passenger door and looked up to the first floor. No signs of life. For a while he sat. Pulling himself together. So he thought. Then it was time. He unplugged his mobile phone, got out, slipped on his linen jacket and dropped the phone into his inside pocket. An instinct. A natural accessory of his life.

37

And yet the last thing he wanted to do was talk. To anyone. He took out a small brass key to let himself in through the green door. Changed his mind. Rang the bell.

Leonard spent most of Sunday in bed, reading. No radio, no television, no newspapers. Johnson came in a couple of times to see if he was all right. Not ill or anything? Didn't look it. Seemed to be fine. Truth was, Johnson didn't much care as long as she got a good supper. Later, when the sun was softer, Leonard, barefooted, wandered into the tiny garden he shared with her and half-dozed in the gentle curve of the old steamer chair. Belloc lay on the grass by his side where it had slipped from his lazy fingers. He dreamed of that last voyage of the Nona, of Belloc in his dark cap, round steel-rimmed spectacles, huge oilskin coat, his bulk plonked on the hatch skylight. Of Wyndham Lewis, the ghost of Chesterton, John Squire, J. B. Morton, Peters there too, all hurling bags of buns at the glass of claret balanced on Maurice Baring's bald head. And as they shouted and laughed, a young girl in a thin dress rushed between them screaming for her lost handbag. And none of them took any notice. No one saw her. No one saw the fat woman stand at the foredeck with the bag held high in her podgy hand. No one saw the girl rushing towards her, no one heard the woman's cackle as she dropped the bag over the side into the ocean just as the girl reached her. And the horrid gash of pink lipstick that now dripped over the weeping girl's soft blue silk. No one heard the screams as she fell or saw the grotesque face beneath the short, tufted black hair and the laughter as the fat woman pawed the naked roly-poly fiancée. And no one saw Leonard, clumsy in boots and tweeds on the rolling deck stretching out, hopelessly, to stop the girl falling.

He woke. Suddenly. Jerked. He heard the echo of the strangled sound from his throat and quickly looked up to the overhanging apartment windows, half-expecting faces peering at his anguish. But only Johnson stared. And she from the safety of the riverside wall where she always sat in the last of the evening sun. Leonard shivered. Stared back at Johnson's green eyes.

'And what, old lady, was that all about?'

Johnson didn't even shrug. Just blinked. Leonard closed his eyes to exorcise his memory. Knew he wouldn't. Got up and walked to the open French windows. Johnson sprang noiselessly to the grass and followed. Brushed seductively against his leg as he mashed fish into her bowl. Her pure white fur shimmered. Her tail held high as he set the stainless steel dish into its usual corner by the door. At last. Supper. And about time. He really had been in a strange mood all day. She wasn't quite sure she could be doing with it.

Sally Keemer spent Sunday writing letters. This and that. No one in particular. Then another card. Fun. To someone very special. She made two telephone calls. One took a long time and afterwards she cried. She then walked down to the columned porch of the main post office and posted the letters. For two hours she walked through the city. Then along the tow-path, back up by Poulteney Bridge, window shopping in the closed Milsom Street and at last the steep climb to the perfect circus of houses. Instead of turning left and home, she turned right and then right again by the Assembly Rooms where a quartet had been clubbing a simple Schubert sonata as she left home. All now gone. It was late. Dark although not properly so, and it was easy to see in the telephone box. But she neither dialled nor searched for coins. She waited, staring first at her small wristwatch, then at the telephone. As she bent her head to look once more at her watch in the dull light the telephone box door opened.

# MONDAY

## *Five*

At ten forty-five on Monday morning, Detective Inspector Leonard walked into Manvers Street police station. His leave period was over.

He'd missed the news that morning. Hadn't seen the papers. But he didn't need the weather forecast or the hottest-day-since-records-began headlines. The skies said it all. It was going to be another scorcher. The Georgian city was already a sad bowl of fumes. The topography was all wrong for the late twentieth century. The shirt-sleeved constable nodded and wondered about the other's green tweed. Leonard didn't see the nod but said good morning anyway and waited for the buzzer that would tell him the door was open and let himself into the narrow corridor. Upstairs, his tiny first floor office was much as he'd left it. Most people came back to a rash of yellow While-U-Were-Out stickers. Not Leonard. He had few friends. None called the office. Any calls were likely to be internal. Usually on administrative matters. He didn't mind those. Leonard liked administration. He was good at it. He had a lawyer's mind for detail. Once he had been a barrister. But not for long. Disillusion? Maybe. He'd been young enough to keep moving. No family. Few friends. Nothing in his own company that made him want to share with others. He picked up a letter from the lawyer. It was signed Hazel G. Donlevy,

Force Solicitor. It annoyed him. Why the middle initial? It was everywhere now. Another American import. He liked Americans. They made him laugh. He thought them more honest than his own nation. He read their literature. Dreamed with their music. But he didn't like their cultural clichés intruding on his life. Middle initials were that month's Leonard grouse. They hadn't been. He hadn't had one that morning. Maybe it was being back.

'Morning, sir. Good leave?'

She was as fresh as Bath was clammy.

'You've had your hair cut.'

He wasn't supposed to say things like that. Sexist. Next year it would probably amount to harassment. She grinned. Pulled at the soft dark strands as if to stretch them.

'It's my new butch look.'

That would be the day, he thought. Didn't say so. Instead he pulled open the top drawer. There it was. Where he'd left it. A half-eaten gingerbread man. He'd meant to stop at the bakers for a fresh one. He prodded it. Really was ten days old. Not even gingerbread men survived that long out of their tins. He swung in his chair, hands clasped behind his head. Across the way, the ugliness of the discount store could only be matched by the blandness of the police station. Detective Sergeant Jack was speaking but he was only half listening.

'. . . So unless anything comes up, you're probably on your own for a couple of days, sir.'

That's where he came in. He swung back to face her. She was leaning against the filing cabinet. Pretty. Make someone a nice sister, he thought.

'What's that?'

She didn't make a noise sighing. She was used to this strange man. They'd worked together for almost a year. Other officers asked her what made him tick. He didn't fit. Never appeared at functions. Wasn't disliked, but wasn't popular enough to have a nickname. They'd tried. Lennie, Lenno, The Professor. But an officer had to be liked or disliked for a nickname to stick. He was neither. Few knew anything about him. Even Superintendent Nash knew very little. Leonard had come to Nash's predecessor on attachment from another force. There'd been something big. Leonard had been right in the middle. Very bad news, involving the Security Service or something. But none of this had been entered on Leonard's personal record. Nash had had a quiet word with Special Branch to see if they knew anything. They'd tried. Made their telephone calls. Been told to wind in their necks. And if Nash couldn't find out, who could? When Madelaine Jack had found herself as his sergeant, there'd been nudging and winking in the canteen. But even that had died out. And yet they all understood that somewhere in the quiet, complex personality of James Boswell Hodge Leonard there was an extraordinary policeman who shouldn't have been a policeman. That was enough to keep their interest. But she told them nothing. She knew little. There was one secret. Neither had ever spoken about it. Not a bond, but it was an understanding. Now he was blinking at her. Cleaning his perfectly clean spectacles on a green silk handkerchief. He hadn't heard a word. She smiled again.

'I said you're on your own, boss. I'm roped into collation on this thing.'

He nodded as if understanding. He didn't. What thing? She must have told him. He hadn't heard. If it were important she'd tell him again. The clerk came in with an armful of files. Plonked them on his desk. They'd heard her coming. Everyone heard her coming. She sang every song in the charts and none of the tunes. She was bright. Lots of fresh lipstick. Roots needed attention. But she was breezy enough not to bother.

'Okay? Had a nice time?'

He started to say yes he had, but she was gone. He looked at the top one. Consequences of Re-Structure. Since when was it spelled like that? He stood, took off his jacket and draped it over the back of his chair.

'Anything you need before I go?'

He smiled.

'Another week off. Can you fix it?'

'With this lot going on? Overtime I can arrange. See you later, sir.'

She was gone. Smelled fresh. She really would make someone a good sister. By eleven-thirty, Leonard was bored. He'd been through the files, ticked them. Sent them on to the next poor devil to read, comment on and initial. In the corridor Ray Lane, still an inspector, long overdue for promotion, was going through a long list with a young Detective Constable. Lane looked ill. Overweight, but more than that. There'd been something about angina? He'd bought a mountain bike. It didn't appear to be doing him any good. Lane glanced in Leonard's direction, raised a hand in salute and carried on talking. At the corner by the FACPU office, one of the two Special Branch officers was muttering to himself and scribbling in a small notebook. Family and Child Probation wasn't exactly his line of business. It didn't take long for SB officers to become caricatures. The clerk was on the rounds again. She was humming. Managed to smile without crashing the Michael Jackson chorus and disappeared into Crime Management. Leonard looked in. Big room, for Manvers Street anyway. Half-empty. Everyone busy. No one looked up. He was beginning to feel unloved. Something was going on. He, a Detective Inspector, hadn't a clue. He continued along the corridor and turned right by the Superintendent's office. His timing was good. The door opened and Nash emerged. Eyes down. In thought. He looked up. Startled? No. Surprised. As if he'd forgotten Leonard was on his strength.

'Oh, hello, James. You're back.'

Leonard supposed that he must be. At least everyone knew that he'd been away.

'Something up, sir?'

Nash looked at him. A keen look to see if Leonard might be winding him up.

'You joking?'

'Sorry?'

'No. You don't, do you. Well, there is a little matter of a murder, you know.'

He started for the stairs. Two at a time. Leonard followed. One at a time. Up and along the corridor, the short cut through the canteen, the Training Room had been taken over. It was now a Major Incident Room. Boards. Screens. Keyboards. Everything including Detective Sergeant Somers-Barclay, blond Tarzan hair in perfectly casual place, a gold cufflink in a blue shirt showing from exquisitely tailored and pressed light-weight suit and, as ever, pouring his own imported coffee in time to hand to Nash. As ever Nash, almost preoccupied, took it, then put it down on a desk and forgot about it. Somers-Barclay didn't mind. He'd make the perfect butler. One day he would be the perfect District Commander, of that his mother was perfectly sure.

The room was too narrow for anything but a Training Room. Certainly never built for this. Old-fashioned blackboard on the right-hand end wall. Plenty of chalk. Nothing much to write. Not at this stage. Tables now pushed against the walls.

Leonard ignored Somers-Barclay's offer of his seat and leaned against the back wall. He'd see what this was about and then retreat to his files. It had to be important. Nash was strategy and policy. The Boss. The District Commander. Murder wasn't his part of ship. He didn't clear the lower decks and do the speeches on these occasions. Yes. Had to be important. Nash stood in front of them, arms folded. Still as slim as the day he'd joined the force twenty-seven years earlier. The voice friendly Bathonian. Soft tones from behind teeth that had a bite that never let go until he was ready. Someone had once drawn a cartoon of him. Called him Rambo. Unfair. But he'd not thrown it away.

'Right. First off, thanks for last night. I know some of you weren't supposed to be in. Some of you stayed on. Appreciate it. The body's now been ID'd with a Bath address. This one's ours. Okay?'

45

Murmurs and nods. Once upon a time something like this meant long days. Long nights. Loads of overtime. Loads of extensions and double glazing to pay for. Yes, sir. A-Okay. Twenty-nine pairs of eyes flicking from blackboard to Nash, from Nash to Lane, from Lane to Madelaine Jack. But they knew once upon a time was just that. Waited for the Boss to say so.

'The only reason I'm up for this morning is that I know a lot of you did good work last night and I wanted you to know it was appreciated, and there's going to be lots more where that came from. The second point is that I appreciate that times are hard. The gravy train's left town. Overtime's officially a thing of the past. But I wanted you all to know that I'll pinch from a budget somewhere if you need it. But the word is Need. Okay?'

Lots of nods. Forget the extensions. Who needed double-glazing? The older hands were already working out the chances of Extra Refreshment Allowances. Subsistence Allowances if there was a chance of getting off the patch. Nash was finishing.

'You should all have a fact sheet as we knew it at eight o'clock this morning. Maddy's done a good collation job, so read it and re-read it.'

He was the only one who called her Maddy. Not even Leonard did. Never called her anything. Most of the time didn't have to. Somers-Barclay had tried it once. Didn't work. To most of them she was Jacko. She was passing out a two-page incident sheet. The new Constable was more interested in her statistics than the ones she'd put on paper. He looked up. Caught Leonard's cold stare. Looked down at the paper with studious brow.

Inspector Lane was against the blackboard wall at the far end of the room. Waiting for them to pipe down and his cue from Nash. Nash had one more thing to say. He put his hands on his hips. The room quietened. No Toscanini. But they'd follow Nash's every beat. Trusted him. Good boss.

'Final thought from me. I want this one and I want it quick.

46

It's different. It doesn't look domestic and pleasure. Not a family affair. Okay?'

The room nodded in unison.

'Right. That means it could be tricky. It will be easy to miss the obvious. It could be that we'll get into politics. This one was well-connected as you'll see from Maddy's sheet. So careful. Okay? Very careful. I don't want size tens trampling all over Gucci deckers. Understand me? We want a quick result. But remember what we're here for.'

They knew what he meant. One or two looked at Leonard. Leonard didn't look at one or two. He knew. Trust Nash to remind them. His mission statement was printed on every forehead. 'We must be compassionate, courteous and patient, acting without fear or favour or prejudice to the rights of others.' Odd time to tell them. Nash looked at the wall clock.

'One quickie. In about half an hour we'll have the regional team arriving. It's going to get bigger. But we're going to be stretched. Now we've got all eleven districts, seems every young tearaway wants to prove something. Detective Superintendent Marsh will run the show, but for reasons I won't go into, he may not get here until Wednesday. When he does, he'll be taking over the briefing room next to mine. Okay? Let's get into this one, and perhaps we won't have to detain him for long.'

There were a few grins at that. No one pretended that Bath could handle a full-scale murder inquiry without the help of at least one of the five regional crime teams. Forty, maybe fifty officers on an inquiry like this. A third of Bath's strength. But instinct said it would be nice to try. Nash had done. He stepped to one side. Inspector Ray Lane straightened.

'Ray?'

'Thank you, sir. Okay, listen up. Inside the hour this place is going to be crammed with imports from ASDA.'

He didn't pause for laughs. But they were there. Superintendent Nash kept a straight face. Just. They all knew. They all knew he knew. Asda, the well-known supermarket chain, had

47

become the name for the new police headquarters, if you didn't happen to be working at the new police headquarters. Avon and Somerset Dream Academy. Nash didn't mind the joke. Used it himself. Privately. Lane's timing was good. This could be a long hard slog. It was the sort of line that brought everyone on board. Good man, Lane. Never be promoted. Pity. But as Nash had told him, it meant that he had a good man at that level. Promotion would have meant a transfer to ASDA.

'You all know the score. What you don't know is in the sheet. It'll be updated on the screens where we can, but don't forget: we can only update if we get it in the first place. So don't hang on to information. Soon as you get anything, put it in. That way it'll get collated. That way we don't go chasing our tails. That way we don't miss anything. Everyone got that?'

More nods. The new generation of coppers loved the screens. Just as they loved to go running in their lunch break. The older generation loved to be on the streets. Not running. Steady. But both knew that the screens were useless unless everyone talked to them. The computer would only tell you what someone else had put in. Computers were informers. Policemen felt collars.

'But we do have one titbit for you – and I don't want any sniggers from you, Hosko.'

A beefy constable with a certain reputation tried to look innocent. The rest laughed. It was a good team.

'We got a picture for you. Jacko?'

Sergeant Jack went to the state board and pinned up a ten-by-eight studio portrait of the murder victim. Hoskins, ever predictable, whistled. The dead woman had been very beautiful. Bobbed Titian hair. Eyes laughing at the camera. Long-necked. Bare shoulders. Leonard blinked. Blinked rapidly. When this picture was taken, she'd not been wearing the silkiest, skimpiest dark blue shift.

# Six

Nash was tapping the desk with a paper knife. It wasn't much of a tap, but the desk was new and, unlike Nash, marked easily.

'Why the hell didn't you tell me?'

'I didn't know.'

'It was all over the papers this morning. Radio as well.'

Leonard shrugged. Gazed out of the window. Roof tops and the George. He fancied a cold Guinness.

'Happens.'

Nash swung in his chair. He liked Leonard. Liked him a lot. But . . . But Nash was a communicator. When the Assessment Officer came from headquarters, he found every officer knew Nash's policy for the district. Nash liked people who communicated. He believed in and understood communities. Born in this community. Grown up in this community. Had policed this community for more than a quarter of a century. He was part of it. Leonard was a loner. That made him an unknown. Policemen weren't loners. To Nash, police work meant team work. Nothing new in that. But too many forgot. Too much television. It was the only way to do anything. Loners were not of his planet. Loners sometimes had a lot to offer, but chose when to offer it. Good policemen offered it all the time and the Nashes of the world decided what to do with it. This was no cardboard tele-figure who played the avuncular fool, the precise bureaucrat to Leonard's supposed genius. Nash was for real. So was being Superintendent and District Commander. The district had just been enlarged to take in the new county boundary. He needed officers around him who understood his mission plan and weren't inclined to read the stars before, or even if, they came to work. Policing was not a pastime with a uniform. That was why you joined. Not why you stayed. He was not annoyed. Frustrated. Nash was no shit. But he could be shitty. He looked at Leonard. Sighed.

'You realize you were one of the last people to see her?'

Leonard turned. Blinked slowly behind the round, steel-rimmed spectacles.

'That was Saturday.'

'That's good enough when we haven't a dicky bird. Anything else?'

'I was one of the last people to see who spoke to her.'

'You mean you didn't? Speak to her that is?'

'No.'

'Why not?'

'I was reading.'

Nash chuckled. A beautiful damsel in distress and Leonard has to be reading. Most of his 140 or so officers would have crawled over each other to get to her. Leonard was reading.

'What were you reading?'

'Mm?'

'Never mind. Okay, James. You'd better take this. But don't forget, we've got visitors, or will have any minute.'

He looked at the silver carriage clock on his bookcase. Needed fixing.

'This is a big number, not a crossword. So stay in touch. Okay?'

Leonard blinked again. It was a sort of nod.

'Sergeant Jack?'

'Maddy? Sure. Now listen, this is day one and a half. You know as well as I do that most of the good news information comes in during the first forty-eight hours. So look at it. Don't ignore it. I want police work, not funny looking man in dirty raincoat and dead cigar stuff. Understood?'

'What do we know?'

'Understood?'

Leonard sighed inwardly. Nodded his head. But Nash wanted sound effects.

'Understood.'

50

Nash looked at him for a few seconds. He probably meant it. But on the other hand . . .

Leonard started to get up, then sat down again. Took off his spectacles and rubbed them on his tie.

'Tell me, sir. Why did you say this could be political?'

Nash shook his head. Wished he hadn't said that. He sensed Leonard believed that Bath was run by a conspiracy of movers and shakers. Wasn't. That didn't matter. It was what Leonard believed. It brought out an aggression in his investigations which didn't match his appearance. People took offence. Nash never forgot that he worked for the community, not the law courts.

'I had a call from that Dover guy, you know?'

Leonard nodded. He knew the editor of the *Chronicle*. Everyone did, even if they'd never met him.

'And?'

'When I told him the name of this woman he actually whistled, you know? Like they did in those old B-movies. He reckoned that a couple of people in this fine city of ours will be interested.'

Leonard got up. He'd talk to Dover later. Turned, hand on the door.

'What was her name?'

'Keemer. Sally Keemer. It was on the board in there.'

He nodded at the ceiling. Leonard thought about it. Sally Keemer. Sally. Pretty. But then she was. Had been. He closed the door quietly. Now he needed to speak to Sergeant Jack.

Madelaine Jack was still upstairs in the big second floor Training Room which had now become the Major Incident Room. Like the rest of the building, there wasn't enough room. By tomorrow the team would tumble into the corridor. Bath didn't get many major incidents. They'd already struggled with one that wouldn't go away. This was extra. Most murders were what Nash cynically called domestic and pleasure, family affairs. All over in twenty-four hours. Straight up and down. No mystery. Just sad and obvious circumstances. The angry spouse. The cheated lover. Husbands, wives, sons and lovers. Daughters? Not that many, although as he thought about it, Leonard supposed that every wife, every mistress, was someone's daughter. Never having known who his parents were, he found it difficult to think families. Families were groups of people one envied in loneliness or avoided at Christmas. He heard people, especially at Manvers Street, talking about wives and husbands, kids and school. Heard, but never listened.

Somers-Barclay was pouring coffee. Did he do anything else? Always pouring coffee. Perhaps it was a family instinct. Sociable. Manners. Laid back. Families with people who called. Friendly. Never alone. Families begat families begat Somers and Barclays. Somers-Barclay's father was now a lord-lieutenant or sheriff, or something. Now *that* was a family. Two peers, a baronet and a distant and loony great aunt who had been mistress to men so famous that they didn't mind who knew it. Many things in the life of Somers-Barclay were like that. Now he ran a hand through his clotted-cream hair, smiled and offered Leonard the china mug. No polystyrene in his life. Not for his coffee. And it was his. Somers-Barclay refused to use the canteen. His first task on any morning was to grind the Kenya Mountain beans sent him every week by an importer in Bristol. Leonard normally refused. Somers-Barclay got on his nerves. The coffee, he thought, came from acorns. This morning, however, Leonard was in a diplomatic mood. He tried a smile which didn't quite come off and accepted the mug. Sipped. Acorns. Said thank you and hoped it sounded as if he meant it. Leonard was in a good mood. This was more than a murder inquiry to him. He had to know why someone would kill such an easy-going and beautiful creature. Having to know was what being a policeman was all about. But most of all, *Leonard* wanted to know. He wanted to know about the woman.

'Very brave, sir.'

Her face was deadpan. He sipped at the coffee, nodded his

head towards the door and she followed him along the corridor and down the one flight of stairs to the cubby hole that he called an office. He opened the top drawer. Still empty. Still no gingerbread man.

'I'm taking over Sally Keemer. That means you're with me. Okay?'

'Mm. Mm.'

She didn't smile, but that was what she was doing. She was used to Leonard. Probably the only one who was. Had the advantage of not trying to understand him. She'd studied criminology at one of the so-called new universities. She reckoned Leonard wasn't a policeman. He was a criminologist. She knew the difference. Wouldn't try to explain it to the others. He opened the bottom drawer and used it as a boot rest. Polished his spectacles. Squinted through them, put them on and then squinted at her.

'Right. What do I need to know?'

Sergeant Jack still had her collation sheet. She glanced down at the clipboard.

'We have very little. Her name is—'

'—is?—'

'—was, her name *was* Sally Keemer. Thirty-two years old.'

Thirty-two? Couldn't be. Late twenties, maybe. But? But what was the difference? She was dead.

'Lives, lived, in Brock Street.'

'Who says so?'

'Address? Her office. Couple of business cards in her pocket. We checked the alarm company and our people. Then the telephone book. It was her all right. Got the picture from her office first thing this morning.'

'What sort of office?'

'Um . . .'

'To have a picture like that?'

'Publicity. Sally Keemer Publicity, office in that cut that runs down to George Street.'

'Bartlet?'

'No, the one above. Saville? Actually, that wasn't an office picture. It happens to be one they had.'

'Why?'

'Why what, sir?'

'Why did they have it? It's pretty glamorous.'

'Sorry. Whoever went up there didn't ask. The need was to get the picture back a.s.a.p.'

'Okay. What happened?'

'Found eleven-fifteen last night in a telephone box by the Assembly Rooms.'

Leonard nodded.

'What was she doing there?'

Sergeant Jack shrugged. They didn't know.

'As far as we know, death was the result of a single gunshot wound to the head. We'll get the full autopsy this morning. No witnesses. Body found by a Jack Smallstone and his girlfriend Tina Tavare.'

'Who says a single shot?'

'The registrar at the RUH. Still alive when they found her. Unconscious, but alive. She apparently lasted forty-five minutes.'

'Next of kin?'

'Not sure. Her mother apparently lives somewhere in Italy. No address at the moment. Maybe Florence.'

'Father?'

'Don't know. But not, apparently, with mother.'

She paused. That, for the moment, was more or less it. Leonard said nothing. Florence. One summer long ago. The most beautiful summer of his life. He looked up. She was watching. Sensing? He wondered why Nash thought her too pretty to be a police officer. No one said a policeman was too slim, too handsome, too quiet. He dropped his boot back to the floor. Closed the bottom drawer and leaned on the desk with both elbows.

'Okay, this is what you don't know. On Saturday night I was

in London. I travelled back on the six-thirty from Paddington. It was delayed. Maybe an hour. Left at, oh, I can't remember. Quite late. Okay?'

She was making notes in the palm sized spiralbound book she bought by the box.

'And?'

'Sally Keemer was in the same carriage.'

Madelaine looked up. Something odd, he thought.

'You've had your hair cut.'

'Yes, sir.'

He paused. Thought about it.

'Did I . . .'

She was grinning.

'Mm. Mm. Yup. You did. But thank you again. Sir, if you don't mind me saying, that's something of a show stopper. You mean you actually know this woman?'

'Never met her in my life. I'll tell you about it on the way. Come on, let's walk the course.'

He was up and heading along the corridor. Somers-Barclay was heading for the same door and stood back.

'Anything I can do for you, sir, anything at all, just sing out. Okay?'

Leonard stopped. There was something.

'Have a word with the *Chronicle*. Tell them we'd like to hear from anyone on the delayed six-thirty from Paddington to Bristol on Saturday night, especially anyone in first class.'

'I didn't know that, sir.'

'Didn't know what, Sergeant?'

'That we'd like to hear from, well, people like that.'

An aggressive senior officer might have told Somers-Barclay to simply do as he was told. Another might have explained why in the first place. Nash would have ranted on about communication. Leonard said nothing. Blinked and was gone, Sergeant Jack following with not even the ghost of a smile.

# Seven

They walked. Bath was that sort of place. Leonard had a bicycle. A big green sit-up-and-beg Rudge. Most of the time he didn't ride it. Too many hills. But it was part of him. It went with the thornproof and brown boots. Eccentric, thought Jack. Tosser, thought Hoskins. On any one day, either could have been right, thought Nash. But now they walked, Leonard lunging at the Broad Street slope. Head forward. Hands in jacket pockets. Jack easy in her stride, sometimes changing step to keep up as he suddenly accelerated with the rhythm of what he was saying. And while they walked, he told her about Saturday night. About the curious drama. The boyfriend with the pony-tail. The Bath matron. The Scottish Hero and Herself. And he described Sally Keemer. Beautiful? Yes. Mischievous? Probably. He stopped by the traffic lights at the end of George Street.

'Tell me, why get screwed up about someone stealing your supper?'

The lights changed. The traffic stopped. They didn't cross. The hands went deeper into the jacket pockets. He wanted an answer. She shrugged.

'You said there was a present in the same bag.'

'But not too important to put in a bag of sandwiches. And she made more fuss about her supper than anything. Why?'

'Maybe it wasn't the cheese and thingy. Maybe it was the theft itself. People talk about being violated.'

'Feta cheese? This wasn't burglary. Couple of louts. Probably threw it away.'

'Or up.'

'Maybe. But it was no big thing. Sally Keemer looked an expensive lady. The carrier bags. High gloss. Expensive thick cord handles. Proper names. Not chain store. The boyfriend

56

looked as if he'd got a time share in *Eldorado*. It was the way she got excited.'

He closed his eyes. There was something else. Something he'd seen but not seen. He wished now that he'd paid attention. Something he'd thought odd. The lights were back on red. The traffic stopped.

'Sir?'

'What? Right.'

They crossed. Yet another slope. Up by Edgar's-buildings where a heroine from another age had watched Miss Tipley and her father the General make their way. On by the antique markets where traders claimed it was quiet and when it wasn't, that they couldn't find anything decent to sell. At the top they paused and looked left. The end of the road was taped off. Blue and white. Clean. Crisp. Properly tied. Neat. Scene of dreadful crime. Men in white boiler suits were on hands and knees. Plastic bags. Everything was going in. The tiniest toffee paper. A spatula of chewing gum full of lovely DNA. The discarded cigarette. Half an elastic band. A torn book-match that had never caught flame. A spinster's hair grip. Everything around the telephone box and for yards beyond. You never knew. Never. Especially when you missed something.

The office was above a shop with coloured paper shapes that may have been for sale. May have been eye catchers. Leonard didn't know, but he liked the colours. A couple of photographers and a local television crew, the blonde eyeing her sprayed hair in the shop window, three reporters, ridiculously young in ventless jackets and a girl, flouncy and noisy, clutching a small tape recorder now that no one bothered with shorthand. They broke off telling lies when they saw him. He recognized the girl from the television station. The blonde hair coloured to imperfection. She was much smaller, slighter, than she looked on the screen. He supposed most people were. The constable stayed where he was by the entrance. Sergeant Jack waved them away. Said something about routine calls and then, with the memory of the blank look on the face of Somers-

Barclay, suggested they might have something to say in a few moments.

As they went in Leonard looked at her. She half-raised an eyebrow.

'Train? Passengers?'

He nodded. Hadn't thought of that. The stairs were narrow. Expensive plum carpet. The door at the top of the stairs white. Solid. Looked original. The brass handle was polished, not varnished. Yellow, not glitter. He knocked and went in. Lots of glass. Tables. Figures. Room divider. Leather sofas. But it looked right. Even the ferns looked right.

The woman at the desk with the mini switchboard did not look right. She looked as if she scratched quite a lot. The hair was bleached and scraped back on an all but fleshless skull. The eyes protruded. Green. Not the green of a redhead. The green of a violent banshee. The beige top was slack over her breastless torso and ran in criss-cross folds as she swivelled on her stool. Leonard showed his identity card. Said who he was. Said who Madelaine Jack was. The woman bobbed her head somewhere between a nod and shake. She didn't say anything. Snatched a cigarette from a packet in the open drawer and snap, snap, snapped with a disposable lighter she didn't understand. She got it to work then dragged on the mentholated tube and flicked non-existent ash at the waste-paper basket. She started to say something when the telephone lit up. She dropped the lighter on the floor because she'd forgotten she was still holding it and stabbed at the console with a nailless talon. The phone went dead. Leonard looked at the machine. Then at her.

'Why not put it on answerphone?'

She stared at him. Dragged again at the cigarette. Coughed almost uncontrollably.

'Because it may be important.'

The voice surly. As dry as a long-forgotten half-Corona. She scrubbed at the side of her face and silver bangles racked back to her elbow. Her name was Cynthia. Cynthia Rathbone. He couldn't believe it had ever been Mrs Rathbone. Leonard nodded at the door behind her.

'We'd like to speak to whoever's in charge.'

'There isn't anyone.'

She didn't look up. She was dealing the morning mail into three dummy hands. Leonard leant with both fists on the desk. She carried on dealing.

'You mean there isn't anyone, or there isn't anyone at the moment?'

'That's right.'

Leonard straightened and sighed to the ceiling. It was ivory. The mouldings picked out in sage greens. Sergeant Jack gave a small cough.

'Lovely flowers. Are they lilies?'

The woman stopped paper-pushing. Almost without turning her head, her reptilian neck rising from her cotton top, she contemplated the white display vase on the corner cabinet.

'Lilies?'

'Yes. I'm never sure.'

''Course they are. Most appropriate, don't you think?'

'I'm very sorry, but we do need some information.'

The woman was now shaking. She stood up. Stared at Sergeant Jack.

'Excuse me.'

She didn't run. The room wasn't big enough for that. She slithered. Her dark green leather skirt hitched in creases about her skinny fishnet-covered thighs. The door banged after her. Neither Leonard nor Jack moved to stop her. They didn't have to. They could hear her crackling sobs from behind the door. The water splashing. They waited. It happened. It would be easier now. The quiet flush of a distant cistern. More water. When she reappeared, Cynthia Rathbone had aged twenty years. The eyes had it. The eyes had it. Harshly repaired with no skill, no pride. The mouth slack. The muscles gone. Puckers of old skin where once there might have been dimples but never had been. She tried a smile. The teeth looked older. Yellow. No longer set, just hanging from red gums.

'Sorry. I'm not very good at this sort of thing. I needed that.'

Leonard tried a smile of his own. He was no better at it than she was.

'There's nothing in the Pitman course that prepares you.'

Her laugh was a short bark.

'Pitman? Girls nowadays learn Pitman? You must be joking. Most of them can't even spell sodding spell-check.'

Leonard didn't want her too relaxed. Too confident. He wanted information, not her opinion. He nodded to the door behind her.

'Tell me, who works in there?'

'That's her room.'

'Where does everyone else work?'

She sniggered. Coiled on to her seat. Leather on leather.

'I am everyone else.'

'Miss Keemer ran this place by herself? Just her?'

'That's right. She hired people as she needed them.'

'What sort of people? Photographers, printers?'

'Them too.'

'Who else?'

The sneer was back. The green eyes starting from their red, smudged sockets.

'Consultants.'

'What did they consult in?'

She shrugged. He looked about him. Green soft leather couches on two walls. Clear, shiny, glass, too low coffee table. Sergeant Jack was looking at pictures. No publicity stills. Didn't publicity agents cover their walls with the good, the bad and the beautiful clients? No filing cabinets. He tried another smile. Needn't have bothered. She was stabbing at the blinking telephone lights.

'I'll need to see your files.'

'Why?'

'Business contacts. Diaries. Anything that would give us an idea.'

DS Jack was peering at the tiny signature on a splashed watercolour. Hartman? Hardman? Lot of apples and other fruit. She liked it. But she was listening. Without turning, she asked the obvious question.

'Do you know who killed her?'

'No.'

'Do you think you do?'

Through the silence, Leonard could hear the laughing and chatter of the waiting reporters. He went over to the half-open window and looked down. A vigilant photographer raised his lens. Leonard turned away. Jack was watching the woman who stared straight ahead. There was nothing to see but a small watercolour. A wisp of white smoke from a chimney hidden beneath old thatch. In the distance, dark hills. Dark with greens and browns and purples. Jack moved between the woman and her focal point.

'Do you think you do?'

The voice was soft. Easy-going. Not officious. Not moving in a southerly direction, your worship. The woman looked up. Hideous eyes. Tiny burst veins. Shadows of yolk where there should have been white. Unblinking green marbles. She discovered Jack. Started, even. Her breath coming from deep inside so that Jack could smell the breakfast cigarettes.

'Do you?'

Cynthia Rathbone shook her head. Her eyes seemed to centre as her head moved.

Sergeant Jack looked away. Tried again.

'What does that mean?'

'Shake means no. Nod means yes. I thought that was sodding obvious.'

Leonard flopped into the leather sofa beneath the seascape.

'Tell me, Miss Rathbone . . .'

'Mrs.'

He paused.

'I'm sorry, Mrs Rathbone . . .'

'Not really, I suppose.'

'Divorced?'

'He's dead.'

'I'm sorry.'

'Why?'

Leonard looked into the sharp eyes. She was right. Why was he sorry? Good manners? That was about it. Why not say so?

'Because I feel it is sad when two people are parted.'

'Bullshit.'

Her eyes were now fierce. He started to say something, but she hadn't finished.

'You people like people dying. It's more interesting. Right?'

Sergeant Jack guessed it was time to return to conventional police procedures.

'Would you mind telling us, Mrs Rathbone, when was the last time you saw Miss Keemer?'

'Saturday, about seven o'clock.'

Leonard looked up. Couldn't have. Sally Keemer was at Paddington station at seven.

'You're sure?'

"Course I'm sure. So would you be at that time of a Saturday morning. Six o'clock. Telephone. Christ! Panic. What's happened? It's her. "Cynthia, darling, be a sweetie and meet me in the office in an hour. Must rush." And that was sodding it. So, Inspector . . . who did you say you were?'

'Leonard, Detective Inspector Leonard.'

'Leonard. Right. So anyway, there I was at seven in the morning, bowing and scraping to madam's most gracious commands.'

'What did she want?'

'Eighty letters out by the lunchtime post so they'd arrive first thing Monday.'

'Eighty!'

'Exactly. It's not so bad with the word processor. The letters were all the same. Just the addresses to change.'

'What did it say?'

62

'Reorganization of the agency.'

'Important?'

'Everything's important to her. I mean . . . well, everything was . . . important.'

Her head dropped to her chest. Leonard thought she was going to cry again. She didn't. She was tearing at a tissue. A small pile of white confetti gathering on the desk top.

'A copy of the letter and names and addresses of all the people it was sent to. Like to see them with everything else she's dictated during the past twelve months. That possible?'

She didn't look up. The tearing had become shredding. She was swinging on the swivel chair like a coquette on a swing.

'You won't find anything.'

'Anything what?'

Now she did look up.

'Anything that'd tell you why she was killed.'

'How d'you know?'

'Because she was clever. If there was anything incriminating she was too damned smart to put it on paper.'

The sentence flicked from her mean mouth one word at a time. The sting was unmistakable. Sergeant Jack was standing by the window. She'd drawn the angle-blind. Now she turned. She too had sensed the spite.

'Did you like Miss Keemer?'

Cynthia Rathbone's eyes were shut tight. Trying to remember? No. The tension. The horizontal lines across her neck. The pain. She opened her mouth as if gasping for air before replying. And then the door opened.

The figure in the doorway was tall, slim, dark haired, dark eyed. Soft, white, loosely buttoned blouse. If the pause was meant to be dramatic, it was. The smile enough to be open. She looked at Cynthia who looked down and then at Leonard and then at Jack.

'Hi. The policeman downstairs said that one of you was an Inspector. Now, let me guess . . .'

She pointed a long blood-nailed finger at Leonard.

'You?'

Leonard rose from the leather couch and took out his ID card. Said who he was. Said who Sergeant Jack was. Deadpan.

'And you are?'

She put out her hand. The grip was firm, not glamorous.

'I'm Jane.'

She didn't wait for a fanfare. An answer. Instead she walked over to the door behind Cynthia Rathbone and threw it open. Until then, everything in slow motion. Now they were swept into the executive suite. Within sixty seconds, Cynthia had been sent off to find croissants, to have fresh coffee ready by the time she was back with them, the answer machine was on, the door was closed, Leonard and Jack were side by side on yet another squashy couch and the woman was seated in a tall-backed ox-blood leather chair behind a glass table which until shortly after seven a.m. two mornings earlier, had been occupied by the late Sally Keemer.

Leonard didn't like losing any initiative. He felt he had lost this one. He took off his glasses and started polishing them on his tie. Hurred on them. Held them high. Squinted at the woman for a few moments before he slipped the steel arms behind his ears.

'I understood that Sally Keemer Publicity was just that, Sally Keemer. I'm still not sure exactly who, other than you, gives you the power to order croissants.'

The woman opened the small, flat, green cheque-book purse she'd dropped on the table and took out two business cards. Leonard dutifully got up and fetched them. *Jane Boxer, Publicity Consultant*. The address was where they were sitting.

'Sally was my partner.'

Sergeant Jack cocked an eyebrow. Jane Boxer caught it.

'My business partner, that is.'

She smiled with an innocence that said everything was now explained. It wasn't. Not for Leonard.

'Mrs, um, Rathbone . . .?'

She nodded.

'Mrs Rathbone told us that Sally Keemer Publicity was run by Sally Keemer. There was no one else.'

'Did she, now?'

Stalling? He didn't think so. Playing. Playing with confidence. Maybe. Why?

'Yes, she did. But you say you're, you were, Miss Keemer's partner.'

'With some confidence, Inspector. I've been closely involved with the company for a very long time. On Friday night we became partners. There was to be an announcement on Monday.'

'Why then?'

'There's a rather large conference here in Bath which starts later today. We have four very important clients at that conference. We thought it would be a good opportunity.'

'You become a partner on Friday, the announcement is due on Monday and she was killed on Sunday.'

'Yes.'

'So the company . . .'

'I didn't know policemen were allowed to wear glasses, Mr Leonard.'

Leonard gazed at her open face. Clever? She gave no hint. Why say that? Curiosity? At another time, yes. But now, being questioned by the police during a murder investigation? When her partner, her friend, was dead. Partner? Friend?

'So the company now belongs to you, Miss . . .'

He made casual play of looking at her business card.

'Miss Boxer.'

Miss Boxer paused. Thought about her answer and looked at Madelaine Jack when she spoke.

'If you mean do I stand to gain by her death, the answer is no. In theory, the company is mine for day-to-day running. But there are finances to be sorted.'

Leonard was back looking at the ceiling. Jack wasn't. When she spoke, her voice had an edge that hadn't been there when she'd questioned Cynthia Rathbone.

'Sleeping partners?'

Jane Boxer might have been smiling behind her straight expression.

'I suppose that is the expression, yes. Sally was the brains, the business, the client getter. But there are, as I say, other financial considerations.'

Leonard was back. So was Cynthia Rathbone. The door opened without a knock and she backed in with a tray of croissants and a cafetiere of coffee. She didn't pour. Didn't wait. Madelaine Jack whispered thank you. Leonard added his. Jane Boxer watched them.

'Tell me, Miss Boxer, what does the company do?'

'Personal publicity. Simple as that.'

'PR, public relations?'

She shook her head.

'Oh no. Absolutely not. We take a client and design a complete publicity package for that individual. Not a company. The person.'

'But you might do it for that person's company?'

'No. Just the individual.'

Leonard wondered who the clients were. Jack wondered still why no photographs of clients on the walls.

'Are your clients famous? Would we know them?'

'Maybe, sergeant. I don't know who you know, do I?'

'Celebrities?'

'No. Not what you would call celebs. Maybe in their own industries. Maybe they want to be. We're very specialized. A client may be someone in show business. Maybe. One or two. But mostly they're in industry, commerce and the professions.'

'An accountant would have a publicity consultant?'

'Why not?'

Leonard shook his head. Yes. Okay. Why not?

'And what do you do?'

'Well, a sales director wants to get noticed and . . .'

'By whom?'

'By anyone, but mainly by another corporation, probably a

bigger one. So he or she, but mostly he, would come to us and we start work on him. New tailor, hairdresser. That's image. That's easy. Do it slowly, so no one gets shocked. Then start making sure that he's in the right places. The right receptions, right dinners, maybe a couple of culture dates where we can bump him into the chairman of ICI or the senior vice-president of Chase Manhattan, or whatever. Soon people are asking who he is; better still, they assume they know who he is. He's got some good sales figures, pulled off some good deals, we make sure that it gets known throughout his industry. Right magazines.'

'You sell him.'

'That's right.'

Leonard looked surprised. He was. Rising starlets. Waning starlets. Politicians. But accountants? Spin doctoring sales directors?

'This is successful?'

She smiled. That same innocence. That same what–else expression.

'It's getting better. And every time we get better, then we're doing exactly what we tell our clients to do.'

'And this is what you were going to do at this week's conference?'

She nodded. Looked at her watch. Small. Gold. Dunhill.

'Not were. Will. I have a meeting in exactly one hour. Okay?'

Leonard looked at his own watch. It took longer. It was on the end of a gold chain in his top pocket. She wondered if it were an affectation. Decided that perhaps once it had been. Not any more. He made no fuss

'Just one important point, Miss Boxer. What was Sally Keemer doing in London?'

She shrugged.

'Haven't a clue. Shopping, I suppose.'

'On the weekend before a major conference. The weekend before the announcement?'

67

'Hardly a weekend. She went up, as far as I know, on Saturday morning and came back Saturday night. We really could live without each other for twelve hours or so.'

'But you weren't surprised when she said she was going?'

'She didn't.'

'Didn't what?'

'Say she was going. It wasn't until I came in on Saturday morning and found Cynthia slaving over a hot keyboard that I knew she was in London and not Bath.'

'Don't you find it odd, Miss Boxer, that your partner didn't mention she was going to London?'

Jane Boxer swung back to Sergeant Jack.

'Not really. If it had been business, she might have told me, but not otherwise. We were business partners. That's all.'

'Not friends?'

Jane Boxer thought about her answer. Her eyes never left Sergeant Jack's. Leonard stared at the cafetiere. Wondered if anyone was going to pour. Wondered about saying no. No, thank you.

'No. I suppose not. We got on quite well, but we weren't friends in the way you might think.'

Later, it was the type of answer both Leonard and Jack would have followed up. But for now there were more important questions to ask. An investigation was like getting up in the morning. If you went through the routine, washed, dressed, had breakfast, went to work, then you got on with the morning. If the routine were broken, then it took the whole day to catch up. Dressing gown breakfasts meant being late for the traffic, bus or train. Essentials missed. Leonard was washed, dressed and working.

'We need a list of all her friends and acquaintances. Will you help?'

'Sure. No problem.'

'Boyfriends.'

'There wasn't one.'

Sergeant Jack looked up from her notebook.

'Miss Keemer was very pretty.'

'So are you, Sergeant. Do you have a partner, special boyfriend or someone?'

Madelaine Jack did not blush. It took a lot of effort. A lot of thinking about buses. About thick-soled shoes running on pavements. Counting the footsteps. Sergeant Jack had a system for cutting herself off. But she couldn't do two things at once. Leonard cut in.

'She had a boyfriend in London. Who was he?'

Jane Boxer shrugged. When she did, the blouse moved with her. She knew it. Watched Leonard's eyes. He knew it.

'Tall. Late thirties, early forties. Dark. Gold chain. Gold necklace. Pony-tail.'

'Pony-tail?'

'Mm. Mm.'

'Haven't a clue, Mr Leonard. Pony-tail? Gold janglies? You sure?'

'I am sure.'

'Well that's amazing. I can't imagine for one moment that she would know anyone like that. Sally Keemer was one of the most conventional girls I know.'

# Eight

Selsey was looking tired. Since Saturday night he'd been both tired and emotional. A very big win. The horse had looked a no-hoper. Selsey knew a lot about no-hopers, especially horses. Why not? He'd backed most of them in his time. This one hadn't run better than fourth in eight races and on that occasion she'd been last. The syndicate were thinking of another trainer. One of them was quietly offering his share to a dog food processing plant. At least that was Selsey's story.

'So you backed it because you felt sorry for it?'

Selsey ran a hand through thick dark hair. Gave Leonard a very solemn look.

'There was no other reason. Wrong season for me. Flat's for ice skaters.'

'Good price?'

'Better than good. Jockey hardly bothered to put his boots on. Form book said it wouldn't have got a job in a panto.'

'No inquiry?'

'Of course. But quick. An objection.'

'Serious?'

'The favourite ran second by half a length. There's always something to say.'

'It was clean?'

'Squeaky.'

'So why did it win?'

Selsey folded his mouth, raised his eyebrows. Why did any outsider win? Leonard knew one reason.

'Funny money on it somewhere?'

'Rainy day stuff? Maybe. I didn't hear that. But then I don't hear everything.'

He looked about him. People were hungry. Woods was filling up. Good lunch-time trade. Regulars as well as tourists. Mostly they wanted to go inside. Leonard always sat in the window corner, in the bar. Never been inside. One day. It was the sort of place where you took someone. One day. Selsey had run the place for years. Except when he was at the races. Except when he wasn't thinking about being at the races. Except when he was taking longer than usual to get back from the races. Or thinking about a bet. Selsey had been thinking bets since his second year at school. Taking them in those days. Clearing a little profit from Bromwich lads. Now he placed them. His staff didn't mind. Good boss. Just as likely to close the restaurant at lunch-time if there was a big rugby match on. Especially England against France. Something to do with the real love of his life.

Leonard sipped. Selsey was still opening Saturday's champagne. Wondered about coffee. Wondered who drank the coffee across the way in what had been Sally Keemer's office. He hadn't. Jack hadn't. They'd left. She'd gone into the outer office to sift the client list. The past five years' worth. Jane Boxer had been nervous. Then why not? Confidential, she'd said. He'd promised it would go no further unless there was very good reason and then he would tell her first. She remained nervous. But not for long. Self-assurance returned. Cockiness? No mourning clobber for her. Untouched. Not even curious. Sally Keemer is dead. Long live Jane Boxer. But would she? Surely she wanted to know. His surely was different from hers.

'You hear a lot.'

Selsey grinned. Puck with a nose for white burgundy and winners. Well, sometimes winners. Always white burgundy.

'About Sally Keemer? I was waiting.'

'Who was she?'

'Sally Keemer Publicity.'

He nodded across the way. They could see the media straggle lolling against the Saville Row wall.

'I didn't mean that. She must have come in here.'

'She did. Surprised you hadn't seen her.'

Leonard hadn't. Wondered why.

'Mind you, she wasn't a luncher. Late night. Then with other people. Lots of them. Fun but never noisy. Long legs. Amazing legs.'

He looked down. Picked up his own glass and sipped.

'I suppose that's wrong.'

'Because she's dead?'

'Because she was murdered.'

'Tell me more.'

Selsey poured the rest of the cold sparkling liquid. The girl at the bar was pouring them coffee.

'Started coming in about ten years ago. Then didn't see her for a year or so. Then she came back. Been abroad, I think. Her French was good. Seven years ago, she gets married. Guy called Sammy something.'

71

'Not Keemer?'

Selsey shook his head. Black tousled hair waved No Way.

'Keemer was her maiden name, I think. Anyway, he didn't last.'

'What happened?'

'Divorced. But some men are born to howl at the moon. Had a habit of getting himself into leg-over situations.'

'So she divorced him.'

'No. I don't think she knew. Everyone else did. She either didn't or was a pretty good actress. No, he took off some place with some woman twice his age and twice as ugly . . .'

'And?'

'Twice as rich.'

Leonard wondered how a man could have driven away from the vision he'd seen.

'This publicity thing. Real?'

'Must have been. She was expensive.'

The girl brought the coffee over. Smiled. She had an intelligent face. Interested. But then all Selsey's staff were like that. They were part of Woods. Not just staff. Leonard smiled his thanks.

'What do you mean, expensive? Frocks? Jewellery? Cars?'

'More than that. I sometimes got the idea that she didn't know any poor people. You know what I mean?'

'Maybe. Boyfriend?'

Selsey didn't know.

'Years ago. When she first started. But not later. Not after she came back. No one she held hands with. No one special. Always a crowd.'

'Any names?'

Leonard was pushing his friendship. He stirred his coffee. Gazed out of the window. Sally Keemer had been shot not fifty yards away. She had been beautiful. Successful. Open. Why would anyone shoot her? He turned back to Selsey. The restaurateur looked tired. It had been hard work winning. Leonard fished out his watch. Pushed away from the table.

'See you later. I'm supposed to be in Brock Street.'

Selsey grunted from beneath the dark mop over his eyes.

'She lived there. I remember. What a terrible, terrible waste. What a crying shame.'

Leonard nodded. He'd arranged to meet Sergeant Jack there five minutes ago. Selsey got up with him and walked out to the pavement. They both looked down towards the taped-off scene of crime.

'Odd isn't it, Jim lad?'

'Go on.'

'You're the robot cop in the family.'

'Okay. Give in.'

'Well, nothing to do with me, but she was in the phone box, right?'

'Yes.'

'Well, she only lived round the corner. Why use a public call box?'


# Nine


The flat was elegant. Creams, beiges, French blues. Long shiny paned windows. Slightly distorted. Old glass. Ceiling to floor heavy curtains tied back with wide brocade. No leather. Very feminine. In the kitchen, the scent of ground coffee. Stainless steel spotless. Unused since the precious char had packed her dusters, soaps and scrubbers. One bedroom was mail order perfect. Not a crease, not a speck. Waiting for a visitor who would never come. The other bedroom was hers. The blue silk dress draped over the shoulder of a delicate chair. Slim blue shoes, one on its side, discarded by their cardboard box. Beige silk and lace across the bed. Ruffled. Disturbed as if she'd rested. As if the shape was her shape. Might still be warm. The bedside telephone tiny, discreet, turned towards the pillow.

Waiting to be used? Waiting for a call? The dressing table with bottles and pots and tubes and brushes lined up and knocked over like so many glass, porcelain and plastic teddies. To Leonard, who had never lived in a house with a dressing table, surprisingly untidy. To Jack, who understood privacy, all very ordinary.

Leonard picked through the drawers, the wardrobe, the cupboard. The same fragrance. A moment as she'd brushed by in the train. He picked up the blue dress, held it to his nose. Didn't sniff. Let the thin fabric lie in his hand. Closed his eyes. Something. What? Another scent? He laid it back on the chair.

'Have them check that, will you?'

'What we looking for, sir?'

'Aftershave. Deodorant. Male deodorant. Or anything else. She was wearing it on Saturday. The boyfriend had his arm around her.'

'And the anything else?'

He looked at her. She looked away. Opened another drawer. She needn't have asked. He hadn't finished.

'And get someone to go over this whole place. Start with the chair. And don't forget . . .'

He closed the wardrobe.

'The sheets.'

He didn't respond. They always checked. Now they did. The dressing table drawers were shallow. Discarded make-up palettes. Unwanted buds. A folding card of unused Bath Theatre tickets. The previous year. The *Dream* away. He wondered why she hadn't gone. Wondered why she had the tickets. Wondered, if she'd known, would she have gone? Would it have been different? The butterfly in the *Dream*. One flutter and her life would have changed? Would be changing still. Instead . . .? They were back in the drawing room.

'Notice something very odd?'

Madelaine Jack looked about. Cream damask, squashy down cushions. The small table spindly-legged, hardly bearing the

74

weight of *Vogue* and *Elle*. Aphrodite in feminine alabaster, not bronze. Soft Chinese washed silk stretched before a flame-effect gas fire. The whisper-thin stereo at home on white almost bookless shelves. The television screen an intruder in the inevitable corner.

'Very neat?'

'No. What's missing?'

She tried to catch a clue from his gaze, but it was not there. He was looking at the whole room through the tall overmantel gilt mirror. She'd seen him do it before. The scene in reverse. Everything in place, but unreal. Mistakes then obvious. He believed it. She wasn't sure. Like now. Shook her head.

'Sir?'

'Photographs. Not a single photograph in the place. No holidays. No wedding. No husband, boyfriend, parents and especially . . .?'

'Her little boy.'

'Right.'

He turned.

'Let's start again.'

From the hall to the drawing room, to the small bedroom, to the large bedroom. To the bathroom, to the kitchen. Nothing. Then the drawers. Nothing. Nice touches. Flowers were fresh. Towels fluffy. Magazines, the latest. An exquisite letter rack on a small Sheraton table. The stationery expensive. The letter head raised enough to tickle a spaniel's belly. Everything expensive. Everything to hand. Just enough. Just enough to be comfortable. A fine hotel would never have taken more care. And that was it. A fine hotel. All that was missing was room service. Leonard walked through the apartment once more. Opened drawers. Opened cupboards. The wardrobe door with its long bevelled mirrors was flung wide.

'Tell me, what does this lot tell you?'

Jack ran her hand along the row of designer dresses.

'Expensive. Nothing more than a season old. Size twelve.'

He pulled open the small dresser. Lace and silk. Unopened packets of tights and stockings. An embroidered silk bag. The wispiest underwear.

'And this?'

She picked up the pile of panties.

'Nothing here from Marks and Sparks. And no bras.'

For some reason she wasn't sure about, she blushed. Leonard was like that.

'Enough of it?'

'Well yes, I suppose so.'

'What about this?'

Another cupboard. Shelves. Neatly folded fine cashmere sweaters. A pair of thin jeans never designed for the Black Mountains. The shoe rack. All boxed. But not many.

'Where's the chunky winter stuff?'

Madelaine opened another cupboard. Two shelves were empty. Leonard was loping back through the flat.

'Clothes, yes. But not too many. Spring and summer. Nothing for winter. And look at this.'

The hall cupboard was now open.

'Two suitcases. Neither big enough to go on holiday with. No photographs. Now that's the clincher, isn't it?'

'You mean it's as if she didn't live here.'

Leonard nodded.

'Oh, she lived here all right. But it wasn't home. There has to be somewhere else. Now tell me, why hasn't anyone said so?'

'Perhaps because we haven't asked. Hardly a mystery, is it, sir? Early days and all that.'

He shrugged.

'Perhaps. Well, we'd better ask. Try her office again. That's the quickest bet. And . . .'

He'd seen something obvious. They both had. What was it? He shut his eyes. Hall. Kitchen. Cloakroom. Kitchen. Drawing Room. Bedroom. Kitchen. Bathroom. Second bedroom. Kitchen. Kitchen. Now where? He walked back to the long

76

thin room. Stood at the open door. Tapping on the frame. Perfect. A show-flat. What was it in here? There'd been something. She was standing at his shoulder.

'Something special in here, sir?'

He didn't turn. He scanned the shelves. The cooker. The glass-fronted cupboards. Fire blanket. Cork notice board. There it was. Top left. Brass hook. A bunch of keys. He walked over, reached up. Nine keys. Two silver Yales. Four Chubb deadlocks. Mini church door. Long mortise. One odd. Old. Clock?

'Try those on the front door.'

It took two minutes. One of the Yales and two of the Chubbs matched. So the others could be the second home. There was still something he'd missed. Maybe not missed. Hadn't connected.

They were downstairs. On the street. He was smelling the flowers tumbling from the hanging basket. Why did everywhere have hanging baskets? No gardens. Hanging baskets. He supposed. He turned, self-conscious. Detective Inspectors liked roses.

'Pretty.'

'Contractors.'

'Cynic.'

She wasn't. But she thought it was probably true anyway. The shambling book man was heading away from them. Feeling in his jacket for the keys. Opening late. Again. Leonard wanted to talk to him. The lost Bennett on Florence. But it would have to wait. Maybe he'd known her. No. Probably not. Just an excuse.

Madelaine Jack was going. Off to confront the lizard lady.

'Just a thought.'

She turned. He was looking at the pavement. Short-sighted and a paper clip gone? He looked up as she returned.

'The kitchen was very clean, wasn't it?'

'Yes, sir.'

'Why?'

'Tidy?'

77

'No. She hadn't used it. So?'

'Where did she eat?'

He nodded.

'Right. Get that picture round to all the restaurants that were open for Sunday lunch. Start with the obvious ones. Where did she eat? When did she eat? Who with? Check her credit card companies. Find out if anything shows up on her bills.'

She'd made a mental note. Started to go. He waved a hand. Still looking at the pavement.

'Tell me, who's talking to the kid?'

'Her son?'

'Mm.'

'Nick was, I think.'

Somers-Barclay would be good. Would feel at home. Be good with the headmaster. Good with the matron. Good with the lad.

'Nothing in your report this morning.'

She hadn't thought of it. Hadn't known about it.

'Remember, sir, until you mentioned you heard her talking on the train, we didn't know too much about her. Certainly nothing about her son.'

He started to go. Stopped again.

'Got it. Those keys.'

She held up the clear polythene bag. Tried to look solemn. But when he was in his stooping, swaying and muttering mood, she found it difficult.

'All present and correct, sir.'

'We sure? No car keys. She didn't have any with her. So where are they? Even if we couldn't find her regular set, chances are she'd keep a spare on the hook. Yes?'

Jack nodded. Then stopped.

'If she had a car.'

'Surely.'

'You haven't.'

Leonard thought about it. Shrugged. Looked up and down the street. Plenty of cars. None with parking fines.

# Ten

The Screaming Skull was in a bad mood. He'd been promised a good bit of beef at a National Farmers Union lunch in Cardiff. Instead, here he was in Bath with an indifferent mug of tea. He'd been messed around by a consultant who for some reason thought he knew better and an administrator whom no one appeared to know, but who was already on the defensive. By the time Leonard arrived, Griffith was slurping his second mug.

'Stoat's piss.'

He threw the rest in the sink.

'If you don't make it, isn't it always?'

Griffith rubbed at his bare skull. The yellowed skin taut across the high cheek bones, and the top lip drawn back to the makings of a snarl. It was his version of a grin.

'Best tea's in the best hotels. That's a fact. Take it from me.'

He was a pathologist. Had to be true. Leonard looked around the room. The attendant whose name he could never remember was squeaking in his white rubber apron and white boots. A long slab. Scrubbed and sluiced down. Next one please. Sally Keemer had been drawered up some time ago. Leonard wondered in which one. He wanted to see her. Officially he should. But this time he wanted to. He rubbed at his spectacles. Squinted at Griffith.

'Anything special?'

'Plenty.'

'Go on.'

'Four bullet wounds . . .'

'Four?'

The Screaming Skull stared hard at Leonard. It was the shafting, piercing stare that had unnerved many a student, many an attendant, many a police officer. Only his customers stared back.

'One, two, three, four. If it had been three, I imagine I would have remembered to say so. If it had been five, I would have thought to tell you. Yes, Inspector, four.'

'I was told one.'

'Are you suggesting I cannot count, or perhaps I don't recognize a bullet wound from a nostril?'

Leonard grinned at him. Partly because he liked Griffith and regarded much of his sarcasm as a game. Partly because he knew that it annoyed the other man.

'Go on.'

'Thank you.'

Leonard shrugged and glanced at the trolley being prepared at the far end of the room. He could see the small, stainless steel electric saw. Stainless steel. Made it different. Made it surgical. We weren't much when we were done. He returned to Griffith. There was the typed report. Came much faster these days. Good summaries from Griffith. Everything was good from him. He was flipping through his notes. Waiting. It wasn't a game. But they played one.

'Tell me. Please.'

Griffith didn't look up. Sub-edited as he went along.

'Wound one. Behind right ear.'

'Which is the one we thought was the only one.'

The Skull paused. Stared. Said nothing. Waited. Leonard waved a hand. The Skull sighed his do not interrupt sigh.

'Behind the right ear.'

'How close?'

'Blackening and propellant tattooing.'

'Close. What happened to it?'

'Wound track.'

'Sorry. Wound track.'

'Struck right ramus of the mandible and then into the right maxilla. I found it in the nasal cavity.'

80

'That it?'

'What were you hoping for, a scouring of the maxillary sinus and a man-sized tissue commercial?'

'What about the second bullet?'

'Was it?'

'Was it what?'

'The second one?'

Leonard waited. Spoke slowly. Softly.

'You tell me.'

'I'll tell you about what I've called wound two. Nothing more.'

It was Leonard's turn to sigh. But he believed he had the picture. First shot from behind. Now what?

'Bullet wound below left eye and left side of nose.'

'Close?'

'Punctuate abrasions. Bullet track through nasal cavity. Damage to lower left nasal bone, zygomatic arch . . .'

'Zygomatic . . .'

'Look it up. Muscle just below the arch. That's where the bullet was.'

Leonard was now getting a picture. But he needed the third piece of the pathologist's jigsaw.

'And bullet number three?'

'Lower.'

'Lower where?'

Griffith flipped over a page.

'I'm about to tell you.'

He looked up. Maybe expecting Leonard to apologize? No. Just looked up. Leonard wondered if this act wasn't some defence mechanism. Decided the Skull was simply a frustrated actor. Liked being a caricature of the cantankerous Home Office examiner. Maybe he was like it for real.

'Bullet wound three. Right shoulder.'

'Why'd the hospital miss it?'

'Pillocks.'

'That a medical opinion?'

'I'm sure I could find a scrap of Latin to cover it if that'd make you feel better.'

'No. Just wondered.'

'They didn't find it because they weren't looking for it.'

'Bullets make holes. Pretty obvious, I'd have thought.'

'Bart's? Guy's? Thomas's? For a moment I seem to have forgotten exactly where you did your postgrad. It is Doctor Leonard, isn't it?'

'Okay, okay, let's get on with it.'

'Mostly there's a hole. But not this time. The bullet entered at the cartilage over the upper arm bone, right in the neck and head point. Now, what normally happens is that the cartilage tears. But this time it didn't. It went back together and covered the entrance.'

'It must have been a very small bullet.'

Griffith got up. Stretched to the ceiling. Leaned forward slowly. Touched his toes. Then up again. Hands behind neck. Gentle massage.

'I was waiting for you to ask. Very small. Point two two round. Three of them.'

He stretched again. As if finished. Leonard knew he hadn't. Prompted him.

'Number four?'

Griffith went back to his notes.

'Oh yes. Very interesting indeed. Track goes in just below here . . .'

Holding his notes away from him like some actor at a first read-through, Griffith stabbed with a long, almost jagged, finger at his collar bone.

'. . . And then tracks to here . . .'

This time the finger was below the collar bone, by the first rib. He dropped his notes on to the stainless steel trolley at his side.

'Quite a journey. Upper lobe of right lung. Sixth thoracic vertebra. Back into the lung. And that, Inspector was that.'

'No other wounds? Cuts, bruises, struggles?'

Griffith's head snapped round. Black eyes unblinking. Unforgiving. Griffith was not a cynic. Was not a fatalist. To him the body had figured enough ways of dying without outside help.

'No, Inspector. No. That was quite enough.'

Leonard shut his mental notebook. Slid off the high stool. He needed to get back to Manvers Street. He'd got the picture he wanted. The first shot in the head. Behind the right ear. Second shot in the cheek, below the eye. So instead of being knocked forward with the first shot, she turned. Second shot in the face. She would have seen her killer. Third shot in the shoulder. Now back against the box. Fourth as she started to fall.

'I'd better have a look.'

'Had you?'

'I saw her on the London train on Saturday night.'

Griffith waved a finger at the attendant. He knew. The routine was the same.

'You mean you knew her?'

Leonard shook his head. Perhaps too vehemently. Wished he had?

'Just another passenger. There was a bit of a commotion. One of her bags had been stolen. Nothing important. Or so it seemed at the time.'

'And now?'

Leonard turned and looked, slightly up, to the tall, lean pathologist. They'd stopped playing the game they both needed on occasions like this one.

'Up to me to find out.'

The attendant was opening a side-swinging panel. Griffith hadn't finished.

'One thing you won't see.'

His voice was soft. Just a trace, the barest trace of the Merthyr. Somewhere. Long, long, long time ago.

'She was pregnant.'

# Eleven

It was late when Leonard got back. The Incident Room was filling up. He wanted to talk to Sergeant Jack. She wasn't there. Nor was Somers-Barclay. And no, he hadn't gone to the school. He'd gone to the hospital. Detective Sergeant Nicholas Somers-Barclay, bob-sleigher, police ski champion of something or other, probably the fastest man on ice as far as Leonard knew, had slipped down the just cleaned and very shiny back stairway. Nothing serious. Leg maybe broken. He'd landed, much to the delight of half the station, rather heavily. There was already a cartoon of him on the state board in the Incident Room. Somers-Barclay going one way, his monogrammed coffee machine the other and a prize for the best caption.

Leonard stood in front of the team. He didn't like standing in front. Didn't like briefing. What he didn't know was that most of them liked him doing it. Quiet. Succinct. Answers short, to the point, clear. He rubbed at his spectacles. Put the green silk handkerchief back in his jacket pocket. Squinted at them, although he could see them perfectly. The incomers, the officers from headquarters, wondered what they were in for. A couple knew and waited quietly.

'Some thoughts for you all. Sally Keemer was shot four times with a point two two. Low-velocity. May not have been a handgun, but probably was. The following is a scenario, my scenario. Okay?'

Heads nodded. They'd learned that Inspector Leonard demanded responses. Didn't like dummies. When he was firing like this, even his speech pattern changed. Faster. Precise. To some it was unnerving. Others reacted with their own change of pace. Which was what he wanted. Leonard's reputation among his few supporters was that he got others thinking. Most said he didn't think like a policeman. Another planet. Whatever they thought, they now listened.

'Okay. She's in the phone box. We think phoning. The receiver was hanging when she was found. But it could have been knocked off. So in phone box, making call, probably, therefore, facing away from door. Go look at the box and you'll see why. Door opens, she starts to turn, gun at back of head, behind right ear. First shot. She turns, is turned, or spins. Doesn't matter. Second shot is to face. Under eye, by nose. Force would have knocked back head. Probably starting to fall. Third shot in shoulder, up here.'

He jabbed at the top of his arm. All eyes watched his finger just as he had watched Griffith's.

'Fourth shot beneath collar bone. Here.'

Another finger. Another twitch of the eyes.

'By this time she's going down quickly, but it seems from how she was found, and remember she was still alive then, she tried to get out of the box.'

'Trying to go after him?'

Leonard stared at the constable.

'Him?'

The young man realized his mistake.

'Sorry, sir.'

'We don't know why she was outside. Simple instincts. Get out. Get away. Get help.'

'Why not phone, sir?'

The voice at the back was big, confident, Somerset. Leonard didn't answer at first. Thought about it.

'Good point. That could explain the phone. Get on to it. Check the emergency service. Dud calls. Someone calling and then not speaking. Hoax. Okay?'

'Sir.'

'Right. Now here's something for everyone. We think Sally Keemer had another home. We don't know for sure. Just think. May not be in the district. Maybe not even in the area. So we need to find out. First thing, someone check the telephone books. No reason to think she's ex-directory. Her Brock Street flat isn't. If there's nothing then someone start putting together a list of all local authorities and telephone numbers. Make it a darts board list. Bath's the bull, then start working out.'

'What we looking for, sir?'

It was a daft question from the new constable. Leonard didn't mind. Someone had to ask it on behalf of the ones who weren't smart enough to ask.

'Good question. Council Tax. Sally Keemer appears to have been the law-abiding type. If she's got another home, she'll pay Council Tax. So start looking. And don't forget, it could be in Scotland.'

That brought a groan. It was meant to. Leonard raised a finger.

'We're already asking the people she worked with. It may be that the answer's on a postcard already. But be prepared. DS Jack will tell you soon as she's back.'

'She's gone over to Clifton, sir. There's a message for you.'

Leonard looked blank. The duty sergeant helped out.

'The school? When Nick S-B did a wheely on the stairs, she said she'd go.'

Lots of laughs from that one.

'Fine. Now, before your questions. I need to know. Anything on the other passengers?'

Ray Lane had just come in. He'd heard the end of the briefing. He was shaking his head.

'I've just been talking to the senior conductor. Man called Sidney Walker. He gives a reasonable account of what happened. But . . .'

He looked at Leonard and spread his arms.

'. . . He's not too good. I think he's worried that he's involved. You know? Good at tickets and announcements, but this is all a bit too close to retirement?'

Leonard nodded.

'I'll have a word with him. Maybe be able to prompt him. But no other passengers?'

Lane shook his head.

'Nothing, I'm afraid. But there was a good piece in the *Chronicle* about us looking for passengers on that train and we can get the local radio people to follow it up in the morning. It'll only take one of us to volunteer to give them a two-way and they'll have us on.'

Leonard tried to remember the other people. He couldn't imagine any of them being likely to listen to the local radio station. But someone else on the train, someone he hadn't seen. Someone might have seen something. If they'd seen her, they'd not have forgotten. He'd need Jack on the Bennett Show, or whatever Radio Bristol called it. Maybe get something on with the morning man. Turner. John Turner? That was it. Big audience. Kids away to school. Husband off to work. It was a long shot. But why just that train?

'Get someone to check the Saturday morning trains. The eight-whatever-it-is. See if anyone remembers her. Who was she with? Where did she sit? Must have been first class. Get the booking office to check first class tickets.'

He remembered his own.

'Wait a minute. Second or standard or whatever it is they call them, and those supplement tickets that uprate to first. She probably had one . . . of . . . those . . .'

Leonard was gazing across the room at his first question. His only question that Saturday night as he cycled away from the station. Sally Keemer had said that she'd bought a ticket at Paddington. Why did Sally Keemer need a ticket? She had, presumably, bought a return in the morning. Cheaper that way. Weekend bargain. So why the second ticket? Extra ticket for Bristol?

'And check with Paddington. See if anyone remembers selling her one through to Bristol just before half six on Saturday evening. And we think she had a boyfriend. Tall, dark, suntan, thirties, gold bracelet, pony-tail. See if anyone remembers him.'

He turned to look at the state board. The ten-by-eight picture had been rephotographed and enlarged. It was a good job. She was very beautiful. Could even have been a film star.

'Try the Paddington taxi rank. They must have arrived together. Hard to forget them.'

There was a lot to do. He started to move away. It was Ray Lane's voice, gravelly from too many cigarettes. Tired from too much weight, stress and thinking about the future and if there was one.

'Just try one on everyone?'

Leonard paused. Nodded. He needed Lane. Needed his simple good approach to policework.

'It's hardly an original thought, but what was this woman doing in a telephone box, when she lived not more than two hundred yards away?'

Leonard was disappointed. Selsey had beaten Lane to it. But Lane hadn't finished.

'I'll offer you a couple of ideas. One: impulse. She was a business woman. A go-getter. Wants to do something. Does it. Doesn't wait. So she has an idea, needs to make a call, sees the box, can't wait until she gets home. Right?'

There were plenty of nods for that possibility. The young constable was about to interrupt. To give everyone the benefit of his thinking. But the intake of Lane's breath told him now was not the time. Lane was off again.

'Two: she was calling home. Someone was there, or she thought there was, and she was checking. Let's remember how she was dressed. Linen jacket, T-shirt and cotton trousers. Trainers. Relaxed. Sunday relaxed. Not partying. Not dining. So far, we've got no sightings. Odd for someone that good-looking and for someone who knew a lot of people. So maybe she hadn't been out for long. Maybe she was on her way somewhere, which would explain why no one had seen her. She hadn't been anywhere. None of the regular restaurants remember her that lunchtime. Maybe she was ringing home because she'd forgotten something. Forgotten to tell someone something.'

He paused. He wanted a cigarette. But not in here. Not these days. It allowed the new constable to get in.

'Make a point, sir?'

Lane peered at him as if noticing him for the first time. Nodded.

'Well, sir. She was, a go-getter, I think you said, sir?'

Nodded again.

'Well, sir. Why did she need a telephone box? Her type never goes anywhere without a mobile.'

Leonard thought about it. Good thinking. He hadn't seen a mobile phone in the flat. And he hadn't seen a charger. Every mobile phone has a battery charger. Maybe in the office. Surely not. She'd have two. So where was it? Where was the phone?

'Good. Check her office. Find out who she used. Must know. She'd have done it on the company. Get a print of every call she's made in the past six months. Her office will have them up until the latest bill. They itemize every account. And double check if her battery charger was at home or the office.'

Most of them looked up. Including Ray Lane. Battery charger? Where did that one come from? That was typical of DI Leonard. Came out with something. No explanation. The dim ones moaned, the bright ones worked it out for themselves. He turned to Lane.

'Anything else, Ray?'

'Mm. This thing about itemized calls. Her home phone would be itemized as well. Maybe she was using the box because she didn't want the call traced.'

Leonard waited for the mutterings and chat to die down.

'Okay, I've another one for you. Maybe she wasn't making a call at all. Maybe she was receiving one. Prearranged. Now we've got a lot of maybe questions. None of them is getting us anywhere quickly. But think them through, they raise questions we can answer.'

Leonard started ticking off his fingers.

'Second address? Telephone accounts? Uptrain tickets? Downtrain tickets? Taxis? Boyfriend? Passengers? The task is to find out what Sally Keemer did, who she saw, who saw her between the train leaving Bath Spa on Saturday night at nine-fifteen and when she was killed at some time around eleven on Sunday night. The only thing we know for certain is that she went to Bristol to see her son in boarding school. Not necessarily the college. But at Clifton. Okay?'

He paused. No more questions. And then the door opened. It had been a long day, but Sergeant Jack looked as fresh as if it had just started. But it was her face. It was bursting, not with good health, but with something to say. Leonard waved a hand.

'And here's our starter. Well? How's the son?'

Madelaine Jack walked to the front of the room. Took a deep breath. The new constable tried to look away. Couldn't.

'That's just it, sir. I've just come back from the school. There isn't one. Sally Keemer didn't have a son at the school. Never has had.'

# Twelve

Nash was in the corridor. The Force Solicitor was talking to him. Talking at him? Her language was precise. Predictable. What she had to say he'd heard before. All in her letter that morning. She was one of those people who concentrated on his lips, not his eyes, when she spoke. Didn't really matter. Nash had only half an ear on what she had to say. There was something bigger going on. Not his part of ship. But he wasn't going to stay in his cabin. He had the feeling that had been there for more than a quarter of a century in the job. Expectation. Expectancy. Not excitement. But close. Strictly, he should confine himself to District Commander things. That was Nash. Strategy. No manpower charts on his walls. Trophies, cartoons, a too small map of the enlarged patch. Think policy. Think community policing. Think about the future. Not the past. Murder was about the past. Who a person had been. What a person had been. Nash talked about the Three Ls. Loves, Lies and Larceny. You could usually find a reason in the Three Ls. But it was up to the Leonards, Lanes and Marshes of this world to find out why someone had departed it.

Superintendent Marsh had called. Courtesy call. It was his investigation. He'd be over in a couple of hours, then maybe disappear. Could Leonard be trusted? Nash had not been at Bath during the last time Marsh had come across Leonard. A difficult time, Marsh had said. Nash could understand why. Marsh was tall, humourless, as spare as an abbot. Immaculately tailored, white cuff and gold cuff-links, glistening, black, slim, toe-capped shoes. Leonard was tall, yet didn't look it. Languid as a well-published poet. Had a tailor. A tailor whose cutter cut with wit. Marsh cleansed of emotion. Leonard confused by his own. A good team. Should have been. If let be. Murder doesn't let any but onlookers be. Marsh understood method, principle, formula. Leonard understood very little. So always asked. Nash held the ring. Now he watched Leonard. Leaning against the wall. Hands in pockets. Red striped shirt softer than Marsh's starched cotton. One heel out, the other cocked against the skirting board. He was listening as Detective Sergeant Jack talked. Head down. Nodding. Biting at his lower lip.

'It doesn't make sense. Why would she say she was going to see him, then stay on the train if she wasn't? She didn't need to make an alibi with complete strangers. Get someone on to every prep school, every boarding school in the Bristol area. It's hardly Smith or Jones, is it? There can't be many Keemers at any school.'

'If any.'

'That's what you think?'

'Possible.'

'What about her office? Asked them?'

91

Madelaine Jack shook her head.

'I will. Haven't had a chance. I'm about to call them again. It's been on answerphone since I got back. Could be our Cynthia has thrown a wobbler at last.'

Leonard looked up. Something he'd forgotten about.

'Conference?'

She flipped open her mini notebook.

'At the Wholmes. Registration this afternoon. Conference proper, nine in the morning.'

'Don't they start with a welcome reception? Maybe tonight. She could be there.'

Jack flipped back a page.

'Seven-thirty this evening, then what they call a casual buffet. You can bet the new leaderine will be there. I didn't get the impression she was in mourning.'

'Jane Boxer?'

'About as much charity as a sparrow hawk.'

He eyed her for a moment. Peering into her face. Remembered the way Jane Boxer had mocked her. What was it the woman had said? Something about being attractive? Lots of friends? No one special? Too personal?

'You thought that, did you?'

'Didn't you, sir?'

He wasn't sure. There was something about Jane Boxer. Sharp. Humorous? But too sharp? Too humorous? Brave?

'Abrasive.'

'Yes, sir.'

'More than that?'

'Yes, sir.'

'Enough to kill?'

Madelaine Jack looked at the ceiling, puffed out her cheeks and blew a triplet of air above her head.

'Too much self-control. Anyway, why bother? She'd just become a partner.'

'We think.'

'But Sally went in Saturday morning. Dragged poor old Cynthia in to type the letters. Big announcement.'

'How do we know that?'

'Cynthia said so. Anyway, it would be easy to get a copy of the letter. We can check the computer. We can check with someone who got the letter. See when it arrived. But Cynthia seemed pretty certain.'

'And if she were lying?'

'Why would she? She certainly can't stand Jane Boxer. Look at the way Boxer treated her. In front of us.'

'Doesn't mean she wouldn't go along with a lie. Plenty of cases where an alibi has hated the suspect. But what happens when the alibi has something to hide?'

'Blackmail? I'm sorry, sir, I can't see what's to be gained.'

'Talking of secrets . . .'

'We are?'

'Blackmail. She was pregnant.'

'Oh my God.'

'Someone's.'

'So who was the boyfriend?'

'More precise than that. Who was the father?'

'Would she have known?'

He looked up. Quickly. What was Jack suggesting?

'Presumably she'd have had to have been sleeping around at a fair rate not to know.'

She shook her head.

'No, didn't mean that, sir. I meant would she have known that she was pregnant? At what stage was it? She'd know if she missed. But would she know for sure?'

'Don't women know these things?'

'So I'm told.'

'I didn't mean . . .'

'But we don't know that she did. There have been cases with women going through stress, missing, or hardly showing, and not realizing that they were. Just a thought.'

He hadn't thought to ask Griffith. Mistake. Bad mistake. Obvious mistake. He was cross. Griffith would have noticed. He'd be awaiting his call. With relish.

'Not sure. When you get a moment, call the Screaming Skull, will you? Find out.'

'What's the legal position, I wonder?'

He might have answered. Then again, it wouldn't have been much use. He hadn't thought it through. He was saved by Nash, who pleaded Leonard's attention to escape from the solicitor. Leonard didn't mind Nash straying. Now he'd said yes three times to the Force Solicitor who was now off to bend another ear.

'James? Superintendent Marsh will be over in a couple of hours. Have something ready for him, will you?'

If Somers-Barclay had been fitter, there'd have been trays of coffee from the front door to the MIR. Nash was there.

'That reminds me. How's Nick?'

'He'll live.'

'Well you can't win them all.'

He laughed. Regretting his joke in front of Jack.

'Keep me in touch, won't you?'

Jack looked very innocent.

'What do we do about the claim form, sir?'

Nash had been heading back to his office. Stopped. Turned. Slight frown? Apprehension.

'Claim form?'

Still innocent. Now the sweet smile.

'Yes, sir. Saw you talking to the solicitor. I assumed it was for DS Somers-Barclay's claim. You know, sir. Industrial compensation?'

Superintendent Nash, District Commander, twenty-seven years in the job, nearly fell for it. Nearly.

'Compensation? I expect an apology from DS Somers-Barclay. Frightened the coroner's officer into thinking he was about to collect a couple of hours overtime.'

A half-smile. Then gone. Quickly. As he swung in his new

94

executive chair, he thought about the leg-pulling he'd nearly fallen for. Leg-pulling. He picked up the phone and dialled the Community Relations Office.

'Roy? Is the legal beagle still with you? Ask her to drop by before she leaves, will you?'

Outside, Leonard was still leaning against the wall. He was humming. An atonal sound that came from the back of his throat and almost never got through his closed lips. But it was there. A musical buzz. He straightened up and took Madelaine Jack by the elbow and started walking back towards his room.

'That's a very good point. Nearly missed it. Nice one.'

She looked perplexed. She was.

'It was?'

He was nodding his head. Rapidly. Bouncing nodding.

'Sure.'

'Well, as my aunt Susie from Arkansas says, "I'm afraid that just got by me." Would you please explain, sir?'

Leonard stopped by the door.

'Compensation.'

'Nick? I was only joking. I was . . .'

'No. Sally Keemer. Compensation for her death.'

'You mean insurance.'

He smiled. Blinking behind round steel-rimmed lenses.

'I mean exactly that. Get someone to go through the office accounts. See what personal insurance she carried. Bound to have something. Personal liability. Car insurance. Anything. We want her insurance broker. Anything we can find.'

'Someone would insure her, or be a beneficiary?'

'Could be. Won't know unless we ask, will we? Seek and ye shall find, as Superintendent Marsh will tell us.'

He was about to say something else. Stopped. Dawning in his eyes. Walked into the office and picked up his jacket. Distracted. Buzzing again.

'Sir?'

He stopped in the doorway.

'Mm?'

'Should I know where you're going?'

'The reception. Most obvious place to start looking for her, isn't it?'

'Jane Boxer?'

He blinked. Already elsewhere in his mind.

'Who?'

'Jane Boxer. You're looking for her?'

He started for the stairs. Head shaking

'Not her.'

'Who we looking for, sir?'

Leonard turned at the stairs door. To him it was obvious. His expression said so.

'Sally Keemer.'

# Thirteen

Leonard stood just inside the door, listening to a Bulgarian talking about networking. She was tall, thin, with the complexion of a day-old cadaver, thick accent and much throat clearing. He wasn't listening to what she said. Key words. That was networking.

'Co-operation . . . development agencies . . . principal negotiators . . . joint accounts . . .'

He didn't care. She didn't notice. She went on until she found the perfect diversion. They'd wandered towards a group. It spoke a different language. American. Like many East Europeans on the new business conference circuit, the woman's commercial sense was caught between the big European market and the instinct that might is right. In her case there was nothing as mighty as the dollar. She made no excuses. Simply abandoned Leonard and announced herself to the surprised but courteous group. The man nearest Leonard looked as if he'd heard it before. Looked embarrassed. He was smoking a cigar.

Quite a big one. That surprised Leonard. Nowadays, he thought, health-conscious Americans only did that in films. The man turned and stuck out a hand.

'Ed Firmani, how are you today?'

Leonard was about the same as he was every day. He tried to look as jolly as Mr Firmani. Perhaps he should learn to hold a cigar between thumb and fingers and smile like George Burns. Mr Firmani could and he looked very successful on it.

'James Leonard, how do you do.'

'Just great, James. Great. Now, you gotta be English. Right?'

Leonard searched for his now-how-did-you-know expression.

'Right. And you, Mr Firmani—'

'Please, Ed, call me Ed.'

Mr Firmani fished for a business card in the breast pocket of his Brooks Bros suit. Take any card. Take this one.

'PanAmerican IT. We tell you what you need to know. Keep you ahead of the game. Okay?'

'Very impressive.'

'And we're getting bigger, James, much bigger. And you know something, James? In this business size sure is everything.'

He punched Leonard on the biceps. Gave a laugh that would have scared a child. Drank rather than sipped his champagne. He looked around the room. The eyes flicking from face to face, group to group. Sizing. Weighing, Noting. The room was filling. Perhaps a hundred, perhaps more. Mostly thirty-some-thing upwards. Mostly well manicured from head to toe. Young vice-presidents of big corporations. Young sales directors of medium companies. Young going on fifty-five. The room was full of money and people who made deals with it. Mr Firmani did another quick sweep and, as he spoke, was looking over Leonard's shoulder at a new group that had just come through the door. In this business, whatever this business was, no one, but no one, stood with his or her back to the door. In the old days it could be life or death. In these days, it could mean an extra zero on a contract.

'What about you, James? What's your line of country?'

'I'm a policeman.'

The eyes homed in. The glass went up again. Perhaps a little too soon. The party-goer's alternative to a mock sneeze into a spotted handkerchief. But the eyes had said enough. This was, said the sign outside, IT-97. Information Technology didn't stretch to talking to policemen, not even partying policemen. Then the shadow went by. There was, in IT, always an explanation.

'I got you. International exchange, mm? It's everywhere. I tell you, James, you people have gotta get organized. They are. They do big laundry deals, you hearing me? Big laundry deals, right in front of our Goddamn eyes. They move more money in one day than some of the big boys on Wall Street.'

He parked his smouldering cigar between clenched teeth. Pulled the conference programme from another inside pocket. As he spoke, the cigar waddled to the side of his mouth.

'What catches your mind on this schedule then, James.'

When Leonard didn't answer, he looked up.

'I think, Mr Firmani—'

'—Ed—'

'I think, Ed, we'd better keep it to Mr Firmani. I'm not here as part of your conference.'

Ed Firmani slowly folded the conference leaflet. Put it away. He nodded his head very slowly. He took out the cigar. Looked at its now dead end. His lips formed an oval any chorister would have envied.

'Oh. You, you with the police department here?'

'That's right. Detective Inspector Leonard, CID. I'm investigating the death of Sally Keemer.'

Mr Firmani looked into his now empty glass with the solemnity of a mourner. Ash flicked as he fiddled with his tie. In the circumstances embarrassed by its garish mock college stripes.

'I heard. Real sorry. You got anything on this yet?'

'We are, as we inevitably say on these occasions, pursuing a number of lines of inquiry.'

Mr Firmani reached for passing champagne and put his empty glass on the waitress's shoulder-high tray. He took a deep breath. Somewhere between a sigh and sniff, nipping his nostrils in and then bulging them as he exhaled.

'Nice lady. I really was very sorry to hear about it. I want to share that with you, James. Really a nice lady.'

'You obviously knew her well.'

Mr Firmani had dumped the salesman. Now he was downtown Ed Firmani, just a block or two away from Gramercy Park. Not his home district. But home it was.

'We'd met a few times.'

'When did you arrive in Bath?'

'Saturday. Why?'

'When did you arrive in England?'

'Like Saturday. I came straight here from the airport.'

'And did you see Sally Keemer?'

'No.'

'At any time?'

'Okay. Can we get this straight? This official?'

'She's dead. Now officially, Mr Firmani, when was the last time you saw Sally Keemer?'

Mr Firmani sighed. He shrugged. Both shoulders. Both arms. In one hand the cigar. In the other, the glass. More dead ash flicked. The glass wobbled. A little wine spilled. Mr Firmani sucked at the back of his hand. Leonard's gaze made him look away.

'I guess it was on my last trip to Europe.'

'Which was when?'

'That would have been last fall.'

'Not this year?'

'No. Last fall. I was in London for a trade exhibition and conference and, well, she did some work for me.'

'What sort of work?'

99

'Regular work.'

'Mr Firmani, at the risk of appearing abrasive, I must say that for someone who is in the Information Technology business, you have a particularly obtuse way of answering the simplest questions.'

'Well, I guess like that guy Shakespeare said, two nations separated by a common language. Right?'

'Shaw.'

'Right.'

'No, I meant . . . Never mind. Just tell me how she helped.'

'Okay, now let's see here. Um. Well you know what she did?'

'Publicist.'

'She was more than that. She understood the way people reacted. It works like this: I come over to Europe, I need to hit the decks running. Sightseeing is for the day I retire. Okay? Okay, I know the best places in Paris, Bonn, London, Rome, Brussels. I know every shaker. But question, James, question. What is the most important question? I know who they are . . .'

'But do they know who you are?'

'Right. We, I, hired Sally to make Goddamn sure they did.'

'Why did you hire her?'

'Pardon me?'

'As you just said, you go everywhere on the Continent. But you hired a publicist who works out of a not very big office in Bath. Why?'

'Right. Well, I guess her partner? Jane Boxer? She knew our people. And Sally did the watch-over-you thing.'

'But you still haven't said why you hired her.'

'Because, Lieutenant, she was Goddamn good.'

'Okay, I believe you. Let me put it another way. Why did you hire her, or Miss Boxer, or however you want to explain the connection, and not someone else? How did you, in New York, know about Jane Boxer and Sally Keemer here in Bath?'

Mr Firmani never got to explain. A voice from behind

100

caught him in full flight and he fell with all the certainty of a driven partridge.

'Why, Mr Firmani. I see you've met our Mr Leonard.'

She was in black. But Leonard guessed it was not mourning. The perfect little cocktail number. After Six, her mother would have called it. Mr Firmani had seen it before. The smile was dazzling. If the whole package was meant to be distracting, then it succeeded.

'Mr Leonard, fancy seeing you here.'

Leonard fished for a friendly smile and hoped it got as far as his eyes. He had no way of knowing.

'Just passing. A few things on my mind, so I thought I'd drop in. I hope that's okay.'

Firmani seemed nervous. Nervous of what? Leonard? Not really. Being questioned? Just a little. Jane Boxer? Maybe. But why? Embarrassed, Leonard supposed. Simple. A visiting fireman being questioned by a policeman heading a murder inquiry was not what he'd imagined. Imagined. Image. Of course. Sally Keemer had been about image-making. Jane Boxer was about image-making. Making Firmani's image. Firmani was flicking at his cigar with a Zippo. The effect would have rated a footnote at the Rio Conference.

'I was telling the lieutenant just how much we admired Miss Keemer and how sorry everyone is.'

'I'm perfectly sure Mr Leonard understands. But if you don't mind, gentlemen, life must, for the moment anyway, go on. We mustn't let everything stop, even for the Bath police. I need Mr Firmani, if, that is, the arm of the law can spare him?'

There was the merest trace of a sneer in her voice. But nothing he could land on.

'It is, Miss Boxer, a murder inquiry. If you wish, I could ask Mr Firmani to come down to Manvers Street with me.'

Firmani now looked alarmed.

'Hey! Just hold on a minute. What is this?'

'As I said, it's a murder inquiry. You, Mr Firmani, happened to be someone on the client list of the murder victim.'

101

'Is it murder?'

Her voice was challenging.

'We're treating it as murder. It is a precise definition. But I don't think you'll find a lawyer who'd argue against me.'

She backed off. But slightly. Looked at the tiniest of wrist watches. Not the Dunhill this time.

'Inspector, will you do me a big favour? For two months we have been trying to fix an interview with the *Financial Times*. Now that may seem insignificant in the present circumstances. But it isn't. On the other side of the room, I have the person who is going to write an article in the *FT* about Mr Firmani and PanAmerican IT. May I?'

Leonard blinked. Took off his spectacles and rubbed at them with his handkerchief.

'Where can I get hold of you tomorrow?'

Mr Firmani looked relieved.

'I'll be right here through till Friday.'

Leonard shrugged. Looped his spectacles over his ears. Jane Boxer was smiling. A professional smile.

'Thank you, Inspector. Much obliged, your honour. I owe you a drink. Let me deliver Ed to the pink press and I'll see you outside in the bar in two minutes. A deal?'

She didn't wait for an answer. She knew he'd be there. She linked an arm through Mr Firmani's.

It took ten minutes. Leonard wasn't in the bar. He'd found a leather sofa in an alcove away from the foyer. She found him. The waiter followed with an ice-bucket. There was no pop. A discrete *phhht*. She thanked the waiter, gave Leonard a glass and raised her own.

'What shall we drink to?'

'Your partnership?'

'Why not? Sally would.'

She sipped. Leonard put his glass down. If Jane Boxer felt put out, she gave no sign. Leonard wiped his spectacles. Looked into the distance at the glass doors that led to the terrace and the garden beyond. He watched an elderly couple, arm in arm, slowly mounting the steps. A stroll before dinner. He in a finely cut lightweight suit, a Brigade of Guards tie. Hat in hand. She, floral frock fit for a vicarage. They paused to admire the bloom of a late, quite pale, rhododendron. Together. Leonard felt deep envy. Deep loneliness. He turned back to Jane Boxer. She was watching his eyes. She'd seen something. For a moment he wasn't simply a policeman with steel-rimmed spectacles. When she spoke, her voice was softer. Not yet on guard.

'You're allowed to drink. It's not a bribe.'

Leonard looked at the glass. Then at her. He sipped. Then replaced it on the low glass table in front of them.

'Tell me, is this a case of the show must go on, or don't you care?'

If there was a moment, then it was gone.

'I care, Inspector. I care very much. I'm not trying to sell you the line that carrying on as normal is what Sally would have wanted. Frankly I don't know what she'd have wanted.'

'And frankly, my dear . . .?'

'Oh no. Of course I do. I liked her. We'd known each other for half our lives. We were at school together. So yes, frankly, my dear, I do give a damn. Of course I do.'

She waved a slim arm in the direction of the reception.

'But all this isn't going to stop for her, nor for anyone else. The conference is the main event. These people are paying hundreds a day to be here. That's got nothing to do with Sally Keemer Publicity. We're just part of it.'

Leonard looked at his glass. Left it there.

'We need to know what she did between ten past nine on Saturday night and the time she was killed.'

'Why ten past nine?'

'Because that was the time the London train left Bath for Bristol and she was on it. It was late.'

'D'you mind me asking how you know she was on it?'

'Because I was. I saw her.'

Jane Boxer should have been surprised. Should have been amazed. Should have shown it. She tried not to. Why?

'Coincidence?'

'Coincidence.'

Jane Boxer crossed her legs. Leonard reached for his wine.

'Tell me, Miss Boxer . . .'

'You often say that, don't you?'

'What?'

'Tell me.'

'Then do.'

She leaned forward. The soft laugh was almost a warm giggle. She playfully patted him on the knee. The colonel and his lady had finished admiring the garden. He held the door for her and they smiled, quietly, at the two young people on the sofa. The colonel thought her legs rather fine. The colonel's lady thought them a lovely couple and wondered if they might see them at a dinner.

'Stop growling. It was only an observation. Nothing special.'

Leonard tried not to like her. Murder was something to growl about.

'Did you see, speak, or hear from her, or hear about her, from Saturday evening until the time she was killed?'

Jane Boxer's smile slipped away. The sigh was a punctuation mark in her mood.

'I'm sorry. I, well, I get on something of a high on these occasions. Working like this, I mean. There's a lot of adrenaline. The interview with the *FT*, if it appears, will keep Mr Firmani on our books for another twelve months.'

'You haven't answered.'

She finished her champagne and poured more. Topped his hardly touched glass.

'The answer is no, no, no and no. I didn't see, speak, hear from or about Sally. We talked Friday, as I've already told you. The arrangement for the partnership was tied up and that was that.'

'Were you due to?'

'No. We didn't see much of each other socially.'

'Bath isn't that big.'

'Okay, what I meant was that we didn't arrange to see each other. We weren't that close. We have a few mutual friends, but that's chance not design.'

'And yet you're partners.'

'Do you see your Sergeant socially?'

He didn't answer. She carried on.

'Anyway, we didn't need to talk until today. The whole thing was fixed. Apart from putting in an appearance, there wasn't a great deal for Sally to do this week. She was actually working on something quite different. Ed Firmani was my client, or rather his company is. I'd fixed the interview. Got a couple of lunches with blue chips arranged for him, plus a warm and wonderful day in London, and that was that.'

She sat back. Looked at her watch.

'I should be getting back.'

'This won't take long. Did you know Sally Keemer's ex-husband?'

'Sammy? Sure. Everyone knew Sammy. He was a regular bastard. Played around. Got caught. Cried never again. Played around some more. You know? Straightforward man.'

'Did they keep in touch?'

'I don't know. She never mentioned him.'

'Tell me . . .'

He paused. She smiled. Licked her finger and ticked off one to herself in the air.

'Tell me, did they, did she, have any children?'

This time the surprise was genuine. Open. The mouth almost dropped. Almost.

'Good God, no. Well, not that I know of. You think she did?'

'Why do you say that?'

'Come on, Inspector. You wouldn't have asked unless you thought she had. You tell me.'

He sipped some more. This time held it.

'On Saturday night, she told other people on the train that she was going on to Bristol to see her son at Clifton. As far as

105

we know, she had no son at Clifton. Now why would she say a thing like that?'

Jane Boxer looked at him for some time as if weighing up what she was about to tell him. She bit at her bottom lip. He wondered how much this was for his benefit and how much for hers.

'Sally and I have known each other since the sixth form. We, well we knew each other well enough. Okay?'

He nodded.

'Sally had fantasies. She had ideas, which by the next day she believed were true. Sally was quite capable of saying that she had a son, simply on the spur of the moment, and then within seconds inventing a whole school career for him.'

'Why?'

'Why does anyone have fantasies? Don't you have them? Something to do with what you really want, or what you think you want, isn't it? Insecurities? Wanting to belong?'

He wondered about the Screaming Skull's final shot. He wondered who the father might be.

'But she wouldn't go so far as staying on the train to Bristol?'

'Having said it, she would play it through. She could hardly get off and say she'd changed her mind.'

'Maybe she was meeting someone in Bristol.'

'It was only . . . what time did you say?'

'About ten past nine.'

'Not exactly time to be tucked up in bed on a Saturday night. Or, well, maybe it was.'

'She had a boyfriend in Bristol?'

Jane Boxer fidgeted.

'I honestly don't know. I don't believe she *did* have a boyfriend, not what you'd call a boyfriend. Someone special.'

'That's what you were suggesting.'

'Look, Mr Leonard, Sally had a lot of friends. You saw her.'

'Very beautiful.'

'Right. So she wasn't the type to sit at home knitting bed-jackets.'

106

'I need to know who her boyfriends were.'

'A lot of them won't like that.'

'Why?'

'Let's put it this way, a lot of their wives won't like you banging on the door asking questions.'

'Anyone in particular?'

'She was too smart for that.'

Leonard thought again of the lifeless form in the tray. Not that smart.

'She was with a man in London. Tall. Thirties, maybe forties. Dark. Lots of gold. Pigtail. Know him?'

'You asked before. The answer's still no.'

She stood. Ran long fingers down the short skirt. Leonard found himself half-trapped by the coffee table. Very close. She smiled. He could smell her scent.

'Now, I'm sorry, Inspector. I'm a working girl. Gotta go. Gotta do it.'

'Just one more thing. Did Sally Keemer have another house? An apartment anywhere?'

'There's a cottage somewhere on Exmoor.'

'You don't know where?'

She smiled. Leaned closer and tugged playfully at his spotted tie.

'You really don't listen, do you? We kept apart. Strictly business. Now I must go. Here . . .'

She took an ivory card from her small, flat, silk bag. Instead of handing it to him, she popped into his top pocket.

'I already have one.'

'No, you don't. That's got my home number on it.'

Her finger was still in his top pocket. Her eyes mocking his. He tried again.

'I need that address.'

'Ask her maiden aunt. She knows everything. Believe about ten per cent she says and you may learn something.'

'Her aunt? Where do I find her?'

She stepped back, gave a mock sigh and shook her head.

107

'My, Inspector, we are not very sleuthy, are we? You've already found her. The foul Cynthia, that's who.'

'Her aunt?'

'Right. Why on earth do you think she employed her? In the days we could afford peanuts we got the monkey.'

She tugged at the tie again.

'Nice tie. Bye now.'

She glided away down the long carpeted corridor. Knowing he was watching her go. He did. He waited for a couple of minutes, emptied his glass. Thought business must be good for her to leave most of a bottle for the waiter. He was tired. It had been a long day. He pulled out his pocket watch. The ivory card came with it. An address among the tall elegant houses and flats of Widcombe. He wondered why she'd given it to him. He stretched and went through the door on to the terrace and headed for the drive. From the first floor window, Mr Firmani watched him go until Leonard disappeared beyond the shrubbery. Then he turned away from the window and back into the room.

'You sure this guy's got nothing?'

Jane Boxer took his hand.

'Nothing to worry about. You have my word.'

# TUESDAY

## *Fourteen*

When Leonard arrived at Manvers Street the next morning, Sergeant Jack was already in. She heard him coming. That slightly out of tune humming deep beneath his breath. When Leonard was thinking, he hummed. When he was agitated, the humming became buzzing. He paused at the doorway and looked to where she was sitting sideways on to the entrance. Something struck him. He wasn't quite sure. Then it dawned. He pointed to her hair.

'You've . . .'

Then he remembered. She tugged at her fringe.

'Yes, sir. But not since yesterday.'

She didn't often see him laugh. But just then she did. Curious. He wasn't humourless. She knew that. But for most of the time, he wore the grave Tractarian expression. He plonked himself down at his desk and looked at his paper bag with all the excitement of finding a parcel. He'd been to what he called The Bakers. His bakers. A gingerbread man. It disappeared into his top drawer and she wondered if it would be forgotten until crumbly and stale, like most of them were. He pulled open the bottom drawer, rested his booted foot on it and began tossing the morning's post into the trays in front of him. Without looking up he spoke in the most casual of voices.

109

'Had a session with Jane Boxer last evening.'

'Yes, sir.'

He looked up. Was there something in her voice? Disapproval?

'What?'

'I said yes, sir. She have anything interesting to say?'

'Maybe. Sally Keemer has, or had, a cottage on Exmoor. But she doesn't know where. But she says her aunt does. And guess who the aunt is?'

'Cynthia Rathbone.'

'How do you know that?'

'While you were with Me Jane, I was with She Cynthia. My God she's a mess. Forty a day and she's cut down. Gin on the corn flakes. Vodka and a straw in the hot water bottle in case of night starvation.'

'It's rum.'

'It is?'

'You can smell it. Must be good at her job. Or something.'

'Or something. She said she'd been there from the start. Began without a salary. Took enough for her rent from the first client and has helped herself to whatever the business could stand since then. Strange arrangement.'

'Anything on the cottage?'

'An address. Couple of miles from Simonsbath.'

'Is that Exmoor?'

'About as Exmoor as you can get.'

'She doesn't own a car. Does it have a station?'

'According to the witch she hires one.'

'Same company?'

'She didn't say.'

'Find out and check when she last hired, what it was, how long she had it. The lot.'

He closed his eyes. The cottage in the country. The picture postcard life. Was she the type? She didn't seem it.

'Jane Boxer said she didn't know where it was – the cottage.'

'Lying?'

110

'On such a small thing?'

She looked uncertain. He pulled out the gingerbread man. Broke off an arm. Offered her the other one.

'Get someone to check the phone book, local Council Tax office, CBO. Usual thing. Then we'd better tell someone we're interested. I'd like to go over there before anyone else does.'

'Like Superintendent Marsh?'

Leonard looked up. Blinked. Rapid blinking. Off came the spectacles.

'Where is he? Here?'

She shook her head.

'He was last night. He's back again tomorrow. But Inspector Lane gave him a full . . .'

'. . . And frank . . .?'

'With respect, sir, he's too experienced for that. He gave him a full run down. The whole team will be here by lunchtime.'

Leonard got up, snapped the gingerbread man in two across his belly.

'Head or tail.'

She gave him an old-fashioned look. He gave her the armless trunk.

'Our Cynthia in?'

'Supposed to be.'

'Good. That's where I am.'

He was off down the corridor, then the back stairs. Nibbling at the gingerbread. Nagging at the thought of Marsh's actuarial stare. His appetite for facts. If he saw a discarded gingerbread man, Marsh would probably outline it in chalk and demand to know the name of the last person to see it. Leonard stopped on the bottom step. Marsh was right.

The newspaper office was old-fashioned enough to be a newspaper office. Downstairs the front window was wood-framed. There was still a counter where the public came. News photographs in the window could be bought. Advertisements placed. The narrow staircase up to the editorial offices bore the footprints of reporters and writers who on any day of the week could come face to face with the people they wrote about. The newsroom had none of the atmosphere of Houston Control built into the mighty broadsheet and tabloid headquarters along London's riverbank. True, the Remingtons, Imperials and filthy sets of carbon paper had long gone. In this office, the computer screens were no longer modern technology. Computer screens had been around newspapers for too long to be called modern. But take them out and the office would have comfortably slipped on a green eye-shield. Raincoated bachelors, skilled in shorthand, nursed in council meetings, ever with cigarettes in the corners of their mouths, would have rushed in screaming Hold The Front Page. All of fictional days long past. And so was all this. The wooden door was about to close. Next month, new offices. On the old gas site. There was justice somewhere. But the *Chronicle* was a good paper. Good in any generation. Good on any site. And Leonard needed its help.

He sat in the editor's office. Dover faced him from the old partner's desk in the middle of the room. Big man. One day he'd be stout. But not yet. Not old enough. A banker's striped shirt stretched over a grumbling stomach. It had been a long time since breakfast. The first editorial meeting was at eight. Dover never held a meeting on an empty stomach. He eyed Leonard with suspicion. Liked him, or at least he thought he liked him. But didn't like being used. Exchange of information was no exchange. Leonard wanted something. Not unreason-able. According to Dover's code, everyone wanted something. That was why people did evil, stupid and good things. That's why everything in the whole world happened as it did. All because everyone wanted something. Even those who wanted nothing more than a quiet life were on Dover's chart. You wanted a quiet life, then you let someone else get on with it, or get away with whatever it was you were avoiding. So Leonard was no different. He thanked God for that. Dover was a newspaperman. He liked being a newspaperman. He even liked the word. Newspaperman. Had a proper ring to it. It had the ring of his hero, H. L. Mencken, the sage of Baltimore. Dover walked with Mencken. Always assume the bastard's lying was about right. Dover waited for Leonard to lie.

'You ran a story about looking for people on trains.'

Dover clasped his hands behind his head. Nodded, slightly. 'Any luck?'

'No.'

'Important?'

'Extremely. I can tell you that Sally Keemer was on the train, in the last first class carriage, at ten past nine or so on Saturday night when it pulled out of Bath Spa for Bristol. Everyone who was in her carriage got off here. She went on to Bristol. We have no idea what happened to her.'

As he spoke, Leonard could see her face. Beautiful. The half-smile. Wished he'd smiled. Dover picked up a pencil. Made a note in tiny letters. He'd taught himself years before to take all notes in tiny letters. He wasn't excessively neat. Just made it harder for others to read.

'If no one's contacted you, how come you know everyone else got off the train and she didn't?'

Leonard thought about it. Blinked at the dirty windows across the narrow road.

'Because we have one witness.'

'Who was on the train?'

'Right.'

'So someone has contacted you?'

Leonard shook his head. He didn't want to tell Dover. Didn't want the headline. Top Policeman Travelled with Murdered Girl.

'No. We knew about one other person on that train. That person told us everyone else got out of the compartment and that the girl travelled on.'

'Reliable?'

'I believe him.'

Dover made another note.

'Him?'

113

Leonard nodded. He'd give Dover that much.

'I could do with a quote.'

'For what?'

'Presumably you didn't come to put a classified in. Is there a story?'

He looked at his watch. Then the desk clock. He had time. An hour. Leonard had wondered about it. Thought about it on the way to the newspaper. Six minutes walking wasn't long to think of something which was bound to annoy the Press Office at Headquarters and therefore Marsh and therefore embarrass Nash. Leonard didn't want to do that.

'You could say that police believe that one of the passengers may hold the secret to the last hours of Sally Keemer.'

'One of them could be a suspect?'

Leonard thought of the overweight matron. The sturdy Mac-whatever. His tightly-curled fiancée. He half-smiled.

'No. None is a suspect. Just need their help. One, a woman, perhaps in her fifties, in a blue skirt with many Harrods carrier bags, lives in Bath. The other two were, I, we, think, Scots. He was wearing a kilt and the woman was probably his fiancée. Redhead.'

'And they live?'

'Don't know. But not Bath. Visiting after a wedding or something.'

He shut his eyes. Trying to remember the half-tones of the conversation. Why had he not listened? Because he hadn't wanted to know and because he'd fallen asleep. Which was the same thing. Dover made more notes.

'Can we say how you got the descriptions?'

'A reliable witness?'

'Nothing more?'

'When I can, you'll be the first.'

Dover smiled. Dropped his pencil on the spiral-bound notebook.

'Not much choice, have you, unless you think a free ad in *Trade It* is going to help.'

114

'BBC?'

Dover's eyes narrowed. But only for a moment. This was his city. Not the BBC's.

'Okay.'

Leonard got up. Didn't wait for anything else. No handshake. No promise of a drink sometime. Then Leonard thought of something. He left the door closed. Sat in the nearest of the row of hard chairs against the far wall.

'Tell me. Who do you think Sally Keemer was?'

'Think?'

'Mm.'

'Curious way of asking about her.'

'Tell me what you think.'

'Why should I think anything?'

'Because you know more than most what people in this town—'

'—City—'

'—City think of themselves.'

'It's hardly I Cover The Waterfront stuff.'

'But you know. Who do you think she was?'

Dover's hands were back behind his head. The chair tilted and he gazed at the attic windows on the other side of the street. Close enough to touch. But they weren't. That was Bath. You thought you could touch any bit of it when you wanted, but apart from the inner circle of lunchers and diners, you couldn't. Who did he think, think, Sally Keemer was?

'I met her a few times at receptions. Said hello in restaurants. Saw her occasionally in Shades.'

'For the wine or the people?'

'Half the Bath team drinks there.'

'She was a rugby fan?'

'Saw her a lot at the Rec.'

'Doesn't fit with what we know about her.'

Dover thought about it. Leonard was probably right.

'Fan? Probably not. She knew a lot of people who were. Proper place to be seen and to see. Anyway, it's fun.'

'Because they usually win?'

'Bath's like that.'

'Full of success.'

'Not full. But more than its share. Anyway, she was part of that success. Someone who didn't need London, but took a bite when she wanted.'

'What was she like?'

'Beautiful. Fun. Deep.'

'How deep.'

'I think very deep. For example, I couldn't tell you who her friends were. Now that's either a very lonely person, or someone who's totally self-contained.'

'Or who has another life.'

'Did she?'

'You tell me.'

Dover eyed the policeman. Why should he tell him any-thing? He dropped his hands on to the arms of his chair and tilted forward. Both feet firmly on the ground.

'I'm not sure I know anything to tell. She was in the publicity business. She ran it from Bath, but got publicity for most of her clients elsewhere. So I met her at places, rather than her coming to me for puffs.'

'You said you couldn't tell me who her friends were. Who did you think they were? Anyone special?'

Dover thought about it. Yes. One or two. But so what? He didn't really know. He'd heard. But then he'd heard that there'd been life on Mars. He shook his head.

'Don't think so.'

Leonard nodded. Blinked slowly. Quartz eyes flipping ques-tions and answers into visual order. Dover was his own man.

'Think so. Think so. Let's go back to my first question. Who do you *think* she was.'

'And just like the first time, I'm not sure I understand what you mean.'

'Well, we both know she was a publicist. We both know, or have a good idea what a publicist does. But that's something for

116

her trade handbook. The CV. When someone's well known, which she was . . .?'

'Yes, I suppose so.'

'When someone's well known, we get an idea of standing, of social circles, of importance, of influence, of something quite indefinable. And so when we talk about a person, we're often talking about who we think that person is, rather than obvious things such as profession, address and credit rating.'

Dover, in spite of his reservations about Leonard, was interested. He was also in control.

'Okay. Let me tell you who I think Sally Keemer was, according to your rules.'

He put his head back, closed his eyes.

'Sally Keemer was just thirty-something, beautiful, designer league, would know everyone she wanted to know and would make sure they knew her. You'd never believe she'd have anything mundane in her fridge. An opened jar of Beluga, yes. An obscure Algerian pepper, yes. A pair of kippers for an overnighting boyfriend. Maybe. Cartons of orange juice. No. Milk. No. Eggs. No. Too ordinary. Butter? Possibly, but Normandy and unsalted and only to cook with, which probably she didn't. See what I mean? You'd not expect to see her in Waitrose. She was someone who got invited to parties, dinners, receptions, and only went to the ones that mattered, mattered to her that is. And I think, now she's dead, and particularly because of the way she died, plenty of people will feel uneasy.'

Leonard sat up.

'Because they were mixed up with her?'

Dover gave a short snort.

'No. Not at all. Because Sally Keemer was everything I've just said, yet she was murdered. That means a lot of people who thought she was just what I've said will know that there was something else. Something about which they had no idea. And that, Inspector, is very scary.'

★

117

This morning Cynthia Rathbone wore mustard leather. Dark mustard that matched what had once been the whites of her eyes. Eyes long-stained by the jiggers of pusser's rum she preferred to tea. Layers of wrinkle cream had left an alabaster mould where there might have been moving skin. Now the mask was ready to be sliced at the neck and slithered on to a revolving turntable and exhibited in a minor gallery. The real Cynthia Rathbone shifted and squeaked in her typist's chair and offered him coffee. He took it. Didn't want it. But it put them on equal terms. The answerphone was on; but she still jumped every time the light flashed.

'You could do with some help.'

He tried to be friendly. She stared at him. The eyes popping. The lips thinner and thinner as she prepared to reply.

'To do what? Tell them she's dead but it's business as usual?'

'You being pestered?'

The hands shook from the elbows as she flicked yet another disposable lighter at yet another cigarette. As she dragged deep into her lungs her right hand flicked out to switch on the small desk fan to blow the smoke into the washroom corridor. It didn't. She knew that. But this was a woman with five toothbrushes and bad gums. Pestered? Of course. The very sunrise pestered her.

'It's the ones who don't ring.'

'Who don't know? Don't care?'

'Oh, they'd care all right. You bet they'd care.'

'Then why don't they call?'

'To say what? Won't see you for lunch after all? Won't be over tonight after all? But they want to call. I know. I really do, you know.'

Her voice had risen. A lonely woman shouting rape when she wanted to rejoice. A bizarre vision. A trembling, lonely, frightened, defiant woman.

'Who are they?'

'Doesn't matter. Not now.'

'Now she's dead.'

'If that's what she is.'

'What does that mean?'

'Obvious, isn't it?'

Leonard raised his eyebrows. She saw his question. She hissed through cigarette smoke and her answer was taut, tight, spiteful.

'Woman like her doesn't die. She knew too many things. Too many people. When that happens, then those people are nervous. Nervous. Yes, that's right. Nervous. Did you hear that?'

She was looking across the room to where he lolled in the corner of the leather sofa. He could have been on another moor. Her voice raised another decibel. He nodded. He'd heard. But he didn't understand.

'You mean nervous that she left some evidence of what she knew?'

'Of course I do.'

'What sort of things did she know?'

Cynthia Rathbone shrugged. It wasn't a shrug of 'don't know'. It was a shrug of 'where do you start?'. Leonard tried again.

'Did she know enough for someone to kill her?'

'You're the policeman, not me. 'Course she did. Must have done.'

'Must?'

'Yes. Must. She was hardly mugged for her Rolex, was she?'

'We don't know that.'

'Albert Street? Yes, you do. If it had been down by the bus station or by the arches, Okay. But here? Don't make me laugh.'

No one had done that for a very long time.

'Tell me, who killed her?'

The eyes bulged like pimentos from stuffed olives.

'The line forms on the right.'

'She doesn't seem to me the sort of person who had enemies.'

'You're a man.'

'You're her aunt.'

'So?'

Leonard looked about the office. Comfortable. Nothing tatty. Nothing worn.

'She employed you.'

'And she made sure I didn't forget it.'

'You didn't like her?'

'Some days.'

'Most days?'

'Most days I don't remember.'

Leonard looked at the eyes. He could believe it, but not the way she meant.

'Tell me about this line on the right. Jealousies? Business deals?'

'Husbands.'

'She was having an affair?'

Cynthia Rathbone stubbed a half-smoked cigarette into a small box. Still no ashtrays. She pulled another cigarette from a bag on her desk and flicked and puffed.

'Little Miss Image Maker didn't have affairs. She had games. She played with men like . . .'

Leonard waited. She was staring at the desk. Trying to remember? Trying to stop? He nudged.

'Chess?'

She looked up. Looked frightened. Surprised to see him still there.

'What?'

'Like chess.'

'No. Played with them for real.'

'You said husbands.'

'That's right. You know what they say? She had six husbands — one of them her own. Well, that was the golden girl of Bath.'

'Who were they?'

120

'Oh no. Not from me, you don't.'

'I'm looking for a murderer.'

She shuddered. Dragged deeply. Her fingers in a long spiked V as she held the cigarette hard into her thin lips. The nails were blunt, bitten, murky lizard green. Next she tried her coffee. It was cold. She started to make a face. Spilled it.

'Sod. Look at it. Look at it.'

She stood. Arms stretched down. Palms towards him. The front of the thin leather skirt was blotted with coffee. The lonely, frightened, spiteful eyes were wild.

'Sod. Sod. Sod. Sod. It's all her sodding fault.'

And then she was gone. Slithering from the room leaving behind bag, burning cigarette and Leonard sipping at his coffee. He could hear her sharp heels dulled on the thickly carpeted stairs. Still cursing. Still blaming.

## Fifteen

Selsey had bought some claret. Not unusual for a restaurateur. But this was special. Some people in Colchester.

'Why not? I'm a big supporter of Boadicea. Didn't you know that?'

'Still?'

'Sure. She was a big wine-drinker.'

'So was Ivan the Terrible.'

'But she was on our side.'

Leonard teased the centre from a white bread roll.

'She didn't have much option.'

Selsey looked from beneath his great dark mop. Sucked at his teeth. Shook his head.

'Jim lad, you're very abrasive today. Try a glass.'

'At those prices?'

121

'Had a fellow last night got through three bottles. Three bottles. Just for the two of them. Mind you, most of it slipped down his throat, not hers.'

'More money than sense.'

'Maybe. He'd have been useless even if he did get her home.'

Leonard ran the side of his hand along the table cloth leaving a dike of white crumbs. He felt guilty. Someone would have to clean up. Selsey was warming to his tale.

'He was three sheets to the wind when they arrived. You remember George Raft? You know, the Yank?'

Leonard nodded, only half-hearing. Who was Cynthia talking about? Who else would know?

'Well, dead ringer for him. Could have been flipping a silver dollar and I wouldn't have given it a second thought. And the girl. Cool as a trolley dolly. You know she . . .'

Leonard looked up from his crumb sculpture. Selsey was peering at him. Dawning. He slapped his hands together and pointed at Leonard.

'Of course, Jim lad. Of course.'

'Don't tell me, it *was* George Raft.'

Selsey looked puzzled.

'What? Don't be daft, he's dead. Ages ago. No, the girl. I know who she is. Worked for that Sally Keemer. I remember now. Came in here a couple of times with her. Wanted an account. Wanted too much discount. I remember her.'

'Jane Boxer?'

Selsey shook his head.

'I really don't remember. Dark hair. Looker. Nice teeth.'

Leonard wondered. Why not? She was a working girl. He was a working client.

'Just good friends?'

'State he was in, I shouldn't think he had much choice.'

'Did he know that?'

Selsey thought about it. The hand on the arm. Hand? When did a hand become a paw? The whispers? Why not? It was busy. Woods was always busy that time of a summer night, even on a Monday.

'Who knows? I didn't get that close. But I tell you something, old George Raft there could have out-gunned Boadicea. Three bottles. I tell you, Jim lad, he'd been practising. And it was close to last orders when they arrived. He hadn't been on mineral water before they got here.'

'She often come in?'

'Sort of. Not a regular. But when they're that pretty, you don't forget. But she never had unpretty ones, did she?'

'Who we talking about now?'

'The dead girl. I see them going in and out of that office of hers. Could have been a modelling agency to look at them. Except the old crow, of course.'

He laughed. Shook his head.

'Cynthia Rathbone?'

'The one with the leather? That's the one. Bet she sloshes it on her porridge.'

He made a pouring motion with one hand and flapped the other in disbelief.

'Eccentric.'

'Eccentric? Is that what she is? I tell you, Jim lad, if she got a part in *Treasure Island* it'd be the parrot. Mind you, if you want to know what went on in that place, she's the one to ask. After all, she was the one with the envelopes.'

'The records, you mean?'

'Do I? No, I don't think so. The brown envelopes. She was the one who paid the girls.'

Leonard shifted in his chair. The one with the shortest skirt and the bottom brought coffee. Poured. Smiled. Took her time walking away. Leonard's weakness. At that age anyway.

'Tell me, who are the girls? You make it sound like a Bluebell line-up.'

Selsey hunched over the table. Face up at an angle. Squinting into an imaginary sun.

'Don't get excited. It's all kosher. From what I hear, she

123

hired pretty girls to look after clients when there was a conference or something. Happens all the time.'

'Who were they?'

'I don't know. I'm a happily married punter. I just look.'

'And listen.'

'No. Don't listen. Hear sometimes, but never listen. Leave that to people like you.'

Selsey leaned back. They looked at each other. Friends. Strange friends. Except by chance, never met each other anywhere but Woods. No invitations. No casual calls. No parties. No Sunday lunches. But friends. An understanding. And now Leonard had asked enough. Selsey had told enough. Best to stay friends. Selsey glanced out of the broad window. Nodded across the street. The smile lightened the moment.

'Now that, Jim lad, is a looker. For her, I'd sign on for point duty.'

Madelaine Jack was swinging across the road towards them. She gave a friendly wave. Not to Leonard. To Selsey.

'You think she'd marry me, that one?'

'You said you were happily married. Remember?'

Selsey nodded gravely.

'Ah, so I do. So I do. But should one day I find myself proceeding in a lonely direction, officer, then . . .'

He shrugged.

'Then?'

'Then, Jim lad, I'd probably remember I was on the rota and which girl in her right mind would marry a man who has to cook for a living?'

They were both chuckling when she came in. Selsey was calling for wine. She was shaking her head.

''Fraid not, maestro. 'Fraid not. We have business to attend.'

Leonard raised his eyebrows.

'New business?'

She dropped the *Chronicle* on the table in front of him. Dover had been busy that morning. The story ran alongside the same head and shoulder picture of Sally Keemer that was pinned to the wall in the Major Incident Room. The headline that went with it was bold enough for the outbreak of war, or the slashing of Income Tax.

## Murder Probe

### Police Hunt
### Bath Woman

Police hunting the killer of Sally Keemer, gunned down close to the city centre on Sunday, want to interview a Bath woman who travelled from London with her shortly before he was murdered.

Both Sally Keemer and the mystery woman are known to have been in the same first class compartment on the delayed 6.30 p.m. train from Paddington.

Sally Keemer, 29, managing director of a top publicity agency in the city, was shot only yards from her Saville Row office just over 24 hours after the two women met.

Today police stressed that the woman is not a suspect, but needed for an informal interview. Also on the train was a Scottish couple, believed to be on a short visit to Bath. Hotels were being contacted this morning . . .

Leonard didn't finish reading. It was what he'd wanted.
'Anything?'
'Better than that. Our Mystery Probe Row New Move lady has surfaced. We're due there in ten minutes.'

# Sixteen

Usually, Mrs Hanbury-Collings would not have seen the *Chronicle*. She never saw the *Chronicle*. The proper paper was the *Daily Telegraph*, although she remembered more from her *Daily Mail*. Mrs Hanbury-Collings was single-minded about what her late husband called The Medja. She wouldn't have known where to find her local radio station on the dial. The proper BBC was the World Service, although she could no longer hear it. She was brought up on the World Service. Everything in the Rhodesia of her childhood stopped not for tea, but Radio Newsreel. Now the BBC was, for some reason she failed to understand, called Radio Four. She never admitted to watching her television set, but curiously knew the latest plot of every soap and could hold forth for quite a long time on the dress sense of almost every woman presenter, and the complexion and signs of drink on and in every male who appeared between seven and eleven each evening. So usually, Mrs Hanbury-Collings would not have known that she was being described as a mystery woman by the *Chronicle*. But these were not usual times for Mrs Hanbury-Collings and her son Ashley.

Mrs Hanbury-Collings was at her bank in Quiet Street. She came out and stood on the corner, wondering if she should walk up the hill and home, or take a taxi. As she turned, she saw the billboard.

**Bath**

**Murder**

**Hunt**

**New Move**

She bought the paper. She tried to appear as casual as possible. She imagined people might notice her. A simple act. Buying a newspaper. It became an achievement. She fumbled with her purse. She nearly dropped it. She couldn't quite make out how much she had. How much she needed. She didn't know how much the paper was. Why should she? She'd never bought it before. Would the man notice? She wanted to be as normal as possible. How Mrs Hanbury-Collings hated fiddly change. Why could not these folk charge a round figure? No one would mind a few coppers more if it made it easier to buy. She tutted to herself and ignored the smile of the news vendor and the muttering of yet another beggar. Really. It was all getting too awful. After all, this was hardly Birmingham or whatever those places were where she knew there were quite a lot of poor. This was Bath. She walked away, quite stern-faced and slipping the newspaper into the large, shiny, green Harrods bag she affected in town. The whole was a furtive act. She could not bring herself to read the paper on the streets. What if she were seen? Her neighbours. She believed the only people who read papers on the streets were people who put money on horses. Mrs Hanbury-Collings was flustered. All because of a paper. All because she felt out of control. All Ashley's fault. Stupid, stupid, stupid boy.

When she got home, she went into her kitchen and laid the newspaper out on the table. Stupid, stupid, stupid boy. And now the police wanted her. What was it they said? Informal talk. She sat down. Got up. Sat down. Got up. Mrs Hanbury-Collings had spent many hours telling others that what the country needed, that is, what others needed, was the wartime spirit. And so, at this point, Mrs Hanbury-Collings did what she believed to be the thing everyone had done when the chips were down in wartime Britain. She put on the kettle. And while it heated, she went into her bathroom and washed, cleaned her teeth, changed her frock and returned to make herself a nice cup of tea.

And as she sipped from a china cup, she knew that she would

have to call the police station. It would be reasonable for the police to want to speak to anyone who had seen the girl. Clearly they knew she had been on the train. How she detested this sort of thing. But, couldn't be helped. Some of her friends already knew that she had been in London – after all, Mrs Hanbury-Collings was not one to keep her spending sprees to herself. She wondered how the police knew. Those funny little Scottish folk? The poet or whatever he was? She thought the Scots. The poet had been a dull little man who had slept most of the way to Bath. And hadn't she seen him as she was waiting for her taxi? On a bicycle? A bicycle in Bath? Whatever next? No, definitely the Scottish folk. The whatever they said their names were. Gordons or something. Or at least he was. And hadn't he talked to the detestable woman? Film star indeed! Imposter. Always had been. Amazing she could understand him. Quite Scottish. Something about business? She really didn't know. But she would.

Mrs Hanbury-Collings finished her tea, rinsed her cup and saucer, went back into her bathroom and repaired her lipstick. She fluffed the sides of her colour-rinsed hair, ran her fingers down the pleats of her blue frock, went into the hall and called the telephone number that had been at the end of the *Chronicle*'s article. Having done so, she went into her drawing room, leafed through the housing advertisements in *Country Life* and waited. The woman had said thirty minutes. Mrs Hanbury-Collings hoped the woman knew what she was talking about. She wanted to get this over.

Thirty-five minutes later, the Bath matron felt alarmed. A policeman? He could not be a policeman. But he was. They had been through the formalities. Warrant card. Introductions. And the girl. Didn't look at all like a police officer. Far too pretty. Should have been doing one of those travel programmes, or maybe the tennis. Looked healthy. The weather, perhaps. For a moment, she'd wondered if the whole thing wasn't an elaborate ploy. But for what? For the life of her, Mrs Hanbury-

Collings couldn't think. On the doorstep she had been, well, as she would tell her very good friend Marjorie, nothing less than shocked.

'Good gracious me. You?'

He'd smiled. A secretive smile. Daring anyone to believe that was what it was. He pulled out the credit card shaped piece of white plastic. Bad photograph. Crest. Avon and Somerset Police, it read. His black felt-tipped signature in the left corner, the Chief Constable's in the other. Their only contact. Still the old card. But Leonard would always be the last to change.

'I'm afraid so. Coincidence, yes?'

'Are you sure?'

'Oh yes. Sadly. Very sure. May we, eh, may we come in?'

And now he was sitting on the other sofa. Why was he looking at the fireplace? Had he not seen a screen before?

'It's from Rhodesia, you know. Antelope skin.'

He looked up.

'Mm?'

'The screen.'

'Oh yes. Very attractive. Very attractive.'

'My late husband, you know. We lived there. But, well, not any more.'

He seemed far away. But she knew he couldn't be. He really didn't look like a policeman. The girl, Detective Sergeant Jack, she said she was, had settled in the corner on the high chair where sometimes Mrs Hanbury-Collings read her newspaper when her back hurt. And now he was asking questions. And she listened very carefully. And she answered very carefully.

'When did you last see Sally Keemer?'

She was quick.

'On the train, of course.'

Too quick.

'You're sure?'

''Course I'm sure. Why shouldn't I be?'

Perhaps not too quick. Perhaps she'd been thinking about it ever since she called. People behaved strangely when they

129

talked to a policeman. Easier talking to a uniformed officer. People more relaxed with a uniform. More a sense of servant to the community. More open. Uniform, it was all there. Badges. Black tie. Cap. Handcuffs, two-way radios, truncheon. Big boots. All up front. Nothing hidden. Friendlier. But CID? Criminal Investigation Department. Criminal. Investigation. Department. Sinister. Stranger people. Something hidden. He leaned back. Tried to relax. To relax her.

'When you left, can you think what she said?'

'You mean like goodbye?'

'Mm.'

'Well I think that was it. She just said goodbye or something. She was rather ordinary, you know.'

'Was she?'

'Oh yes. Very attractive in an obvious way, I suppose, but of course, rather common. Didn't you think?'

Leonard's eyes were closed. He remembered the smile. The half-smile as the train pulled away. He was trying to remember something. Couldn't. He didn't answer for a moment.

'And you're sure that was the last time you saw her?'

'I've just told you.'

'Mm. But well, you know, living in the same place. You might not remember a stranger, but coincidence of the train journey, you might see her again. Church. Walking. Waitrose.'

'According to the paper she was killed the next night.'

'Yes, I suppose so. D'you mind telling me what you did on Sunday?'

'Me?'

'Yes please.'

'You surely don't think ... Really, Inspector, this is out-rageous.'

He put a hand up.

'No, no, no, of course not. Badly put on my part. Forgive me.'

'Well, I must say ...'

'It's a pure formality. Procedure. When we talk to a witness

130

or a potential witness, we always ask what that person was doing on the day the, the um, the crime was committed. After all, if you said you were being attended by a doctor for a regular bout of amnesia or something, then that of course would have an effect on the way your evidence was recorded. Modern times, I'm afraid, Mrs Hanbury-Collings. Modern times.'

She seemed, seemed, reassured. Even agreed with him on the oddities of modern times. But he didn't let go.

'So if you could just tell me, briefly, of course?'

'About what?'

'Sunday.'

'Well, I'm afraid it was the usual tedious old Sunday. I went to the eight o'clock service – in the abbey, of course . . .'

'Of course, and then?'

'Well, then came home and started to prepare Sunday lunch. Mrs Much isn't here at the weekend and I do have to rather fend for myself.'

'Very difficult.'

She peered at him for a moment. Did she sense something other than social sympathy? His face was straight. His eyes, waiting.

'So, well, I cooked Sunday lunch and then Ashley, that's my son, came as he does every Sunday, for lunch with my grandson. He's divorced, you know?'

'Mm?'

'My son, Ashley.'

'Right. And then?'

'Ashley had to go out for a while. He came back and collected Richard, my grandson, and his young friend – they had to be back in school, you know – and then came back for the evening.'

'Here?'

'Why yes. Where else?'

'You didn't go out at all?'

'Of course not. I had company.'

Mrs Hanbury-Collings sucked at her lip. Lipstick on her top

131

teeth. Leonard looked away. Spinach or lipstick? Which was worse? Neither unless you knew. He waited. Wondered if there was anything else. Nothing came.

'Tell me, what did Sally Keemer talk about on the train?'

'This and that, I suppose. Once we got over the, eh, well, you know . . .'

He nodded.

'Well, I suppose just general things. She'd been up to town for just the one day, I think she said.'

'You're sure about that?'

'Well, yes.'

He didn't say anything. Just stared at her.

'Well, I suppose I am. It is very difficult you know, Inspector. I mean we talked about the young folk today. You know, how they have no respect. And she said she felt violated, which if you ask me was going a bit far. After all, just look at her – she was clearly pretty loose herself, now wasn't she?'

'Was she?'

'Of course she was.'

There was a snap in the carefully modulated tones of Mrs Hanbury-Collings, who had not always been a Hanbury-Collings and who hadn't always lived in Bath. Much further north. Much further. Leonard heard it somewhere beneath her vowels. Just a hint.

'Why of course?'

'Well, the way she was pawing over him.'

'Who?'

'The man, of course. I saw them, you know. On the station. I mean he was actually, well . . .'

The grunge of blood-red lipstick set in a tight cut across her face.

'Well . . . ?'

She stared at him. Seeing it again. Seeing her. Film stars indeed. Trash!

'He was actually feeling her. And, and she let him. There! I've said it. Said it.'

Mrs Hanbury-Collings seemed very upset. Detective Sergeant Jack sensed something. Couldn't quite understand what was going on. But then the most respectable were often the most police-fearing. She could never understand why. She was told, of course. There was even a line in the handbook on interrogation. Perhaps this was just that. Nothing more. Perhaps.

'Tell me, did she mention her friend? Name? Who he was? Anything?'

The matron shook her head. There was the merest smudge of powder on the collar of her dress. He wondered if it were a frock. He could smell it. The same smell as all those years ago. The smell he'd wanted on his pillow. Then. Now? He looked at her. Realized she hadn't answered. Or had she?

'I'm sorry?'

She in turn looked puzzled. Hadn't he been listening. No, couldn't be a policeman. Not a proper one.

'I was saying that she said nothing more than she'd met a friend. Mm. A very close friend, I would say. Wouldn't you?'

He didn't answer.

'But no name?'

'That's what I've just said.'

'She didn't seem nervous, apart from the incident with the carrier bag.'

'Excitable.'

Excitable. Leonard nodded. That's what he'd thought. It was there at the back of his mind. Strange how someone so high-powered could become so agitated over something so small. But small to whom? Him? A policeman. She? Not a policeman. But was that what had excited her?

'Because of what had happened?'

'I suppose so.'

'But she didn't mention it again?'

'No, I suppose she didn't.'

Leonard shifted in the sofa. Thick down cushions. The long

133

window slightly open. A slight breeze on the ceiling-to-floor net curtains. Peaceful. Yet something nagged.

'Tell me about the Scottish couple.'

'The Gordons? Actually, she wasn't a Gordon, was she? Not yet anyway.'

He snapped his fingers.

'That's it. I remember now. Whisky or something, wasn't he?'

'Odd name for a whisky person. I'd have thought gin was more his line, wouldn't you?'

'It's a very Scottish name. What did they talk about?'

She shrugged. Her corsetry squeaked.

'Just the same. Small talk. Nothing more. You wouldn't expect them to have anything else, now would you? I mean, look at them. Awfully provincial folk.'

'They didn't say where they were staying, did they?'

'Of course they did. Wholmes.'

'Well, well. You're sure?'

Mrs Hanbury-Collings tutted. For a moment forgetting her caution.

'Of course I'm sure. I said I thought it rather grand and they said they didn't know. It had been recommended by the people they were going to see. A brother, I think. And they were giving them dinner that night. They wanted somewhere where they could book in and know the dining room was good, should they need to stay in.'

'Did they say how long they were staying?'

'Sunday afternoon, I think. Something about a night sleeper to Edinburgh. Strange couple, you know . . .'

She was interrupted by Jack who was now up and moving towards the door.

'Would you excuse me a moment?'

'Of course, dear. If you want the . . .'

DS Jack was taking a small mobile telephone from her pocket. Smiled. Mrs Hanbury-Collings looked nervous. They could hear Jack in the hallway. She was asking someone if the Gordons were still there.

'If she's asking the Wholmes, I tell you they've gone. And they're not the Gordons. He's a Gordon. She isn't.'

'How do you know they've gone?'

'Well, they said they were going. On Sunday. Why should they stay? Look, if you want to know where they've gone I can help you.'

She got up, not without some effort, and went to the sofa table. A small, dark blue, soft leather handbag. She fiddled with the gold clasp and then took out a small card.

'Here we are. Spey Gordon, Iain Gordon, that's with an "i", Iain Gordon, Director. Here you are, telephone number and address.'

He took it. An address on Speyside. Archiestown. He wondered how the name was pronounced.

'He just gave you this?'

'Well you'd hardly expect me to ask for it, now would you, Inspector? Or perhaps you would.'

Mrs Hanbury-Collings seemed to be gaining confidence.

'It's just that when people give cards, it's quite often in return for other cards.'

'Oh, I see.'

She did. She remembered.

'Of course, you're right. Well naturally I don't have such things. Mostly trade, I believe. But she had one. Gave him one of hers. Said to call her if he needed her services at any time. Well, I can tell you, his young lady didn't think much of that. Oh no. Not at all.'

Sergeant Jack was standing in the doorway. Eyebrows raised. There was something. It was time to go. He rose to his feet and ran an eye along the mantelpiece. Half a dozen invitations. Mostly heavily printed. None from Sally Keemer.

'Well thanks very much, Mrs Hanbury-Collings. Thank you indeed.'

'Is that all?'

'For the moment, yes. Thank you indeed.'

Hope in that voice? Expectancy? Urgency? No. A widow going through an ordeal. A stranger on the train. Twenty-four hours later that stranger is dead. Not a normal death. Murdered. Now two police officers in your drawing room. Read nothing from a smudged page, once said a very correct inspector. The only man Leonard had respected. Mrs Hanbury-Collings was very smudged. For the moment.

He was by the door. They'd see themselves out. Of course they would not. She was following. Mrs Much was out. Perfect hostess? Or priceless knick-knacks to be found on the way out? At the door he smiled into her eyes. She looked into his. Defiance. He'd surprised her. Just another passenger. No. Not at all. The door was closing when he remembered.

'Ah, just a small point, madam.'

Her smile was bright. Freshly prepared.

'Tell me, I seem to have heard Miss Keemer mention that she was going on to see her son at boarding school.'

The smile was still there. The blood-red grunge was fixed and smile-shaped.

'I really don't remember.'

'Didn't she say that was why she was staying on the train?'

'Did she?'

'Yes. Or at least so I thought.'

'Well, Inspector, you have the advantage. It was something that I must have missed in all the excitement.'

He waited for her to go on. She didn't. Wasn't going to. He gave a half-salute. But she wouldn't have seen it. The door was already closing. For a moment Leonard said nothing. Hands in pockets, legs slightly bent at the knees, he was examining the pavement. Not for clues. For thoughts. He looked up. Squinted into the afternoon silhouette of the house opposite. Blinked at the edge of the sun. Having found the latitude of his thoughts, he wondered about Mrs Hanbury-Collings. But perhaps he wasn't the right person to wonder. He had taken an instant dislike to her. A long time ago, there'd been a visitor. He knew there'd been talk of adoption. He didn't want it. Wanted to belong. But not to her. He couldn't remember him. Only her. But it was the mouth. The frock. The pearls. The powder. Yes. He was the wrong person to think about Mrs Hanbury-Collings.

'Well?'

'Blue rinses aren't used to murder are they, sir?'

'Who is?'

'What I meant, sir . . .'

He nodded. He knew what she meant.

'What the hotel say?'

'Mr Gordon and Miss Wilson left on Monday.'

'Not Sunday.'

'No, sir. Monday afternoon. But — and this is the interesting bit — your Mr Dougal Gordon has a reservation with them for tonight and tomorrow night.'

'Has he indeed? So the McTavish of McTavish did not take the low road.'

'Sir?'

'Before your time, don't worry. Single or double?'

'Alone — as far as we know, of course.'


# Seventeen


It was three-fifteen in the afternoon. She was in the bath. It was a large bath covered with a soft mountain of bubbles. The silly trill from her mobile telephone brought her back from the half-sleep that was slowly rinsing the champagne cocktails of lunchtime. She could hear the agitation in his voice as soon as he spoke.

'We've got to discuss this. Can you come over? This evening?'

She was relaxed. Almost amused.

'Don't be silly, darling. Of course not. I'm a working girl.'

'Just for a few minutes?'

'I'm sorry, darling, but I really don't have a few minutes.'

'But I need to see you.'

She said nothing. Waited. Teasing.

'Are you there?'

'Of course I am.'

'I said I need to see you.'

'That's nice.'

'I don't mean that.'

She pulled the still stiff loofah across her flat belly. Put on her kittenish voice. All part of her act. It was good.

'Oh. Are you sure?'

Good enough to make him angry.

'For God's sake.'

'Darling, don't get so, so worked up. Remember what we agreed. Do nothing. There's nothing at all to connect you. As far as anyone's concerned you were here in London. Miles away.'

'But suppose someone saw me?'

'But no one did, my darling. We'd know if they had.'

'How?'

'Because they've got a very sweet policeman who's not at all like a policeman and he tells me everything.'

'Why? Isn't that suspicious?'

'No, darling, it isn't. He's simply a little unconventional. Anyway . . .' She stretched out a long leg through the bubbles and turned on the warm tap with her toes. '. . . I think he's got the hots for me.'

'What's that?'

'Now don't be silly.'

'I'm not being silly. I know you. Don't play games. We're talking about my neck.'

'They don't do that sort of thing anymore. But don't you worry. Won't be long. Let it all die down and then we'll be together. All right?'

She could hear him breathing into the mouthpiece. She knew what he was going to say, but she let him say it.

'Listen, perhaps it's better if I go to see them, the police that is. Tell them that she and I were friends.'

'And what do you think that would do?'

'Someone's bound to link us. They'll get round to me eventually.'

'Maybe not.'

'Of course they will. They'll think it odd I haven't contacted them.'

'Darling, it's hardly the Boston chainsaw massacre. It's a tiny murder in dreary old Bath. There's absolutely no reason for you to know anything about it.'

'Yes there is. There was a bit in the *Telegraph* about it.'

'You might never have seen it.'

'But I did. Don't you see? That's the whole point. Better I go to see them than have them knocking on my door at two in the morning and me having to explain.'

'There's nothing to explain.'

'But what if someone did see me?'

'There was no one there to see you. Remember?'

'I don't know that. Not for sure.'

She stretched again. Turned off the tap.

'I'm sorry, my darling, but it's already been a long day and I'm about to change for the third time. I do really have to go to work.'

'Please?'

'Now, darling, you know I would. I'd love to, but I really am working, and this evening.'

'I'm worried. It's, well, it's okay for you.'

She heard in his voice another level of his anxiety. He was on his high board. Perhaps ready to dive.

'Look, let's not worry at the moment. I'll call you when I've finished tonight.'

'Come over.'

'Perhaps, my darling, it's better that we're not together for the moment. Not until it's all died down.'

'What does that mean?'

'Very well then, I'll call you tonight and I'll try to come over. But it'll be very late.'

The relief was audible in his sigh, then in his voice.

'Thank God for that. Don't let me down. Not now.'

She blew him a kiss into the mouthpiece and made more promises for that night, then pressed the off button and let the phone drop to the cork-topped stool. For a few minutes she lay back, her eyes closed. No longer dreaming. Thinking. God, why were men so weak? Slowly she stood up in the water. Pulled the curtain and allowed the stinging shower to wash away the foamy bubbles from her body. Then, wrapped in the outsized white towelling robe, she opened the door and went into the bedroom. The man dozing on the bed opened one eye and raised a hand.

'Hi. How we doing?'

She smiled and rubbed at her neck with a small towel.

'We're doing just fine, Ed, just fine.'

He swung his feet to the floor, came across and slipped his arms about her waist. She struggled to pull away, but not very hard.

'Come on, heart-throb. It's culture time. Remember? Wild West Show and crayons by numbers? We're due there in thirty minutes.'

'No problem. No problem. It takes ten minutes in a cab.'

He ran his hand down to the tie of the fleecy gown and pulled her on to the bed.

# Eighteen

The hotel was not very helpful. McKittrick, the manager, kept asking for Leonard's personal guarantee that Dougie Gordon was not a fugitive.

'You must understand, Inspector, we have to be quite certain in these matters.'

'Mr Gordon is, as far as I know, a perfectly law-abiding citizen who just happens to have been on the same train as the woman who is now dead.'

'But you're sure he is not involved?'

Leonard sighed. Detective Sergeant Jack took over. Smiled. Reassuringly.

'All we need to know, sir, is if he can remember anything on the train journey that may help us.'

'With your inquiries.'

'With our inquiries.'

'I do understand these matters, you know.'

'I'm sure you do, sir. Now, we understand that Mr Gordon was due to leave on Sunday but delayed his departure. Do you happen to know why?'

The manager sniffed.

'Perfectly simple, Sergeant. She, she was quite incapable of getting up. She'd drunk enough to float the Queen Mary, the night before that is. Quite a display, I'm told.'

Leonard blinked. Rubbed at his spectacles with his tie. The future Mrs Dougie Gordon had taken a drink? Could this be true?

'You mean she was a little worse for wear?'

McKittrick raised his eyebrows and left them there.

'Let's not beat about the bush, Inspector, she was rat-arsed. There! I've said it. Totally and utterly incapable. Had to be carried to her room. I'm told she was doing Scottish exercises in the foyer at one o'clock.'

Leonard slipped his spectacles on.

'So still burns run very deep.'

'I beg your pardon?'

'Nothing, sir, nothing. Just a thought. Do you have her name?'

'Wilson. J. R. Wilson. Separate rooms, you know.'

'And this, this occasion, took place Saturday night?'

'So it did. So it did. Or early Sunday morning if you want to be pedantic.'

'Can you tell me where Mr Gordon made his new booking?'

'I'm not sure I follow you, Inspector. He made it at the front desk, where else would he make it?'

'You mean before he left?'

'Oh yes. He was very fortunate, you know. We don't have many vacancies at this time of the year.'

It was warm. Almost too warm. They were walking back to Manvers Street. A droopy young man came out of the paper shop quickly stuffing a magazine into his carrier bag. He eyed the long-limbed figure strolling with the curly guy, quickly looked away from her breasts and hurried on, wishing. Clutching his plastic bag. Leonard wasn't hurrying. He was nagging.

'So if he booked on Sunday afternoon, what happened between Saturday night and Sunday afternoon to make him come back?'

'And why not just stay on?'

'Maybe his fiancée had to get back to Scotland. Maybe a row?'

Instead of crossing at the lights into Pierrepoint Street and heading to the police station, Leonard turned left and they walked down towards the river. He wanted time to think before facing the routine of the Incident Room, the team, the need to feed into the system which he knew was right yet detested.

142

'Odd. On the train, they were tourists. They'd come from a wedding, as far as I remember. Kilt. The lot. Just a family evening in Bath. I wasn't listening. But that was it. All very innocent.'

'It may still be.'

He looked at her. Intelligent eyes. Saw things he didn't. She could be right.

'But why come back? Why not stay? Why not go home?'

'Well, suppose he's what he appears to be. A stereotypical whisky distiller—'

'A what?'

She ignored him.

'Let's suppose he met someone at this party of theirs. Miss Wilson was hardly likely to get in the state she did from a quiet evening out. What I'm saying, sir, is that he could simply have found a potential customer. Coming back could be strictly business.'

He nodded. Okay. Okay for now.

'And what I'm saying is that an innocent enough guy in a kilt suddenly becomes more than a witness. And what about the old girl? Same thing. That should have been a straight-forward interview. You know, "I wonder if you can help us" and five minutes later "Thank you very much, you've been most helpful." But it wasn't, was it?'

'Nerves, sir.'

She was probably right. And yet. Leonard was certain that Sally Keemer had mentioned a son. His Sergeant had said no son. But Sally Keemer had said so. Sure she had. Now Mrs Hanbury-Collings had said she didn't notice. Mrs Hanbury-Collings wasn't the sort of matron not to notice. So how could he have been wrong on something so simple?

'So no son.'

They crossed the road, walked along the worn stone pavements of Duke Street. The sun's heat was coming off the blackened Bath stone walls. He stopped. Took off his glasses. Rubbed at them. Waited.

'Well, sir, that's what the school said.'

'Wrong school?'

'We tried every boarding school in the Bristol area. Nothing.'

The voice was wrong. Jack was strong. Probably played tennis. He should know. He didn't. He sometimes wondered about her. Wondered why she'd once saved him when she could easily have stood back or by. But he knew more about her voice than about her. Curious mixture. Home Counties from her family. West Country from background. Teesside from her three years at college. He supposed he heard her voice when he thought about her. He woke up. She was watching his face. Waiting for him to prod. Nudge. Reassure? It was there in her voice. Evidence said he'd got it wrong about the kid. Misheard. Half-asleep at the time. Fact and fiction, like dozing when the news was on and mixing it into a dream. But she was willing to believe he'd got it right. There had been a son. Or at least Sally Keemer had said there was. So she was uncertain. What about? What she'd been told or why he believed he was right? And if he were?

'Okay, then why say it?'

'Fantasy?'

Shook his head.

'The Jane Boxer school? No. Tried that. Too obvious.'

'Fantasizers are. They dare you not to believe them. Dare themselves not to, I suppose.'

'We're missing something here. If there wasn't a son, then why did Sally Keemer stay on the train? Why was she going to Bristol at gone nine on a Saturday evening?'

He clicked his fingers. He knew there'd been something niggling.

'That's it. Who was she going to meet on Saturday night, who not only would wait for her, but didn't need to be told that she was late? Because not once did she try to call anyone from the train. I'd call that odd. Wouldn't you?'

She would. She was smiling. He'd nudged.

★

In the Incident Room, nothing. Officers had been out at Bristol Temple Meads station. Talked to station staff. Taxi drivers. Put up notices. So far nothing. Sally Keemer, a beautiful woman in a thin summer dress who had attracted so much attention at Paddington, had apparently got off a train at a busy InterCity station without being noticed by anyone. None of the officers thought this odd. They'd all looked for missing girls. Girls pulled into bushes, into taxis, into oblivion. They'd all pounded streets, carrying pictures, asked questions obvious and obscure. They'd all learned how easy it is for someone to disappear. For someone not to be seen. But that was usually when an act of horror was committed. Sally Keemer was different. She'd not been abducted. She'd not been murdered. Not then. That was Saturday. Sally Keemer had gone home and apparently led a normal life until around eleven o'clock on the Sunday evening.

Superintendent Marsh was sitting on one of the table edges in front of the whole squad. Immaculate. Could have sold anything from Gieves & Hawkes's window. The white cuff was starched. The new Mrs Marsh was relieved that her husband had absolute faith in three institutions: The Law, The Church and The Bristol Laundry. From the first two she'd always know where he was and by the third she'd be relieved of the tedium of washing and ironing. From one of these immaculate cuffs a flat gold link gleamed as he rubbed his temple with a very white and very thin manicured finger.

'Right. DI Leonard tells me that one of the three people on the train on Saturday night, Mrs, Mrs eh . . .'

'Hanbury-Collings,' supplied Jack.

Marsh looked at her. Wondered why Leonard had left it to his DS.

'Mrs Hanbury-Collings claims that she remembers nothing about Sally Keemer saying she was off to meet her son. DS Jack says there's no Keemer registered at any of the boarding schools in the area. So, either DI Leonard's got it wrong, Mrs Wotsit has got it wrong, or what?'

145

There was an apologetic but well-bred cough from the centre floor. Detective Sergeant Nicholas Somers-Barclay, complete with plaster cast leg, crutches handy by his side and somehow with fresh coffee on his table, was beaming.

'Excuse me, sir. I've managed to put together a couple of points of interest on this one. I've talked to the registrar. He went through his lists for a couple of years either side of the mystery son's age group. Certainly in this area, there's nothing registered.'

Marsh nodded slowly. Thoughtfully.

'Well done. That may save us all a bit of, eh, legwork.'

The room gave an appreciative chuckle. Somers-Barclay tapped his jolly old cast and Marsh realized that he'd made a joke. His face remained severe.

'However, let's not throw this one away. If DI Leonard says Sally Keemer told everyone that she was going to see her son, then I think we can accept that's what she said. Mrs Hanbury-Collings may have forgotten or not noticed. So the question is why she would say that. We need to get to someone else who was there and to someone who knew her.'

Jack looked across to where Leonard was leaning against the wall. He was looking down at his brown boots. Hands in pockets. Didn't look up. She cut in.

'One of the other people on the train, a Dougal Gordon, will be back in Bath this evening. DI Leonard and I will be seeing him.'

'James?'

Marsh would never call him Jim, Jimmy. Only Lane was anything but formal with Leonard.

'We've this blank period. Bath ten past nine on Saturday night, then nothing. Maybe she stayed in. I don't expect Gordon can come up with much on this. He appears to have been at a dinner party, then waiting for his fiancée to, well, get herself ready for them to leave. We don't know why he's coming back. It could well be a business contact. We'll know soon enough.'

Somers-Barclay gave another of his coughs. Leonard ignored him. Marsh didn't.

'Nick?'

Somers-Barclay liked that.

'Being somewhat hampered, sir, I've gone through some of the files we brought in from her office. There's nothing very much to go on. Inland Revenue seems up to date. VAT is. Interesting that the client list only goes back six years, but the business has been going for about ten.'

'Anything special on that list?'

'Not that I can see, sir.'

Leonard was interested. But he wasn't sure how interested.

'Tell me, is there anything under Firmani, an Ed Firmani from New York? It would be quite new.'

Somers-Barclay looked through his notes. Scanned the list. Shook his head.

'No, sir. Nothing.'

Leonard thought about it. Why? Marsh was looking at him.

'Firmani?'

'Maybe nothing, sir, but I met him at the conference reception. He said he was Sally Keemer's client.'

Somers-Barclay was going through the list again.

'No, sir. Nothing. Maybe her partner can help.'

'Jane Boxer?'

Somers-Barclay ran a deeply tanned hand through his very blond mane.

'No, sir. Cynthia Rathbone.'

Now Leonard was interested.

'Partner? You sure?'

Somers-Barclay looked a little startled. Of course he was sure.

'Checked out the company at Companies House. Standard business. One hundred pounds nominal capital. Two directors. Sally Keemer and Cynthia Rathbone.'

# Nineteen

Today was a black leather day. Her breath reached him at four paces. It was a mixture of long and darkly drunk rum, cigarettes and diseased innards. She looked little better on the outside than she must have on the inside. Her latex face hardly moved as her mouth twisted to hold the smouldering cigarette. She gave a half-cough and half an inch of ash dropped into her lap. She seemed not to notice. The eyes, screwed against rising smoke, popped as she turned from the desk-top screen to face him.

'Firmani? Here he is. PanAmerican IT. What's the problem?'

'He doesn't appear on the latest client list and accounts.'

'If your people had asked instead of behaving like the sodding Gestapo, I could have told them. He's new. Wasn't one of Sally's. Plain Jane brought him in. One of hers. Or at least PanAmerican IT is. Up to now she's kept all her contacts on her own file.'

'Was that usual?'

'More or less.'

'More, or less?'

'Usual. Someone working as a publicist gets a client, wants to act up big, get the office behind them, then it goes on their account and we take a cut. Twenty per cent.'

'What do you know about him?'

'Nothing much. He's hers. We worked for him a couple of times. Must be paying his bills.'

'When I met him, he said he'd met Sally.'

'That's right. Couple of times. Last time he was here. Jane introduced him, Sally took him on. Something to do with European media, I can't remember. I don't take too much notice, I just keep the office going.'

148

Leonard walked over to the window. Down below empty but for passers-by. The photographers were long gone from the black railings and tall white wall. He turned back into the room. She was watching him. Slightly hunched as if she was being continuously kicked in the stomach.

'Where is she now? The conference?'

'Her? No. They've done that bit. She's in London with your friend Firmani.'

Leonard was mentally reaching for a telephone. He hadn't finished with Ed Firmani.

'He's going? He said Friday.'

'Day trip. Still got his big speech to do. If we ever get round to writing it for him.'

'Why they in London?'

'All part of the treatment. Get on this, on that. Seen here and there.'

'Can you do that? I mean, just like that?'

'If you're good.'

'Is she?'

Cynthia smoked and nodded. Reluctant to do so. But yes, Jane Boxer was good. She looked down at the desk diary. Scanned it. Then him.

'12.30, drinks and lunch at The Ivy with one of those nearly-Royal rent-a-Sloanes. That'll catch the lazy diary writers.

'3.30, Cork Street. American Civil War Art. Not too much good stuff around so it'll get the good and great out. Flesh gets pressed and more diary writers. Drop a rumour that our Ed's about to set up an Afro-American art gallery on the Internet or something. More diary writers drool. We've got another tart with him just in case there's a photo-opportunity.'

'My God.'

'Wait for it, Inspector, save your bucket for later. There's more.

'7.30, Leicester Square. Film première. She's got him there with some actress. More was than is. But still looks good in next to nothing. Big picture with her boobs hanging out and a

149

caption saying something about him putting up money for an Anglo-American production of one of the Churchills.

'10.30, at première party. That's at the Hilton. Mostly picture stuff. Plenty of opportunity for a picture with something younger in something smaller. Then unless he gets going with something who wants more than her picture in the papers, it's back here and tucked up with a hot-water bottle by three in the morning.'

'Is he going to put money up?'

She sucked on her cigarette. The eyes peeled out of her sockets like blanched grapes.

'Shouldn't think so for one moment. But the papers want tits and a story. We give it them. He gets noticed, which is good for business, happy, which is good for our bank account and, if he's a lucky lad, laid, which is good for someone depending on how good he is.'

'This is all very cynical.'

'Thought you were a policeman.'

Leonard dropped into the sofa. Legs straight out. Hands behind his head. Blink. Blink. Blink. She squirmed on to her high seat and stared back.

'Tell me, who owns the business?'

'I do.'

'You're a partner.'

'Always have been.'

'What's all this about Jane Boxer becoming a partner?'

'That's right.'

'But you say you own the business.'

'Eighty-one per cent.'

'An odd figure.'

'I had fifty-one. I've always had most of it, for what it was worth. Then I get Sally's thirty. Boxer's partnership is the rest. The bit she bought last week. Nothing more.'

'But I thought you hadn't any money.'

'Half the businesses in Britain start without the partners

150

having any money. They use someone else's, usually the bank's.'

'Miss Boxer seems to think that you take what you can.'

'Miss Sodding Boxer's got a lot to learn.'

'So you've done well from the business?'

She stared at him for some time. Her tight mouth moving silently. Talking to herself. Sorting the argument. Sorting her own argument.

'I killed her for the sodding business?'

'I didn't say that.'

'Then don't. I came into this at the beginning because she needed me. I'd have done anything for her.'

'She needed money and you didn't have any.'

'Sodding right. I was skint. But as I told you, she needed me. She needed someone she could trust.'

'And you were family.'

'She was my sister's daughter.'

'Does she know Sally's dead?'

'I haven't told her.'

'Why not?'

'Why should I?'

'She's your sister. Sally was your niece.'

'Someone'll tell her. Can't think she'll be that interested. She never has been.'

'I understand she lives in Italy.'

'Right.'

'For how long?'

'Twenty-odd years.'

'Did Sally live there?'

'Not really.'

'What's really?'

'She went over there for a few months.'

'As a child?'

She spluttered on more smoke. Seemed to enjoy it.

'Oh no. She'd been running this thing for about eighteen

151

months. Had a few clients, but she was too young. Sodding stress, you know. Like a lot of kids. Couldn't handle it. So she just took off. Came back, started again. Like a lot of kids.'

'Where did that leave you?'

The eyes stuck out. Thinking back. Anger? Something more. He couldn't place it.

'Up shit creek without a paddle. Where she always left me. But I kept the name plate polished and when she came back I gave her a hug, as I always did.'

'And she started again?'

'We did.'

'Sorry.'

'That's all right. It's always been like that. Since her so-called mother pissed off.'

'How old was she?'

'Thirty-two.'

'I meant Sally.'

'Oh. Nine.'

She gave a big sigh. The silk T-shirt wrinkled and flattened like a becalmed cotton mains'l. She reached into her handbag and lit another cigarette from the smouldering stub.

'Tell me about it.'

'You need to know?'

'It makes it easier to understand Sally. It may help.'

'Okay. Sally's mother was a sodding slag. Probably still is.'

The venom in her voice was spat with precision.

'That's a devastating judgement about your sister.'

'I'm big on understatement. Try this: she screwed her husband's best man during her own wedding reception. Still had her wedding dress on. She was married twice. Neither of them was Sally's father.'

'I see.'

'More?'

'Mm. Mm.'

'When Sally was born, she wasn't interested. She wanted her to go to one of those care centres. To be adopted one day.'

152

Leonard took off his spectacles. Rubbed at their clean lenses, polished the grey steel arms. Slipped them back on. Blink. Blink. Blink. Waiting.

'But she didn't.'

Cynthia Rathbone took a great gulp of smoke and spluttered into the roof of her mouth with the sound of a sneezing whippet.

'No. I wouldn't let her.'

'Why not?'

'You ever see one of those places? My God, you've got to be kidding. Maybe they do their best, but can you just imagine putting a kid in there? Go on. Can you?'

Inwardly, he sighed. Outwardly, nothing.

'I can try.'

'I doubt it.'

'So what happened?'

'I said I'd look after her.'

'And you did?'

'Yeah. Yeah, I did.'

Her hand was shaking. She stubbed the cigarette into a tin. It wouldn't go out. Broke in two. One half smouldering. The other wet with nicotine and her saliva.

'Fat lot a good it did.'

He didn't ask why. Waited. She'd go on. She was unloading. Downloading. Off-loading.

'Anything in trousers, she wanted to get them out of them as soon as pronto.'

'Like her mother?'

'Oh no. Oh no. Oh no. Not at all. Her mother's like I said she is. A slag. With Sally it was something else. Simple: over-sodding-sexed. You only had to look at her. Chemistry. Sodding chemistry. She'd shudder at the sight of a stick of rock.'

Leonard got up. Paced the room. This wasn't the woman he'd seen. This wasn't what he wanted to hear. This had nothing to do with the respectable imagery of the Georgian

153

city. But why should it? As Cynthia had said, it was easy. People wanted an image, there were enough people to make money out of that want. He leaned against the wall with his head on his forearm. Not weeping for what he'd heard. Wondering. Looked up. Behind the too-polished glass in the ox-blood frame, the peace of the distant hills. The thatched cottage with its gently rising plume. A warmed hearth. Home. Uncomplicated home. A time for sitting. A moment of not having to hear images built. And built, then cruelly broken. As he looked and longed for the peace in the watercolour, it dawned.

'Where's that?'

'Barledge Cottage.'

'But where?'

'Where it's always been. Up on the moor. I gave your girlfriend the address when she was here. Didn't she tell you?'

'Sally's real home?'

'Sodding right. It's the only thing the bitch ever loved.'

The final eight words were spat on the floor. He watched her reflection in the darkest sweeps of the hills. Mouth twisted. Not a sneer. Something infinitely more cruel.

# Twenty

Leonard returned to Manvers Street determined that first thing in the morning they would find Barledge Cottage and see for themselves the only thing Sally Keemer had loved. He'd have liked to have gone there and then, but it would have taken too long. His main interest that evening was the return of Dougie Gordon. Leonard wanted to get to him as soon as he arrived. He'd even considered finding the Flying Scotsman's train time and joining the InterCity from Paddington. It had been an idea. He thought the melodrama unworthy. But he didn't want

Dougie to settle in without seeing him first. He wasn't sure why. Yet.

Madelaine Jack was in his tiny office going through a list of Sally Keemer Publicity clients. He waved her to stay where she was.

'What about Whisky Mac?'

'Gordon?'

'What time's he arriving?'

'Sometime after one in the morning. Last train down from London.'

'Sure?'

'According to McKittrick.'

'Okay. We wait for him. That okay with you?'

She was nodding and flipping the tiny leaves of her mini notebook.

'Anything special on tonight?'

She looked up. Even, clear eyes. Long lashes.

'Sir?'

'I mean, did you want to get away?'

It was an odd question. Murder was like that. The investigation was all anyone had 'on tonight'.

'No. No. Fine.'

He sensed his own embarrassment. Perhaps it was more than that. His throat-clearing sounded artificial. Corny. Ham. It was.

'And we still haven't seen this cottage of hers.'

She went back to her notebook. A little quickly. A little unnecessarily. She'd already found what she was looking for. The name of the officer she'd spoken to at Minehead.

'I've got the map reference. We could get over to Exmoor, find the house and be back in time.'

'We could?'

He wasn't sure why he bothered to ask. Leonard did not have a motor car. Detective Sergeant Jack was the driver in the team. And any chance to get out of the city and far away, she grabbed.

155

She turned back a page.

'Here we go. I spoke to . . .'

He waved a hand, leaned on the desk with both fists. He smiled. It was real enough.

'Tell me, where's the Red Dragon?'

She was fishing in her bag for the keys.

'Car park, sir.'

'Promise not to kill me?'

'Promise.'

She was swinging out of the door and along the corridor to the back stairs before he could change his mind.

Now they'd crossed the Brendon Hills, coming up to Wheddon Cross. Wheddon, the valley where wheat grows. He saw no signs. Nor would he. Next week, it would be the longest day. The light was good. The Sergeant at Minehead had said it would take two and a half hours, maybe longer. It had taken under two hours. An open-topped Alfa Romeo was not a very police-like car. Of that he approved. It had style. He approved. Detective Sergeant Jack's life's savings had gone into the car. That was her problem. She drove like the wind. That was his problem. They'd crossed the country as if she were mastering Monza. She wore thin brown leather gloves. Not an affectation. Nothing about her was that. He watched, almost mesmerized, as the rev counter swung swiftly as she changed down, then up, then down. The left hand flicked at the gear lever, the long sinews beneath the cotton skirt never still. He understood the sensuous display of a woman doing what he regarded as a male pastime. But did not understand why he should think so. A woman pilot. A woman premier. A queen. Power and sexuality. He lost himself, perhaps hid himself in its possibilities. A woman and image. He pondered Sally Keemer's own image. When he had seen her he'd thought her beautiful. If he had known that she was a manipulator of images, a behavioural sculptress, would he have felt anything else? More? Less? And he wondered what others felt. Her clients. How easy was it to fall in love with Sally Keemer? How much easier to fall in love with the manipulator?

He thought as she drove and he thought without interruption. He had learned that Jack did not speak when she drove. Total concentration. Was that, he wondered, single mindedness? Was that the sexual attraction? Was that Sally Keemer? Who else had thought so? A couple of times she'd asked him for map directions. The first time he was lucky. The second, she had to stop. Her driving was smooth. But looking down, peering through his steel-framed spectacles at the tiny scale map, Leonard felt like a novice Cape Horner. Car sickness was not a dignified moment for a Detective Inspector.

He breathed in the early evening summer air. Better now. The signpost said Simonsbath. Not far. Two miles south, she had said.

'Wonder who Simon was?'

'Sigemund.'

'Who?'

'Sigemund, sir. Most of these names are Old English.'

'Oh.'

He seemed to remember. Hoped he did

The moor road was narrow but well metalled. The car was at home far away from the clogged filter lanes that didn't filter. The one-ways that didn't much go anywhere. He felt free. She looked relaxed. In command. Capable. He liked that. He didn't like having to be capable. She sensed his look, shared a half-smile, then changed down a gear and started to slow. The gorse and stubbled undergrowth came down to the sanded verge. Shorn sheep with their prehistoric faces, chewing at nothing very much, stared at them. Too moorwise to scamper. She pulled over to the verge and flipped down the sun visor to read the directions from her tiny notebook clipped at eye level. Satisfied, she accelerated for a quarter of a mile, slowed and pointed. A track to the right. It dropped away from the main moor road, twisted by a yard of huddled barns where a man in

157

a blue boiler suit was unhitching a trailer from a Land Rover. But this was not what they were looking for. Further down, the moor had disappeared behind them. Now there were broadleaf woods. A grey weathered stile into a deep watered meadow. Somewhere below the sound of a breeze through strangely planted poplars.

Then Leonard saw them. Not the cottage and its smoking stack. Nor the roses at the windows. He saw the hills. Dark, purpled and blue as he remembered from the watercolour in that other world of neuroses and perfect decorations. Now the hedging spiky. Tiny white flowers picking June instead of May. Scentless tall fronds of campion, charlock. Stinky Jack-by-the-hedge and coarse and hairy dogwood. For a moment, in his searching, he wanted this for his real world. Didn't want cramped offices, villains and forms MG 1 to God knows how many. Didn't want to be told to Tick If Attached. Didn't want to be on first-name terms with Manual-General Numbers. Wanted to know each page of Manual-Wild Flowers, or Manual-Nothing Really Useful.

She braked. So did he. Across the cattle grid, and there was the cottage. Disappointing. No ducks in the yard. No maid mending in the evening sunshine. A low, flat-faced, unremarkable stone house with slate where once there had been old thatch. Windows black. Baleful panes with their backs to the sun. Boot scrape, stove blacked and unused. Milk churn long dried out and now decorated by two truly super girls in Fulham. Thickly white-glossed door tight shut. Lacquered shiny Yale keyless. Chubb top and bottom. Heavy levered and anonymous. The back sunny, but no curtains drawn. Small back door. Flimsily locked but heavily bolted. The upstairs windows closed. Curtains. Unaired. No smoke. No smell of bread from the range. No Sally Keemer in the one thing she loved.

The barn was open fronted. Empty. Odd boxes and old doors stacked at the back. Out of the way. A barn still used. Leonard, on haunches, peered at the dirt floor.

'What have you got, Geronimo?'

He looked up. She was very tall from down there. And smiling.

'What?'

'Sorry, sir. Couldn't help it.'

'Don't worry. Could be the squaw's turn to get us supper on the way back.'

He pointed to the ground in front of him before she could say anything.

'What you think? Two cars? Quite different. Look at these. One's got very wide tyres. Very wide treads. And the lines are wide apart. Jaguar. Mercedes. One of the big ones. But these other ones? Tiddly. Thin. Mini? One of those French things?'

'Renault? Citroën?'

'Probably.'

He got to his feet before his knee joints gave him away.

'Got any tape in the car?'

'In the boot.'

'Good. Get someone out here. I want moulds of all the tyre tracks.'

'Now?'

He nodded.

'Mm. But let's have a look inside first. We could need a whole team.'

She had the keys she'd collected from Sally Keemer's flat. Not labelled. But obvious. Inside it was cool. Damp in the narrow hall behind the stair turn and tongue and groove. The one big room with windows front and back. Flagstones. A kingpost. The smell of charred wood in the inglenook. An empty wine bottle propped in the granite hearth. Two eggs on a stand in the kitchen. Leonard took one, cracked it in the sink. Put his nose to the shell. Fresh. The waste bin was almost empty. Shells, a crust, cheese crumbs, a cork, an empty toothpaste carton.

'Odd. Fresh eggs, but no box.'

'Maybe they're not that fresh, sir.'

159

He didn't reply. He trusted his sense of smell. She didn't say any more. For the moment she didn't see the significance.

The living room was big, low and comfortable. Two long chintzy sofas either side of the inglenook. Magazines old and new. A book on herb gardens. Horse brasses, a copper warming-pan, chestnut pot and willow basket of spark-dry logs. A dark refectory table at the other end with an empty fruit bowl at its centre. A dresser with willow pattern plates, cups and saucers and an undisturbed film of dust. A cabinet of china. A round table of soapstone bottles and jade. Over it all, a grandfather clock with its solemn eight-day tick.

'Notice?'

She nodded.

'Still no photographs.'

'Right.'

The first bedroom would have left a friar undisturbed. A small bed covered with a white spread in one corner. A washstand with a bowl and ewer on its marble top in another. The curtains thin and closed.

The second with two single beds and an empty stripped pine wardrobe. Then the bathroom straight out of the latest interior design magazines. Expensive. Heated towel-rails, glass-doored double showers. A long Victorian bath with brass taps in the middle of the floor.

Then up some small steps and into the main bedroom. Low ceilings with heavy beams that had once been charred and were now painted instead of burned black. A big Victorian wardrobe with the top removed and the feet sawn to allow it to stand upright. Oversized white and fluffy down duvet across a mighty wooden bedstead. Piles of white lacy pillows puffed and scattered with all the casualness of a carefully prepared photographic session.

Jack was going through the wardrobe. Dresses and blouses, trousers, designer labels on each one. Boxes of shoes at the bottom. She pulled open a chest of drawers. Softly folded jumpers. A tiny drawer of lingerie. A bottom drawer of jeans

160

and cords, thick socks and scarves and gloves. She turned. Leonard was sniffing the pillows. Now the duvet. Now the sheets. He stood back, walked to the landing and blew through his nostrils. Came back to the bed and sniffed again. Then to the landing. Took out a small, green, silk handkerchief and blew his nose. He crossed to where she was standing by the wardrobe, took out a thin summer day dress and sniffed it. Then another. Then the jumpers. That was it. The train. He stopped. Looked at her. Blinked.

'Tell me, do women wear more than one scent?'

'Sometimes. Depends on the woman.'

'Do you?'

'Um. Well, I don't much wear anything, sometimes in the evening and for special things, but not for work, of course.'

Of course. Wasn't that sort of job. But image making was that sort of job. He went to the dresser. Organza. Givenchy. Nothing else.

'Is that odd?'

'No. Plenty of women do use more than one perfume. Plenty of women don't.'

'Right. Smell her clothes then tell me what she used.'

It took a couple of minutes. The traces were there, but quite different smells. The scent was a scent. It changed its form with age, with temperature, with materials. Jack wasn't entirely sure.

'Well, if it's any one perfume, I suppose it really is this.'

She dropped a tiny spot on a handkerchief from the dresser. Rubbed it. Held it in her cupped hands. Allowed the scent to waft by her nostrils.

'Organza. Definitely. Trouble is, sir, the more you smell, the less you can tell. I mean, I could tell you it's not Balenciagga.'

'Why?'

She looked away. Why did she sometimes feel so embarrassed with him? They'd worked together for more than a year. She shouldn't be.

'Because that's what I use and, well, I just know.'

'It is. Organza. It's what she was wearing on the train.'

161

'You know that for sure?'

He did. It was the sort of thing he did know.

'Okay. I want you to go downstairs, into the garden and then come back and smell the pillows and duvet.'

She'd been gone sixty seconds when he heard voices. He looked from the low window, the cill only just above the crooked floor. The man they'd seen with the trailer along the lane was talking to Jack. She was showing him her ID Card. He said something Leonard didn't catch, looked up to the bedroom, then turned with a wave. Jack returned smiling.

'Trouble?'

'No. No. Believe it or not that was Mr Archer. He's the local farmer – keeps an eye on the place.'

'Archer? I don't believe it.'

'Honest Injun.'

'Right. Now try it.'

He waited. Watched. She puffed at the pillows. Ruffled the duvet. Pulled back the cover.

'Well, sir, I'm not a Labrador, but there have to be a couple of smells there. One of them's quite sharp. And it's nothing that's on the dresses.'

Humming off-key to himself. Bobbing his head. Tapping the side of his leg with his fingers. He knew that. He remembered her scent from the train. She'd gone by, grabbed the top of the seat where he sat as the carriage swayed. She returned, slowly. He would never forget that scent. It was hers. No one else would have worn the same scent with the same smell.

This was Sally Keemer's bed, but she hadn't been the last woman to sleep in it. He was staring at the bedside table, trying to imagine. Trying to see beyond the telephone and bedside lamp. Dusty. No cleaner. Dusty? The dust was hardly disturbed except for one line. He walked over, staring at the small table as if mesmerized and pulled open the drawer. Face down, he found what they had been looking for. A photograph frame. At last. He turned it over. But it was not the image he'd looked for since that first visit to the flat. No gap-toothed schoolboy. Smiling at him was the bronzed face of a dark-haired man. Very even, white teeth. The face part-hidden by heavy dark sun-glasses. Long smooth hair. No pony-tail. But he was certain. The man on the train.

## Twenty-One

While they waited for a borrowed constable to get over from Minehead to stand guard on the cottage, Jack took timed and dated photographs and went off to talk to Archer while Leonard went through the cottage with bags and labels. The wine bottle from the inglenook. The scent bottle. Into plastic bags. The pillow, the bolster, maybe with scent, maybe with saliva. A couple of dresses. One with a faint stain on the inside front of the skirt. A small hair brush. The sheet from the double bed. The white, not quite clean, duvet cover. A toothbrush. These all went into the big brown paper Barrow sacks from the boot of the Alfa. Never be without brown paper sacks. You never know. If you don't need them, great for carrying groceries. But best for anything that was going into the DNA test office. Never plastic. Put a semen-stained sheet or dress-front in plastic and what happened when the bag sweated? Best keep evidence in paper sacks. Best keep the DNA team happy. Best keep the defence lawyer unhappy.

Leonard put calls into Manvers Street. He wanted the itemized phone account on the cottage for the past two years. He wanted the photographic unit at Portishead to reproduce the bedside picture ready for circulation and the standard trace procedures. Something at last to show the London cabbies. He'd finished and the constable from Minehead had just arrived when Jack came back in. She'd been talking to her farmer.

'And?'

'Well, sir, I've got your car for you. White seven series BMW, a 730I to be precise. K reg. Electric everything, damaged petrol flap, poser phone aerial. The tyres are . . .'

'Wait a minute. How does he know all this?'

'He's got one himself.'

'Archer?'

'Right. An older one, but it's the same toy. Anyway, he says the guy who drives the white one was Sally Keemer's regular guest. Certainly for the past eighteen months. Not sure of his name, but he thinks it was Rick.'

Leonard nodded. Getting warmer. Much warmer.

'Anything special?'

'Would you believe a pony-tail?'

'When did he last see him?'

'Sunday. He reckons he must have arrived late Saturday. Very late, because when he came by at nine-thirtyish, it was still light and the car wasn't in the barn or anywhere. What's more, he reckons he left late Sunday afternoon.'

Leonard scraped a foot on the flagstone floor. Hands in pockets. Thinking. Humming again. Same noise. Could have been a different tune, but not even Birtwhistle would have known.

'The boyfriend I saw on Saturday night stayed in London.'

'Evening.'

'What?'

'It was evening, sir. And you don't know that he stayed in London.'

'Therefore he was deceiving her?'

'Not necessarily. I was looking through your report notes again. There was something about her saying that she'd ring when she got home, or was it the other way round?'

'Go on.'

'Well, sir, what if she, they in fact, regarded this place as home? Or what if she knew he was coming down and meant that she'd ring here?'

'We don't know, do we?'

164

'No, sir. That's what I meant.'

'And we don't even know if he did come here.'

'Archer does.'

'Does he? All he knows is that he saw the car. He doesn't say he actually saw this Rick fellow.'

'He says he saw the car driving off late on Sunday.'

'But he can't swear who was in it.'

'No, sir. But he did come up with something else. Archer reckons he wasn't alone at the house. But a bonus ball it isn't. He saw another car there in the morning. A small Renault Clio. But he didn't see anyone, although he thought he heard the car early on Sunday morning.'

'The Renault?'

'He thinks so. It went away for about half an hour and then returned. He thinks.'

'I thought people in these parts knew the moment a stranger crossed the county line.'

'Slight problem here. His eyes aren't brilliant. Pebbles. And he's an ex-gunner. Ears are a bit unreliable, as he puts it.'

Leonard made a mouth. He could imagine the fun a defence barrister would have with that information. Brilliant in a stolen vehicle hearing. Not so good at a murder trial. Mr Archer was beginning to have the stamp of a sympathetic but unreliable witness. But witness to what? Leonard didn't know. Infidelity wasn't a crime. Murder was. And his instincts told him there was a connection. He wondered how many tuppences Marsh would give for his instincts.

The drive back was no less fast than the drive there. Lanes became straights. Bends became chicanes. Slow in, fast out. The Alfa Romeo was having a day out and enjoying itself. Madelaine Jack said nothing. Leonard slept. Or appeared to. With each corner, another conundrum swerved into his mind.

The mysterious man in the white BMW had to be the boyfriend at Paddington station. But was he? He was in London on Saturday evening. Why would he have driven to Exmoor? Why had he come to the cottage? And who was driving the

Renault? It would be too easy to assume it was a woman. Why should it be? So that it matched a new scent? And even if it did, did it have to be a woman? Too easy to think so. Too easy to fit in with the scenario forming in Leonard's mind. And what about that scent? Why not Sally Keemer? Rick could have bought it as a surprise. The Screaming Skull might help. Too late. Did scent linger on a corpse? He didn't know. He'd never asked. And whose car? Sally hadn't got a car. But it could be a hire car. Hadn't Cynthia Rathbone said she hired cars? He wanted to ask Jack if she'd checked out the hire firms as he'd asked her to. But he didn't want to open his eyes. Didn't want to push her. Not at ninety on the not so straight road. The hood was up. False security. And why nothing on the son? He still believed she'd said she was going to visit her son. Back to the fantasy hypothesis. And why didn't Mrs Bath Matron remember? He'd forgotten to mull it over. Too much to mull over. That was the problem. All those things left undone. Car hire. Schools check. List of itemized phone calls. Mobile phone numbers. Jane Boxer background. Client list. Ed Firmani's background. Sunday lunch restaurants. Hadn't asked her aunt if she knew Sally was pregnant. Should have done. Should have done a whole lot more. Someone would ask why they hadn't noticed something. Why something obvious had slipped by. The answer was simple: twenty-four hours equals one day and that was all.

By the time they reached Bath it was late. The MIR was abandoned except for one young constable going through forms. The place was already a mess. The mustard curtains closed. Even tattier than when they were open. The dark parquet flooring scuffed. The whole place took on the atmos-phere of the nastiest 1960s high-rise lounge. Wire filing trays overflowing with unclaimed messages that would have been cleared in the joyful days of unlimited overtime. The black-board covered with names and phone numbers. When the investigation started, a model of first form neatness. Now over-chalked with notes, comments and letters. Bracketed witness references. One group looked good but wasn't, the A 26300 file would be meaningless. Blank. Worse than blank because someone had to check it. The N 420030s were Nominal numbers. Checked out. Cleared. But equally worthless.

Somewhere in the white chalk jungle, perhaps a name, a connection, a gap, a date, a number, a missing number. There had to be something on that long board that suddenly made sense, or, perhaps more important to the team, didn't make sense. Leonard stood looking at it all. Humming his own rain dance. Foot tapping. Not in time. There was none. Just tapping as a small boy might who's frightened of the school lavatories. Waiting for the right moment. There had to be a moment. There was always a moment. There was that second, out of the hundreds of thousands of minutes, of the thousands of hours, of the hundreds of days, when the weary, sightless officer would suddenly see. The flat of the hand banged against the forehead. The number, the name, the time, the blank space. Whatever it was, it had always been there. But now, nothing. Einstein might have made something of the hidden equations. For the moment, Leonard could not. He couldn't even tell if there was anything to be made.

Jack looked in, said something about going to the DPR. He didn't hear her. So she went anyway, fetching and carrying the plastic bags and brown paper sacks they'd brought back from Barledge Cottage. Took their bags of Exmoor plunder downstairs. There was no one in the Detained Property Office on the ground floor. She didn't expect there to be. Not at that time of night. Long past the DPO's bedtime. The maroon-covered book she was looking for was in the Uniformed Patrol Sergeant's office. Looked ordinary. Wasn't. Everything that was evidence went in here. Detained Property Register it said on the cover. Detained was about it. Could take months before a trial came up. Evidence was hung on to. It was all in here. The bags were labelled and registered. The duty patrol sergeant took charge. The most important were the brown paper bags. By the morning they'd be over at the forensic science laboratory at

Chepstow. DNA testing on the same day. Jack had got it organized. She wouldn't wait for the courier service. She'd strike someone off from the team upstairs. Get it done. Don't wait. Meanwhile the test material could go in the freezer. No chances. Wait for the match. She was sure there'd be one. She had no more idea than Leonard who had lain in that bed with the mysterious Rick. But she was certain they'd know pretty soon. When they did, what Chepstow told them about the sheet and duvet cover could make this case in a moment. But that, for the moment, was for another day. It was still today – or was it tomorrow? There was still work to do. Dougie Gordon was about to arrive in Bath.

He met her on the stairs. Even she was looking tired.

'You want to duck out of this one? I can see him.'

She hesitated. That was good enough for him.

'Take those client names and telephone numbers home with you. You can read them in bed.'

She was about to say she'd come with him, but he was already on his way. Head forward. Leaning into a wind that didn't blow. Creating his own cyclone wherever he went. He paused at the swing doors. Looked back.

'Stop by first thing. I'll make you coffee.'

He didn't go straight to the hotel. He guessed Dougie Gordon was locked somewhere between Reading and Swindon. Plenty of time. In ten minutes Leonard was home. In fifteen, he had showered, discussed the cricket scores with an apparently disinterested Johnson and nibbled at the remains of some dates and Greek olives. He lay back in the long, teak-slatted deck lounger. In his lap, a small wooden box. His occasional companion. Johnson sat where Johnson always sat on these occasions, on the wall. A white puff of fur. Green slits slowly opening and closing as she eyed this odd companion.

'Okay. Tell me. Why would a lady like Sally Keemer get screwed up by a silly bag of feta cheese?'

Johnson blinked. There seemed no reason to these speeches.

168

'Simply excitable?'

An imperceptible purr. It seemed a reasonable question.

'What else was in the bag? Money? She'd have said so, wouldn't she? Wait a minute. Did she say something about a present? For her son?'

Who could tell these things?

'Sure she did. Or am I? Too damned tired to be sure. Yes?'

The purring slowed. Didn't really understand the question.

'Something very important. Far more important than Greek cheese. This was a beautiful lady with carriers of designer labels. Cheese. Doesn't make sense.'

Nor did it. Music from an upstairs apartment floated through a summer's window. Johnson did not care for other people's music. Two, three, four, sweeps of her tail. The music continued in its own tempo. Leonard's voice droned in unison.

'Something else. Notebook. List of clients. Organizer. Then why not say so? Present for son? There had to be a son. Where, though? Where?'

The music rose in pitch. A woman laughed. Not amused. Defiant. The spell broken. Leonard swung to his feet. Went inside and left the box, unopened, on the dresser. Questions unanswered. Too many of them.

# Twenty-Two

When Leonard arrived at the hotel, Dougie Gordon had just registered at the desk and the night porter was taking away his bag. Gordon caught sight of Leonard. He was either very good or absolutely amazed. For the moment, Leonard went along with the first option. This time, no kilt. Sensibly shod, grey flannels, double breasted blazer and Royal Naval Reserve tie.

'I remember you. On the train. How are you?'

169

He stuck out a hand. The hard grasp of a war veteran, not a whisky salesman barely in his twenties. Leonard tried to look friendly.

'Fine. Just fine. You?'

He'd slept badly on the train which had taken for ever from London and really he wanted to go straight to bed. But he was a polite young man.

'You staying here?'

Leonard shook his head.

'No. You obviously are. I thought you'd left.'

Gordon's eyes narrowed. Young. Tired. Polite. No fool.

'Seemingly you're well informed.'

Leonard took out the white plastic ID card he kept in his shirt pocket. Many of his colleagues had invested in the new American leather wallet complete with warrant card and silver badge. Leonard still had the simple piece of plastic. He held the card at eye level.

'I try to be.'

Gordon peered at the card, then at Leonard. Neither looked real.

'You don't look like a policeman.'

'Without being rude, Mr Gordon, you don't look like a whisky salesman. It's best you believe me and for the moment it's best for you that I believe you.'

It was too late to be polite. He pointed to one of the sofas. Gordon didn't say anything. Followed him. Leonard stretched out from one corner. Gordon perched on the edge.

'I suppose this is not a coincidence.'

'No, it isn't.'

Dougie's face suddenly lit up. His mouth opened in a big smile. White teeth that had somehow survived academy and university rugby. Dougie Gordon didn't look the type to avoid trouble.

'I don't believe it. What was it you are? Inspector?'

'Detective Inspector, yes.'

'A Detective Inspector! Investigating missing sandwiches. At two o'clock in the morning. I knew Bath was seemingly – by English standards, anyway – quiet, but not that quiet.'

Leonard looked about the foyer. It was deserted except for them and the night receptionist. His sigh was the sort of sigh that comes after a long day and a night that won't give in.

'Do you mind telling me why you've come back to Bath?'

'No. Not at all. But before I do, do you mind telling me why you want to know? It's got to be bigger than cheese sandwiches.'

Leonard looked Gordon straight in the eyes. A confident young man. You had to be. It wasn't easy selling a rare single malt in an age of mineral water. Especially in Bath. The Celts, certainly the Romans, would have approved. Gordon tried looking away. Couldn't. The blink, blink, blink, through stainless steel rims. Unnerving. These were not the vague eyes of the crumpled figure on the train. No humour in them. No kindness. No person. Something, well, almost sinister, about this lean, curly haired man in a tweed suit. And those eyes. The shutters continuing to blink. The image recorded. Now Gordon did look away. Then back. As Leonard knew he would.

'I'm back here on business. Um, personal business.'

He wondered if that would do.

'Tell me, Mr Gordon, would that be family business?'

'No, it would not. Not that sort of personal.'

Leonard waited. He was tired. Gordon was nervous. Gordon would bend.

'Very well. I've a very private business meeting first thing in the morning. At eight-thirty. Very private.'

'Whisky?'

'No.'

'With whom?'

Dougie looked down at his shoes. Big black shoes with toe caps and thick, leather, steel-studded soles. Sensible shoes. He tapped them together. Rubbed his hands. Capable hands. Capable of what?

'Is it important?'

171

'Could be.'

'But is it?'

'Is it a secret?'

'I'd hoped so.'

'Why?'

'Och, well, because it's a very personal meeting and I simply don't want to talk about it.'

Dougie Gordon looked into those eyes. No response. From somewhere deep down he heard a humming. A tuneless humming. The face was sad. The eyes drooped at the corners. The lips still. The hum persistent. Leonard leaned further into the sofa. His head dropped back on the soft down cushions. His eyes closed. When he spoke, the voice was quiet. Horrid. The humming punctuating the menacing message.

'Let me tell you something, Mr Gordon. You're right, Detective Inspectors don't investigate missing sandwiches. I could not care a single fuck whether you want to talk about it or not. Now, just once more, why are you here? Who are you meeting?'

The silence between the two men lasted no more than five seconds. In it, Dougie Gordon looked about and then back at Leonard who had not moved. Had not opened his eyes. Had not stopped humming.

'The lady on the train. The one who made all the fuss? Well, her. We've an appointment at eight-thirty in the morning. Her name's Sally Keemer.'

Leonard stopped humming. Opened his eyes.

In Dougie Gordon's room, the top was off a bottle of his single malt. Dougie was still shaking his head from side to side. More than disbelief.

'How can this be, Mr Leonard? How in God's name can this be?'

The head went back and a slightly more than generous dram slipped down his throat. Very dramatic. Leonard didn't believe him. But Leonard believed no one.

172

'Tell me, what was your connection?'

The Scot stared at the carpet, tracing the non-existent pattern of the maroon fleur-de-lis.

'Nothing.'

'You came all the way back from Scotland for nothing?'

'Oh no. London. I put Herself on the train. The night sleeper—'

'Miss Wilson?'

'Aye. We had to go from London. It was the ticket. The special fare.'

'When was that?'

'Last night.'

He looked at his watch. Rubbed his eyes. Splashed Spey Gordon into both their glasses.

'I suppose that's two nights ago.'

'Monday night.'

'Right.'

'Tell me, then what did you do?'

'Got a room at the Naval Club and saw some people today. Business people.'

'You could tell me who they were?'

Gordon squinted from beneath his black bushy eyebrows,

'Aye, I could. But seemingly, Inspector, you're telling me something I'm not hearing.'

Leonard said nothing.

'Am I under suspicion for something? Is that it?'

'Let's go back to your meeting with Miss Keemer. As far as I was aware, you'd only met on the train.'

'She said she was a publicist and told us what she did. We made a joke of it. I said something about publicists only being able to handle people who were already publicly known. And she said that was show business and that ninety per cent of her clients were not publicly known, but needed to be better known in their industry.'

Leonard had heard it all before. This at least rang true.

'So you decided to let her work on you?'

173

Gordon's eyes shifted. Away. What had Leonard said? He tried to work it out as the other man spoke.

'Oh no. Not just like that. Anyway, it wasn't that simple.'

Leonard remembered the tightly-curled redhead at Gordon's side.

'I imagine not. Go on.'

'Well, my brother stays here. A job at the university, you know. And we'd promised a visit. Which was why we were here in the first place.'

'Why didn't you stay with your brother?'

'It's just a wee place.'

'That was on Saturday night.'

'Aye. That's right.'

'Go on.'

'Well, we had a party. You see we've just become engaged and, well, I suppose it was the first celebration.'

'Who was at the party?'

'Just my brother, a girlfriend of his, well not a girlfriend, just a friend who is a girl, you know?'

Leonard nodded. Waved him on.

'Then we came back here. It was very late. Maybe two o'clock.'

'Who came back?'

'Well, me, Herself, my brother and his friend and, well we then met these nice people. Well he was nice. And he was staying here.'

'In Bath?'

'Right here in this hotel.'

'What time was this?'

'About two o'clock.'

Dougie closed his eyes. Remembering late nights? Remembering something else?

'It's late to be meeting someone.'

'Och no. He'd only just come in himself. An American. It's true, I'm telling you. He said he would be here all this week. He'll tell you.'

'What was his name?'

Dougie started searching his pockets, then went to the bedside table for his wallet.

'I've got his card somewhere. Something like Ferrari.'

'Firmani?'

Dougie had found it. He walked, not quite steadily, across the room. Reading it.

'How did you know that?'

'Go on.'

'Oh. Right. Anyway we all had a drink and that's when I got talking to Ferrari. Sorry.'

He still had the business card in his hand. He read it very slowly. He was tired. He was drinking.

'Firmani. Ed Firmani.'

'Why did you talk about Sally Keemer?'

'Coincidence really. The American's girlfriend—'

'The one with him?'

'Aye. A really wonderful looking girl. Very pretty, knew my brother's girlfriend.'

The Scot paused. Looked intently at Leonard.

'Is this confusing?'

'Go on.'

'Well, it turned out that they both worked for Sally Keemer. And then the American made a big joke that Sally Keemer worked for him and so they must work for him. We all laughed, but then it got very suggestive. Now, I don't care for that sort of talk, so we went to bed. Not together, you understand.'

'I do. Tell me, Mr Gordon, what sort of suggestive?'

'You know.'

'No, I don't.'

'Well, something about that at this time of night perhaps they should be thinking of going to bed.'

'But you were.'

'Oh no. His ideas and mine weren't the same, I promise you.'

'Do you remember the name of his girlfriend.'

175

'No, but my brother's friend would.'

'Was she very slim and dark?'

'Slim? Aye you could say that.'

'And dark?'

'Och no. Very blonde.'

'Dyed blonde?'

'I really couldn't say. I don't think so. But you'd best be asking the lassie herself.'

Leonard looked at him. Lassie? Herself? Och and aye? Was it the real thing? Why not? Saturday's kilt had been the real thing. Not at all self-conscious. Leonard yawned. This should have been much simpler. He should have got the information he wanted and then gone home to bed. But there was something that didn't ring true. The long way round was through detail. When he came back along the route in a couple of days, then it was in the detail that Gordon's devil would lurk.

'Did Firmani fix the appointment with Sally Keemer?'

Dougie shook his head. It was full of sleepiness and not a little whisky.

'No. I did. I telephoned her on the Sunday morning. Herself, you know, well, was feeling a little poorly.'

'She'd given you her card?'

'Aye. But it only had her office number and a mobile, which was switched off.'

'So—'

'So I looked her up in the book and there she was.'

Leonard sipped at the whisky. He promised himself to buy a bottle.

'And fixed the appointment.'

Again, those shifting eyes. Again the niggle in Leonard's head. What was it?

'In a manner of speaking, yes.'

'Which manner of speaking, Mr Gordon?'

'Well, that's what happened. Yes. That's it.'

Another swig. Not a sip. Swig. Another pouring. Leonard shook his head.

'Tell me exactly, Mr Gordon. Exactly.'

Gordon got up. Pointed to the wooden door. Shrugged an apology. Leonard listened to the cistern flushing. The washbasin filling. The face being scrubbed. The bowl emptying. The toothbrush scrubbing. The tap running. Spitting. More water. More spitting. More time wasting. When the door opened, Dougie Gordon looked no fresher. The eyes still couldn't meet Leonard's.

'You were saying.'

'No, Mr Gordon, you were *not*. So you decided to fix an appointment with Sally Keemer. You called her. What happened?'

'She said to come over to her apartment. Straight away. She was going out, she said, lunchtime, but she could give me half an hour.'

'When was this?'

'Sunday morning.'

'And what happened?'

Those eyes again. They wouldn't hold still.

'I went to see her, just before lunch. We talked about me, what I do, what I want to do. Who we sell to. How we sell. She recorded the whole thing on a wee tape.'

What 'wee tape'? There'd been no tape in the flat.

'Go on.'

Gordon spread his hands. End of story.

'That was it. She said she had a conference to attend, but she would have what she called a Publicity Profile ready by Wednesday and we'd meet at her office at eight-thirty.'

'You're sure there was nothing else?'

'Nothing.'

The eyes. Leonard couldn't let go. There was something. He was tired. But so was Gordon. If he was going to get anywhere, then it was better tonight. He was used to this. Gordon wasn't. If he had anything to say, then he would say it tonight. Leonard was the professional at this. Gordon wasn't.

'What else did you talk about?'

'Nothing. She said she was going out.'

'What time did you leave?'

The eyes.

'One-thirty?'

'You didn't notice?'

'Why should I?'

'Presumably Miss Wilson would be wondering about you.'

'She didn't say.'

'Nothing at all?'

'Nothing, Inspector. Nothing at all.'

The voice was stronger. Gordon had broken his pain barrier. Leonard had lost it. Too much thinking about it. He sighed. Took off his glasses. Massaged the bridge of his nose with thumb and forefinger. Sighed again. Struggled from the comfort of the sofa. He'd got as far as the door, when one last question struck him.

'Tell me, do you know why Miss Keemer didn't get off the train at Bath?'

'Of course. She was off to see her son.'

Leonard came back to the centre of the room.

'She told you that?'

'Aye. She told everyone on the train.'

'Including the elderly lady?'

'Mrs Collins?'

'Hanbury-Collings.'

'Oh, I'm sorry. But yes. Strange woman.'

'In what way?'

'Well we saw her on Sunday night. A little gentle exercise for Herself, you know.'

'Where'd you see her?'

'By the Royal Crescent. We'd decided to walk up there. Have a look at the view. And there she was.'

'What was strange about that?'

'Well, she was very surprised to see us. She seemed upset and then said that she was going the wrong way and off she went.'

'Strange?'

'Well, we thought so. As Herself said, someone who lives in the place ought to know which direction she's going. Now, wouldn't you have thought so?'

'What time was this?'

'Nine-thirty. Tennish?'

'At night? In Royal Crescent?'

'Aye. A beautiful place. But terribly expensive they tell me.'

Leonard didn't answer. He was thinking about coincidence. Royal Crescent led into Brock Street. Sally Keemer had lived in Brock Street. Where was Sally Keemer at nine-thirty, tennish that night? He didn't know. But he did know where she was about an hour later. Not three hundred yards away. Dead.

# WEDNESDAY

## *Twenty-Three*

It was four o'clock before Leonard got to bed. The alarm went at six-thirty. He was still in his bathrobe, his jaw damp and shiny, rubbing at his wet hair, when Madelaine Jack rang the bell. She apologized. Said she'd come back.

'Don't be so daft.'

Silence. Just for a moment. Then it was easy. Too many regulations. Too many forms. Too many suspicions. By the time he'd dressed she'd ground the beans and the aluminium pot was bubbling and she'd heard most of the story from a distance. She was feeding Johnson when he came into the kitchen. She'd done so before. Johnson approved of the Other One. Always made sure the stainless steel dish was thoroughly washed. Slightly warm. Johnson considered that rather thoughtful.

'So what do we have?'

He carried his dish of coffee into the garden. Another day to be stretched out, riding on a gentle breeze and wondering which island to make by nightfall. The perfect life. But his lot was that of imperfect lives. She sat in the shade. The garden surprisingly quiet. The tinkling of Johnson's name-medal noisy as she set about her breakfast. Madelaine Jack sipped at her coffee, put the dish on the grass. Ticked off the scores with her fingers.

181

'We know she was in Bath between about twelve-thirty and say two on Sunday afternoon. Gordon says he was with her then. We don't know that she was here before then.'

'He phoned her.'

'Said he did.'

'Check the hotel phone record.'

She nodded. Made a note in her tiny pocket book.

'Okay. We also know she planned to be at the conference on Monday and also to see Gordon for a breakfast meeting on Wednesday.'

'We've only his word.'

'Why would he lie?'

'He's lying about something.'

'He came down on the same train as you did. He appears never to have met her until then. He says he met Firmani and decided to make an appointment. He says she said come now. He says he stayed about an hour, until sometime between twelve-thirty and one maybe. Not much there to lie about. And, and he says he came back, apparently, apparently expecting her to be alive.'

Leonard sipped and nodded. Nodded and sipped.

'He's still lying about something. Check the times he left the hotel. They might remember. Room service will have times if he used it. Usual stuff. Okay, what about Hanbury-Collings?'

'Told us she didn't go out, but she did. No crime so far. Appears to have said she was going in the wrong direction, but she may not have said that. Gordon could have misheard.'

'Possible, but . . .'

'But possible.'

He closed his eyes. Trying to remember Mrs Hanbury-Collings's face. Trick or treat?

'And she was in Royal Crescent. Almost next door to Sally Keemer's flat.'

'But then so was Gordon, sir.'

'And the girlfriend.'

'A double act?'

182

He didn't think so. But he did know that Gordon was lying about something.

'Tell me, what do you make of this phantom son? Gordon says he remembers, but Hanbury-Collings says she doesn't. Gordon says she must have done.'

'No, sir. Gordon says Sally Keemer told everyone. Could be Mrs Hanbury-Wotsit missed it. Still not crime.'

'No, but it's social gossip. She's not the sort of woman to miss something like that.'

Johnson had done. She lay stretched by Jack's feet, a paw bent to be licked clean. Good breakfast. She wouldn't mind if the Other One stayed. Never did, of course. Life was like that. Jack leaned over. Tickled Johnson behind the ear. Gently. Briefly. Not one to advance any affection, Johnson approved. Carried on washing.

'What about this Firmani, sir? The girlfriend? It's all something of a coincidence.'

Of course it was. There were always too many coincidences. That's why the obvious went by without anyone seeing until everything else had been eliminated. That's why missing children were found three sheds away after months of searching the kingdom.

'Which girlfriend?'

'La Boxer with a wig?'

'Why? She was with him earlier. No secret. Better have a word with Madam Cynthia. Presumably they'll have a record.'

He stood. Stretched. He really could have done with a morning dozing in the garden chair.

'You look tired. You okay, sir?'

He ran his hand through his hair. Needed cutting. Started pacing the tiny garden. Johnson looked alarmed. Perhaps time to escape to the wall.

'We're missing too much again. Hanbury-Collings says she stayed in, with her son, wasn't it? Gordon says he saw her out. Gordon says he saw Sally Keemer about lunchtime and that was it. If she's lying, why shouldn't he be? We know that this Rick fellow went to Barledge Cottage – or at least his car did. We know that your farmer friend thinks he was there on Sunday morning. But he didn't actually see Rick. Only the car. We know someone else was there. We're guessing it was a woman. But we don't know because no one actually saw who it was. You know what I think?'

'Shit.'

'Sorry?'

He stopped. Almost open-mouthed. Almost.

'That's what you think, sir. If it all came true it would be neat. But we don't know any of it for sure. And even if we do, we're missing the one thing we need.'

He thought about it. She was right.

'Motive.'

'Yes, sir.'

'So you're right. Shit.'

'Yes, sir.'

She was laughing. Quietly. It found it's mark. Snapped him from his gloom. His tiredenss. He grinned. Johnson thought that unusual. Rather cared for it. Thought the Other One good at that sort of thing. Instead of pacing. Instead of making more coffee. Instead of theorizing. Headed for the open French windows. A tie. A jacket. He was tying his tie when she came in with the bowls.

'Make sure they strike off someone to get those pictures back. Don't wait for the messenger.'

'It's done.'

Sideways look.

'Oh. Good. Um, tell me, who is Hanbury-Collings junior?'

'The son? I think he's a lawyer, accountant, something like that.'

'Find out, will you?'

She nodded. Remembered not to be clever. Mental note in the tiny book.

'By the by, sir, I went through those client names. Only two of them local. An estate agent and someone who appears to have been, or is, a scriptwriter. No one particularly interesting, other than Randy Bowen.'

'Who?'

'Randy Bowen? The writer?'

'Porn?'

'Not really, sir. Not by today's standards. But yes, softish, by, well, yesterday's. Sex life of single-minded tycoon. Sex life of single-minded lawyer. Sex life of single-minded doctor. You know, the sort of thing no one says they read, but they sell in their millions just the same.'

'He was on the books?'

'Until last year.'

'That sort of person need publicity?'

'Depends how many millions they want.'

He was patting his pockets, lifting discarded newspapers, moving a tea cosy, feeling down the side of the sofa. She picked up his wallet from a mug on the dresser. He smiled his thanks.

'That all?'

'Until we get the list for the first five years, 'fraid so.'

He was off to the hall.

'I'm going walkabout. Mrs Hanbury-Collings, Firmani. I'll call in. Anyone wants to know, I'm on the case – whatever that means.'

'Yes, sir.'

The front door closed. He was gone. She looked around. What was she supposed to do? Whose apartment was this anyway? Did he have his keys? Burglar alarm number? Johnson blinked from her sunny wall. Maybe the Other One was staying. No. She was closing the French windows. Pity. The Other One settled his moods rather quickly. Cats understood these matters.

# Twenty-Four

Shortly after a breakfast of pure lemon juice and buttered croissants, Mrs Hanbury-Collings sat at her writing desk and, with a characterless but utterly legible fist, wrote to her grandson's headmaster. The message was quite simple: her grandson would be leaving at the end of the summer term. She felt no earthly reason for an explanation to the head, whom she suspected of having an unhealthy interest in the younger boys. But to save later explanation, she wrote that she was arranging for Richard to attend a school in Geneva where his languages would progress beyond common conjugations in good time for him to return to England and his public school. She signed her name boldly, but not fluently. It was a curious fact that Melissa Jones, as forty-three years ago she had been, had never quite got used to Hanbury-Collings. But she was used to spending the Hanbury-Collings money, including the amount she spent on school fees. And since she paid those fees, she felt no need to consult her son. Especially now. Especially now.

At nine forty-five, Ed Firmani of PanAmerican IT stood in front of his hotel mirror. He pulled his gaping bathrobe closer to his throat and moistened his unusually dry lips. He'd shaved. Patted hot towels on his puffed face. He still looked as old as he was, which wasn't at all his style. Monday had been a hard day and night. Tuesday had been a harder day and night. Getting laid at three in the morning used to be his idea of fun. Not any more. Not when he had this thing hanging over him. He picked up the four sheets of carefully typed double spaced foolscap. Looked at the opening lines. Cleared his throat. Opened his mouth. Closed it. Shook his head. He looked at her reflection behind him in the mirror.

'Listen. I don't know.'

She came up behind him, put one arm around him and rubbed her hand across his bare chest.

'It'll be fine. Don't worry.'

'You can say that. It's not you who's going to be standing there. My neck. Their block. You read me?'

'I promise you, it'll work. And remember, they'll be surprised. Say it once, then call your lawyer.'

'This is no wise-crack. You sure it'll play?'

'Mm. Mm. Perfect. And remember you've got all the time in the world.'

'Forty-eight hours. I don't call that all the time in the fucking world.'

'Ssshhh.'

She ran her nails lightly across his stomach. He eased away. This he didn't need.

'Okay. Here goes. Let's try it.'

She gave him a light kiss on the cheek. Stepped back.

'Okay, Tarzan, let's hear it.'

He stared at the lines for a moment. Then at the mirror and did as she'd told him. Think sincerity. Think hard at sincerity. That was going to be the only way anyone'd believe what he had to say. The involuntary glance at her in the mirror. The reassurance of her wink. The final throat-clear. The rustle of the paper in his hand was the signal. Think sincere. Think it. Think it. Think it.

'What I have to say won't take long. But what I have to say is the truth, the whole truth and nothing but the truth. I promise you.'

At ten forty-five Dougie Gordon was back in his hotel room. He'd eaten a good breakfast. He hadn't enjoyed it. He'd asked for brose. They'd brought him porridge. Milky. Smooth. He liked it watery. Lumpy. A dash of whisky. Brown sugar. But he'd eaten it. Then the bacon, eggs, sausage, black pudding, mushrooms, fried bread. He'd tasted none of it. His mind on

187

other matters. He'd asked for a copy of the *Chronicle*. Not until lunchtime, they'd said. He'd asked if they had the previous day's paper. No. Maybe Monday's. They hadn't. And so Dougie had gone to the library. Asked for the *Chronicle* file. Looked the other way as he did. As if he was asking for something off the top shelf in the most public newsagent in the islands. The woman who pointed him in the right direction had barely noticed him. He imagined she'd taken in every detail. He read the Monday edition. Where she had been found. When she had been found. Then Tuesday's late edition. So they'd got on to her at once. Why her? Why not them all? They knew about her. Must do. But not about him. Or did they? He got to the bottom of the page. There it was.

> . . . Also on the train was a Scottish couple, believed to be on a short visit to Bath. Hotels were being contacted this morning . . .

Dougie wanted to rip out the page. Wanted it hidden. All too late. Utter misery. Why, oh why, had they come to Bath? Why, oh why, did they happen to get that train? Why was she on that train? Why had he gone to see her? Why had he not simply walked away? Forgotten it all. Bad mistake. Rush of blood. How could it have happened? And they would never believe him. Never believe why it had happened. Dougie Gordon walked back to the hotel without seeing a thing. He must have stopped at lights when they told him to. Must have stepped to the kerb when ladies approached. Dougie was that sort of person. Instinctively law-abiding. Instinctively cour- teous. Deep down there was an instinct that until that weekend, that evening, he believed to exist in others, maybe, but not in Dougie Gordon, eldest son of Mr and Mrs James Hamish Gordon of Archiestown, Speyside.

For long moments he walked the bedroom floor muttering to himself. Hands rubbing together. Rehearsing what he knew he should do. Then he sat on the edge of the bed and dialled the direct line he'd been given during the early hours of that horrendous morning. When the phone was answered, it was not him. A woman. A DS Jackson or something. But she would take a message.

'Thank you. Um. Would you please tell Inspector Leonard that I must speak to him. I think there's something he should know.'

Shortly after his fourth cup of black Colombian coffee of the morning, John Smith tried for the twelfth time during the past hour to call her mobile. He knew she was on it because her office had said so. She wasn't taking calls because her answering service said so. Each time, he had left a short message. 'Please call me when you have a moment' had come down to 'Please call me as soon as possible' to 'Call me, we need to talk'. This time, the same voice told him to stand by because his call was being diverted to the message service. This time there was no more please, no more call me. A deep breath then his message.

'I'm going to talk to the police. You should have called me.'

## Twenty-Five

It was better to make an appointment. It was better to have a woman officer with him. Leonard had not and did not. He waited in the hall and went through the charade of the cleaning woman telling him that she would see if Mrs Hanbury-Collings was in. He waited three minutes. He was shown into a living room called a drawing room. A room with too much white brocade. A room with a marble fireplace and a French Gothic clock that did not tick but kept perfect quartz time. Magazines in neat piles of two and three. Perfectly dusted porcelain, silk orchids and a lacquered Chinese cabinet. Over it all presided not Mrs Hanbury-Collings, but the fireplace portrait of a man in a steel grey three-piece suit, with steel grey hair and cold blue eyes. The artist's or his? Leonard did not guess. Posed at the unlit fireplace, pleated in royal blue, one elbow on the corner of the mantelpiece, was Mrs Hanbury-Collings. Leonard wondered why.

'I hadn't expected you, Inspector.'

She didn't ask him to sit down.

'My apologies.'

'One has such a busy diary.'

'I appreciate that.'

'I wonder if you can. Position you know, Inspector. So many people expect so much of one.'

He said nothing. Waited. He'd done his curtsy. Bent his official knee.

'Well, you'd better tell me, hadn't you?'

'Small point but I thought it best to get it straight. You said you stayed in on Sunday evening.'

'Did I?'

'Yes, madam, you did.'

'Then I suppose I did. I really couldn't say.'

'You said you stayed in with your son.'

'Then we both must have "stayed in" as you call it. What a lovely expression. "Stayed in." I must tell my friends. I shall ask them if they "stayed in".'

'You're quite sure about that are you, madam?'

'About what?'

'That you didn't go out. You're certain?'

The planted elbow came down from the mantelpiece. The pose must have been arranged with some difficulty. Mrs Hanbury-Collings almost toppled. The mouth twisted without pleasure. Leonard wondered how a woman with such money and one who paid so much attention to herself could not find someone to tell her about lipstick.

'Do you mind telling me what you're implying?'

'Well, you see, I have a statement from someone who said

190

they saw you in Royal Crescent on Sunday evening. Out, perhaps, for a stroll.'

She stared at him. Past him. Through him. Didn't matter. He wasn't there. Only what he'd said. She was getting rid of what he had said. Quite unaware of the time. Her eyes grew distant. Retreating into her lie. He'd seen it before. This one was quite good.

'Impossible. I never stroll. I mean, one simply doesn't stroll. What a silly thought you have.'

'Not mine, I'm afraid. Perhaps you missed what I said. I said that you were seen.'

'But I was here. In this house. With my son. Obviously a mistake. Someone who they thought looked like me.'

'They?'

'Well, he, or she, or whoever this person was. You're confusing me. Aren't there rules for this sort of thing? You're being intrusive, Inspector. Now I must ask you to go away.'

'You were identified by a Mr Gordon and a Miss Wilson. Both of whom, madam, you met on the train on Saturday evening.'

Some stay out in their own space for a long time. Some keep the lie in their heads even when they think they've abandoned it. Mrs Hanbury-Collings' mental re-entry vehicle brought her back to earth within the click of a hypnotist's fingers. She came back. Smiled.

'Oh dear, I'm quite forgetting my manners. Won't you sit down, Inspector?'

'That's all right, madam. I won't keep you. If you could just tell me.'

The eyelashes fluttered. Didn't fall off.

'Of course, of course, of course. How dreadfully silly you must think I am. Of course. I took a little stroll. Such a lovely evening. And didn't I meet those funny little Scottish folk? Mm. 'Course I did. Quite forgotten them. But then between you and I, Inspector, they are, as my late husband would have said, sublimely forgettable. Don't you think?'

191

She gave a half-glance to the portrait above the fireplace. Wanted to sit down. He wouldn't. She couldn't.

'Do you remember what time this was, madam?'

'No, not at all. It had been a long day. My grandson, you know. Quite tiring. I imagine it was at about the time Ashley, that's my son of course, was taking him back to school.'

'Which was?'

'About six o'clock?'

'I see.'

He said nothing. Flicked over the leaves of his diary. A reminder to order the new *Fowler's* on one page. The date of an organ recital in the abbey. Madelaine Jack's birthday. Didn't remember putting that in. Couldn't think why. An appointment with his dentist. Something about adjusting his bite which he did not understand. That would do. He peered, somewhat theatrically, at the dentist appointment note.

'It seems that you must have taken two strolls then, madam. Mr Gordon says that he met you at around nine-thirty. Maybe as late as ten o'clock.'

'Man's a fool.'

'A very certain fool.'

'I would never be out at that time of night – on foot.'

'You're sure?'

'I've said so, haven't I? Look, Inspector, I do remember seeing those Scottish folk. It slipped my mind. If you must know, and I'm not sure it's any of your business, I had a great deal on my mind that evening, still have, in fact. It is very tiresome since my husband died having to take decisions of the most sensitive nature without the support of a partner. But then perhaps you wouldn't understand that.'

'You're saying that you now remember that after all you did go out, but it wasn't as late as Mr Gordon says?'

'That is precisely what I am saying. Now, if there's nothing else, I've a very important appointment.'

Leonard looked at her for some moments. Stared into those

small, round, piggy eyes. She never flinched. Never moved her eyes away. But then, why should she?

'Tell me, as a matter of routine, would you mind telling me where I can contact your son?'

Now the eyes did move. The slightest flicker. It was enough. A good morning's work.

Ashley Hanbury-Collings replaced the receiver. A policeman in reception. He knew a few, but as a rule Hanbury-Collings rather avoided the company of policemen. He was, after all, in company law. This one he did not know. But the instructions from his mother were clear. He was to say that on his return from taking Richard back to school, they had spent the rest of the evening together until a little before midnight. He was, of course, to say nothing of their conversation that evening.

'Do you understand, Ashley?'

'Of course, Mother, but why midnight? It's quite unnecessary and you know I never stay that late.'

'Ashley, will you please do as you're told. I hardly think you're in any position to argue, especially now.'

'But what if someone saw me leaving?'

'Did they?'

'Well, no, as it happens, I don't think so.'

'Ashley, you are on occasion a quite ridiculous boy. On too many occasions. We talked of this and that. You're not obliged to remember what I said. After all, I am your mother.'

'Yes, Mother. But . . .'

'Ashley, simply do as I say. And as your father would have said, keep it simple. Don't get flustered. After all, he's only a policeman. They're not very bright. Telephone me when he's gone.'

'Mother, you must tell me, what has happened? What has this, this policeman said?'

'Nothing has happened, Ashley. I'm thinking of the family.'

193

'I cannot believe, Mother, that I'm hearing this.'

The telephone had gone down. He had waited. Sure enough, his receptionist had announced the arrival of Leonard just twenty minutes later. Just as Mother had predicted.

Green tweed suit. And brown boots. And glasses. My God, what next? Yet Hanbury-Collings was not the fool his mother believed him to be. Leonard was off-putting. Silence. This wasn't the way the police worked. Mrs Hanbury-Collings' son decided that this was a policeman not to be trusted. His mother's assessment was questionable. There was too much at stake. Far more than she realized. Leonard finished looking about. Finished yet more polishing, slipped his spectacles over his ears, popped the handkerchief into his top pocket and gave Hanbury-Collings a brief smile. Even the smile. The sort customs men reserve for green channel fat cats just before turning them over on Christmas Eve. Leonard sat sideways on to Hanbury-Collings. He gave that smile again. You had to be quick.

'Tell me, sir, what did you do on Sunday evening?'

'Inspector, please. No games. You know full well that my mother would have telephoned me after your visit. I did exactly what my mother said I, we, did. We spent the evening together. May I ask why you wish to know? Is my mother under any investigation?'

'Not at all, sir. I'm investigating the death of Miss Sally Keemer; your mother was one of the last people to see her alive. I'm simply trying to pin down times.'

Again, that brief smile. But was it? The lips turned upwards. The eyes moved. He did not like this curly-haired shortsighted policeman. He liked policemen with razor-cut hair. Conventional suits or blazers from high street chain stores. Shoes. He liked the sort of policeman who could pass for what he understood to be successful soccer managers. He touched the knot of his black and silver speckled tie and gave the discrete cough he always imagined he would have employed to great effect had he been a criminal barrister.

'I have to say, Inspector, that my mother senses a certain harassment.'

'Senses?'

'Yes, I believe so.'

'Does she?'

'Inspector, this is not a matter of words. My mother is a widow, with all the anxieties and vexations that sad state may bring. She volunteered herself as a witness to events on a train from London. Now she feels she is more involved in your inquiry. I really would care to know why.'

Leonard sighed. Glanced about the room. Slowly. Lots of deep-buttoned leather. Reproduction. The large mahogany table that Hanbury-Collings used as a desk was real enough. The walls dark green and silk covered. Expensive. Long time ago. Nineteenth-century legal caricatures. A portrait of Denning. A copy, he thought, and not very good. Grand. Not good. Now what did that tell him about Mrs Hanbury-Collings' son?

'As I've said, sir, simply trying to pin down some times. We have a witness who saw your mother in Royal Crescent later in the evening than she remembers being there.'

Mrs Hanbury Collings hadn't told Ashley this

'My mother is of a certain age. But she is perfectly agile in her mind and particularly, Inspector, her memory. If she says she was in Royal Crescent at—'

'Yes, sir?'

'At, um, at whatever time she said she was, then I'm perfectly certain that she was and that your witness is mistaken.'

'Actually, two witnesses, sir.'

'Then, Inspector, both of them.'

He picked up a silver paper knife and tapped it on the perfectly clean blotter in front of him. Leonard didn't understand. Why the tension? Why not something nice and easy from the devoted son? Why not a confidential aside about his mother sometimes not remembering at her age? Why so screwed up? No. Leonard didn't understand.

195

'What time did you leave?'

'Where?'

'Your mother's house.'

'Well, I suppose I went out at five-thirty or so, maybe earlier, to take Richard, that's my son, back to school. He'd had Sunday with us. Always does, you know.'

Something there? Tightening of the eyes. Second lick of the dry lips?

'And what time did you get back?'

'Not sure. An hour?'

'An exceptional drive, sir?'

'Not that I remember. Why?'

'Well, you say that your son – Richard?—'

Hanbury-Collings nodded. Not testy. What then?

'—spends Sundays with you, so I would have thought there might be a routine and you'd know what time you leave, how long it takes, what time you get back.'

The tapping increased. Not harder. Quicker.

'I really couldn't say. But as it happens I do remember that when I did get back, Mother said she'd been out for a walk. Very hot on Sunday evening, you know. Airless. Then we had a cocktail and we talked for the rest of the evening.'

'About anything in particular?'

The tapping stopped. Hanbury-Collings tossed, nearly threw, the paper knife on to the blotting pad.

'What the hell's that got to do with your inquiry? We talked of this and that. Mother and son. I don't think either of us much listened to the other. What is going on, Inspector? Or do I have to telephone someone in greater authority to find out?'

Pompous? Scared? Okay. Why?

'Just trying to get a clear picture, sir.'

Leonard stood. Another of those smiles. And then a long shot.

'Just a quick one, sir. Did you know Sally Keemer?'

'Of course not.'

Too quick. Too irritable.

'Why of course, sir? She was a well-known business woman in the city.'

'Not to me she wasn't.'

'You're sure?'

The eyes that looked up at Leonard were not frightened. They were not on the defensive. But they were weak eyes. Didn't go with the smooth grey and black silk tie. Nor the stiff collar. The voice was strong enough. Yet it said very little.

'Perfectly sure, Inspector. Never met her in my life.'

It took Leonard fifteen minutes to walk to Ed Firmani's hotel. All the way, he wondered to himself why he didn't believe Ashley Hanbury-Collings.


## Twenty-Six


What Leonard hadn't expected was Jane Boxer. He didn't call from the lobby. He went straight up to room 212. He knocked. Waited. Knocked again and leaned against the soft cream wall opposite. Mr Firmani, he guessed, was one of those safety-conscious Americans who wouldn't let in the New Year without first checking the spyhole. Leonard was rubbing his boot across the deep blue nap of the corridor carpet when the door opened. But not Mr Firmani. Not at all Mr Firmani. Jane Boxer in a white towelling robe with the hotel's name across the left breast. She was very wet. He made no move to go in. DS Jack. It was essential to have a DS Jack on these occasions. She did move. Swung back the door to let him in. The smile was professional. But real. Mocking. Very real.

'Don't stand there, Inspector. You'll give room service a bad name.'

'I'm looking for Mr Firmani.'

197

'Come in, we'll see what we can do.'

Leonard wished he had a hat. At least he could have taken it off as a sign of gentlemanly intent.

'I understood this was his room.'

The door closed. She pointed to the only easy chair in the room and flopped on to the bed, gently towelling at her short dark hair.

'So it is. I'm just using his shower. Quick change for the half-time dwinkies.'

'The conference.'

'Right, Holmes. The flesh pressed, fifty per cent of the weary wallahs wend their ways to airports and a full day's expense accounting.'

'Is it really like that?'

She crossed her legs.

'Isn't everything? But you didn't come here to talk to me. You want Big Ed. Why?'

'Few questions.'

'Mm mm. But why?'

'He had dealings with Miss Keemer.'

'You could say that about a lot of people.'

'I was getting round to you.'

'That's not very flattering, Inspector.'

'Takes time. Investigations don't run for fifty minutes with three commercial breaks.'

She leaned across the bed for a water glass. Robes only cover so much. Maybe she did it deliberately. She sipped and looked at him across the rim.

'What are you looking for?'

Her look went with her pause. Daring him.

'Could you tell me who Mr Firmani's escort was on Saturday night?'

Another sip.

'Why?'

'Miss Boxer, it would simply be helpful if you answered my questions.'

198

'For whom?'

'For the investigation. Unless you have some reason to impede the inquiry.'

She swung off the bed. Very long legs. Not a very generous robe. She tapped his nose with a warm finger and then went to the minibar.

'That was not very subtle, officer.'

'Murder isn't.'

She handed him a cold bottle of mineral water.

'D'you mind?'

He opened it and she poured two glasses. When he took his, her hand lingered quite a time.

'Nor was that.'

She gave a mock pout. Flopped back on to the bed. This time she didn't rearrange the robe.

'Okay. Saturday night? That was Nikki, Nikki Dunn. Two Ks and two Ns. Part of the deal is that we provide a minder for the client. Quite often it can be a long job, so there's a day girl, or man, and someone for the evening if necessary.'

'Who decides necessary?'

'The client. It's like any beauty treatment, face or car. If you want the full wax, you need a more expensive token. It's all up front. No hidden deals. Why do you need to know?'

'On Saturday night Mr Firmani and his, um, minder, met a couple staying at the hotel. By chance, the couple had met Miss Keemer on the train. They talked. I simply need to check out times. Most of this trade is about checking times. Who was where and when. Who wasn't. Who thinks they were.'

'So dear Nikki's in for a grilling. The third degree. She'll love it. You will rope her, won't you? She's into bondage.'

'I need to talk to her.'

'She's a freelance, but Cynth'll give you her address. But, as it involves the company, would you mind talking to her at the office?'

Leonard never made deals.

'What time did the night shift come on?'

199

'Evening shift.'

There was a tightness in her voice.

'Okay.'

'Ten–thirty.'

'That's late. That's night.'

She sipped from her glass.

'Let me tell you what happened. We'd fixed for Big Ed to meet a few people. Quite late. One of those after-supper recital things. You know?'

He didn't. She didn't wait to find out.

'So we arranged for Nikki to mind him. She knew the people, she'd been briefed on PanAmerican IT. All very professional and above board.'

'He'd just arrived?'

'Late afternoon. Yes.'

'I understand that he is your client, not Miss Keemer's.'

'Not exactly. PanAmerican IT is my client. Ed Firmani happens to be Senior Vice-President, sales. The first time I saw him was on Saturday evening.'

'You mean you were there too?'

'Oh no. But I was his Welcome Wagon. You know? Meeter and greeter? Said hello. Glad to meet you. Anything you need?'

'When was this?'

'About eight. Right here at the hotel.'

'How long did you stay?'

'Two minutes.'

'Not much of a greeting.'

'Nikki was with me. She's a warm and wonderful greeter.'

'As good as Miss Keemer?'

She shifted on the bed. This time she did rearrange the robe.

'You don't know too much about her, do you? Sally was one of those people everyone thinks they like. Everyone thinks she likes them. It's only later that you begin to wonder what it was you liked and she liked. If you're a woman, maybe you come to this conclusion quicker.'

'Because she was attractive?'

200

'You don't have to be a behavioural psychologist to figure that. Really pretty. Sometimes beautiful. I watched her with men. When one talked to her she had a look that said he was saying the most original things ever said. He was the most important person in the room.'

'Teaser.'

'Oh no. She believed it. Talk to her and she's watching your lips. A hundred per cent concentration. She could pick up on any line of thought, repeat anything you'd said. Until the next day. It had gone. The only thing that ever stayed in her head was how she looked at any given angle in any given light.'

'Vanity is not unusual.'

'It was what she was best at.'

'And the business. It seems to be very successful.'

Jane Boxer drained her glass, stuck out her arm.

'Would you be a pet?'

Leonard had never been a pet. But he got up and opened another bottle from the minibar. As he stood over her, pouring the sparkling water, she leaned forward. Teasing. Wasting her time. Something had caught Leonard's eye in her open hand-bag. It would wait. He sat back in the chair, waiting for her to continue.

'Five years ago, this business was going under. Sally was brilliant at knowing people and could think of the most outlandish and original ideas for getting publicity for any client. Sally believed she could have got Herod an audience with Il Papa. Okay? What she was lousy at was organization.'

'Which was why she needed Cynthia Rathbone?'

'Partly. Dear old Cynth did more than hold the filing and invoices together. She held her precious niece together. Don't forget it was Cynth who kept it going while the most beautiful woman in the whole wide world went off to find herself.'

'Did she?'

'Shouldn't think so. She didn't want to. She simply wanted an image.'

'Which one?'

'Depended on which magazine had impressed her.'

'But that's the business you're in.'

'Tell that to Cynth when she was putting her own lollipops into the bank account while madam was in a darkened room. There were times when Sally used her like some Edwardian nanny. She'd put her head in that scrawny lap of hers and cry for hours.'

'About what?'

'Mostly her ego.'

'You didn't like her, did you?'

'Not at all. But we got on well.'

'You said five years ago. What happened?'

'I was three years out of university – late starter, you know. Worked for a year as a researcher for the BBC, then a year in political PR. Hadn't seen each other since school, but even then we were never friends. Different set. You know how it is.'

He didn't.

'We met again—'

'How?'

'Party, here in Bath. One of those things. Like meeting someone from a part of England you've never even heard of in darkest Africa. School connection. Becomes a big thing. We clicked. Fancy seeing you after all these years sort of thing. About a month later I started working as a minder.'

'Like a Nikki Dunn?'

'Exactly. It took about three months. She needed me. She was the ideas. I could make them happen. Sally knew every inside leg measurement in every boardroom and in every television studio that mattered. According to her, that was all she had to know. I take the Ed Firmanis of this world and make sure they get where they're supposed to be, make sure they're wearing the right clothes, had their hair properly cut, make sure they're in bed on time and if they're not alone, I make sure I know who they're with.'

'That's a very full service.'

She laughed. The sound came from the back of her throat. A rich sound. Very wet. Juicy.

'Don't start getting the hots, Inspector. We're not the only ones. We, I, charge these people between two and seven thousand pounds a day. A day, Inspector. Depending on which token they have, remember? But we want them back. When the Ed Firmanis get back to the office, the reason they'll call again or recommend us is not because they had a good time. It's because they met the right people, the right people met them, because they're bigger men than when they came to us. We make midgets ten feet tall, Inspector. You want to be Chief Constable? No problem. We'll build you a profile that'll make sure the job's yours in ten years.'

'A lot can happen in ten years.'

'I'm a realist. If I said you'd be Chief Scout in a week, you'd laugh. But ten years? Makes sense.'

'You get to know a lot about your clients. Can you know too much?'

'Not from our point of view. From theirs, perhaps. But don't get any ideas about little black books, Inspector. That wasn't Sally's style. She liked what she did and she wasn't about to foul it up by putting the arm on someone.'

'Tell me, where were you on Sunday night?'

That same laugh. The head went back. Came forward very quickly. The bathrobe performed. She pulled the collar together. Performance over.

'I'm a suspect?'

'Elimination.'

'What's that a euphemism for?'

'Sunday evening?'

'Right here. I had supper with Ed Firmani. The food was tired, so was I and I was in bed by ten-thirty.'

He said nothing.

'Alone, Inspector, alone.'

'No one who could confirm that?'

'Unless you speak pretty good Paddington Bear, then I'm afraid not.'

Leonard needed a little help. Out again came the diary. This time he skipped the dental appointment. Madelaine Jack's birthday would do. He took his time flipping through the pages. He sensed her watching him. Looked up. The eyes. Not so relaxed. Never were when the notebook came out. He learned that in his first week.

'Did you know Miss Keemer's boyfriend?'

The eyes again.

'Which one?'

'The same one I asked you about before.'

'Now why ask again?'

'His name is Rick.'

The eyes were under control. Not the bathrobe. The heave beneath the white towelling was real enough.

'Sally's private life was her own.'

Back to the diary. He ran his finger down a blank page. Flipped another. Nothing but a note that it was the feast of Corpus Christi. Peered as if deciphering his own writing.

'What sort of motor car do you drive?'

'Renault. Why?'

'Just clearing something up, that's all.'

There was one more thing to clear up. It was lying on its side in Jane Boxer's open handbag.

'Tell me, what scent do you use?'


## Twenty-Seven


The Incident Room was a mess. Too many people, too little space. A couple of desks were in the corridor. The Training Sergeant had been moved out of his office on the other side of the canteen. He'd been 'relocated'. He didn't mind but he did. Leonard saw the office cleared for Marsh. He'd hardly be there. On the bright side, the Training Sergeant would get noticed. He'd left his framed degree on the wall. Exeter. Leonard hadn't realized that. Upper Second. Mm. Better than his. He'd mention it to Johnson.

It wasn't the first time that Manvers Street had overflowed. Since the county restructuring programme, it was worse. Thank goodness, yet again, for Detective Sergeant Somers-Barclay. Slipping on the shiny floor and breaking his leg was good for morale in a too-crowded room. Most believed that one day Somers-Barclay would be in the top branches of the police tree. But for the moment he was DS S-B and, when a few felt like it, the butt of their humour. Now the offended leg was stuck out in its much-signed cast on the only spare chair in the room. But the coffee had been delivered by his importer and was bubbling in the filter machine, a small bunch of flowers from a charmed young doctor at the RUH was on the cill and he had taken over the arduous duties of running the Major Incident Room. He was in considerable pain, but was pressing on. They'd have been proud of Somers-Barclay in any nineteenth-century campaign. Indeed, there had been a point when it seemed that no Peninsular engagement was allowed to begin until a Somers arrived. Later in the century a Barclay could always be relied upon to be wounded with honour in practically every Afghan skirmish. Had the Barclays and the Somers not waited until 1914 to marry, the whole history of nineteenth century punitive warfare would have been changed, certainly more bloody.

When the latest in the long line of the family's walking wounded looked up and spotted Leonard standing in the doorway, the beam on his young aristocratic face was broader and insufferably engaging as never before.

'Hello, sir, I think I may have something for you.'

He was waving the top copy from a box of photographs. Leonard doubted it. Wished he hadn't. He liked Somers-

Barclay and wished that he did not. The picture was the head and shoulders he'd brought back from Barledge Cottage. The mysterious Rick. Complete with heavy shades. But they couldn't be back already. Twenty-four hours at least, they'd said.

'Managed to have a word with a chum over there, sir. Got him to push through twenty-five on the scanner by return courier. The proper ones will be here by noon tomorrow.'

Leonard took the offered picture. It was thin but good. Even the felt tip inscription was clear. A strange script. Even. Almost printed. With the capital of his name very large, but not flamboyantly so. Just big. What sort of person was this? Stylish but not flashy? Self-contained? Organized?

> To the very end, all my love,
> *Rick.*

Somers-Barclay was about to say something. Leonard cut in.

'When did they arrive?'

'This very minute, sir.'

'Good. Don't hang on to them. Get them circulated. Into Paddington station. He must have taken a cab Saturday night. Let's find him.'

He smiled his thanks. Started to read the jumble of messages across the blackboard. Nominal numbers spilling into telephone numbers and contacts. Only just up to date, but not for long. Somers-Barclay hadn't finished. He sensed Leonard's mood. The voice was nearly apologetic.

'But, sir, um, I think I know who this is.'

The room turned as Leonard did. Somers-Barclay was wincing as he moved his leg on the chair.

'Go on.'

'Well, sir, his name as far as I know is, well, Randy Bowen.'

The Sally Keemer file.

'You kidding me, Nick?'

'No, sir.'

One of the detective constables from headquarters sauntered over. Picked up another copy. She nodded. Tossed it back on the pile.

'That's right, sir. That's him. Big piece in the weekend mags two, three weeks ago. Exactly this picture of him. Made a million out of soft porn for libraries.'

Leonard pulled up a small chair. Sat opposite Somers-Barclay who bore the sad smile of a smitten ancestor. The leg was getting worse. Swelling inside the plaster.

'I think they call them bodice rippers sir. He writes them. Period romances. Quite hot stuff. Lots of romping and yomping. You know, *Tom Jones* for the illiterati?'

Leonard did know.

'That a real name?'

'I think so, sir. Well, that's what it says on the books.'

'You've read them?'

'Oh, rather!'

The room broke into a laugh. Leonard glanced around. He thought they'd all read them. Somers-Barclay had done it once more. Bath's Daisy had pulled it off. The constable from headquarters was already calling her flatmate to look for the publisher's name on any of the five Randy Bowens in the bedside cabinet. Somers-Barclay picked up his own telephone. While he was dialling he waved at a constable who'd come in to check the message trays.

'Find a copy of *Who's Who*. See if Randy Bowen is listed. We want an address and telephone. Okay?'

He didn't wait for a reply. His call was through.

'Charles? Nick Somers-Barclay. How are you?'

He tapped impatiently with his pencil, conducting the formalities of old friends' greetings.

'Now, Charles, a little guidance, please. How do I get hold of Randy Bowen? . . . 'Course I know he's not one of yours. But I thought . . . what? . . . Okay. Give me that again.'

It was always worthwhile to have old school chums in publishing.

It was late. The time of day for answerphones. Leonard needed answers that evening. She was checking a list with someone in Crime Management. He raised a hand and a minute later she followed him into his room. There was only one desk. One chair behind it and a stacking stool she'd managed to find somewhere. At the new headquarters she'd seen more new desks and chairs and tables than they knew what to do with. Bath was still in the 1960s. Even the identity parade corridor they'd built in the basement had been sponsored by a local glass company.

'I was looking for you, sir. You've had a call from—'

'Tell me, what does 24, Faubourg smell like?'

He wasn't listening. Staring from the window at the electrical store. Was the whole world at a bargain sale? Made him angry. And that made him angry.

'It's a perfume?'

'Mm.'

'Sorry. Never heard of it.'

'Hermès. And something called Individuelle.'

'This Jane Boxer?'

He nodded. Watching for her reaction.

'Now that is her. Charles Jourdan. It's, well, it's cheeky. She'd wear that.'

'Okay. In her handbag was a squarish bottle. Not in a case. Just the bottle. That was the Individuelle. I asked her what she wore. She said 24, Faubourg.'

'Perhaps she wears both. Women do. I told you. Depends when and what for.'

'But she only told me about the 24, Faubourg.'

DS Jack said nothing. It was a good enough reply. Why should Jane Boxer have gone into a long explanation? Wasn't the type. He was leaning on the wall. Thinking. The buzzing

208

from somewhere below his throat. He pushed himself off the wall.

'Tell me, out of those two, which one would you wear in bed?'

He wasn't even looking at her. Yet again. Uneasy. Disturbing? She didn't know.

'I wouldn't. I don't. But Boxer? I'm not sure. I don't know what they smell like. Again it depends what time of day. It . . .'

This was getting complicated. He pushed off the wall. Wagged his index finger. Working something through in his mind.

'Go and buy some. Both of them. Send them over to Chepstow. See if it's still possible to match them against that pillow and the duvet cover.'

'You think Jane Boxer was the mystery visitor?'

'She drives a Clio.'

'Sir, if you don't mind me saying so, this is all guesswork.'

He was blinking. Rubbing at the spectacles. Shaking his head.

'You've seen the blackboard in the Incident Room? More numbers than an anorak's convention. And what have we come up with so far? The identity of Rick. Why? Because DS Somers-Barclay reads mucky bodice rippers.'

'We have? Who?'

'Your Randy Bowen. Ask peg leg. What was that you were saying? A call?'

There were moments when she wondered if the fogeyism, the absent-mindedness, the distractions, the buzzings, the gingerbread men, the green bicycle clips, the stainless steel framed spectacles and everything else of the Leonard she could see, added up to one huge game. But she didn't know. There were times, like this one, when she wanted to scream at him. But she was not sure what she would scream. She drew a deep breath.

'The Flying Scot. He called. He wants to see you.'

'Say why?'

'Thinks there's something you should know. He sounded nervous.'

He was back on the wall. Hands deep in pockets. Fists clenching. When he spoke, he was looking at his tapping brown boot.

'Curious, isn't it? A woman gets on a train and meets four strangers. The next day she's murdered. But each of those strangers is connected to her, although at the time they meet they don't know that. Me because I'm the copper. Mrs Hanbury-Collings because she emphatically denies hearing her talking about visiting her son, when she must have heard. And now it seems she was seen within a hundred yards of the dead woman's address shortly before the murder. The feisty Miss Wilson because she's engaged to our Flying Scot and because, whether or not she remembers it, she danced with a man who had danced, not with the Prince of Wales, but Sally Keemer. Ed Firmani.'

'And now Gordon.'

'Right. He went to see her on Sunday morning. They talked and that's that. You believe him?'

'Actually, there is something odd, sir. You said to check the hotel. He claims that he called her. Right?'

'Mm.'

'There's nothing on his itemized bill for her number. But the receptionist did see him making a call from the lobby.'

'Definitely him?'

'The kilt.'

'Why would he use the lobby phone? Impulse? Not wanting the call recorded?'

'Maybe. But she said guests often do. Can't be bothered to go back to their rooms or more likely because a public phone is about a third of the price of the bedroom one.'

'And he's Scottish.'

'In a kilt.'

He paced the two steps back and forth across the tiny office.

Outside it was hot. The electrical store was still there. He wondered about buying a fan.

'So nothing odd.'

'Only the timing, sir. He says he was there when?'

'Can't remember. Between one and twoish?'

'The girl says he went out at about eleven o'clock. The time is recorded because he extended their rooms for another day.'

'He didn't say where he was going? Ask for directions?'

'I didn't ask. Sorry.'

'Ask her. See if she remembers. She on now?'

'Will be. She's on the Hello Goodbye Hello turn this week. Greet guests in the morning in or out. Take a break. Be there for the evening. They like the same face. This is her last day, then she's off for twenty-four hours.'

He picked up yet another wadge of files.

'These important?'

She nodded. He dumped them on his seat. It was known throughout Manvers Street as DI Leonard's Pending Tray.

'Come on, I'll see what Gordon wants. You can find out what intrigues your receptionist about a man in a kilt.'

They were going out of the front door when the constable behind the glass hailed him. He was waving the telephone receiver at Leonard.

'Somers-Barclay here, sir. Randy Bowen. Got his telephone and address. What d'you want us to do?'

'Where's he live?'

'South West three, sir. Rather smart, I should say.'

'So you would. Listen, call him, tell him I want to come and see him tomorrow evening. Seven-thirty. If he gets uppity, tell him, tell him um . . .'

'We'll have his books banned from Bath Library, sir?'

'If you have any problems call DS Jack on her mobile. Okay?'

He didn't wait for a reply. Jack was waiting for him on the steps. Face to the late sun.

'You should have a hat.'

They walked across the narrow front car park crammed with more vehicles than anyone imagined possible.

'Tell me something, has young Somers-Barclay got a sense of humour?'

'He's very funny sometimes. Why, sir?'

'Dunno. Something he just said. It made me laugh but I don't know if I was meant to.'


## Twenty-Eight


Dougie Gordon sat sipping. Leonard watched and waited. The Scot had taken a drink. Leonard eyed the bottle. He supposed it appeared on Dougie's expense return as Sample Used in Sales Promotion (Bath). Much of the sample had gone. Mournful, he looked. The whole weight of his life on his shoulders. A man born of the longest of winter nights. A man whose instincts told him the freshest of summers were nothing but illusions. Smugness and melancholia. Nothing in between. Dougie was the worse for the drink.

'You see, Inspector, there are some things that seem natural. You know that?'

He looked up from where he leaned forward in his chair. Forearms along the tops of his legs. The bathroom tumbler clasped in large hands as if smuggled there during prayer.

'You do see that, don't you?'

Leonard's head bobbed slowly. A rocking motion that would not gybe the course of Dougie's thoughts. Best leave it to him. He had something to say.

'You see, when I went up there, I thought this was my opportunity. My chance. This was different. Can you understand that?'

Leonard raised his eyebrows.

'Well you should, Inspector. You should.'

Leonard blinked. Said nothing. Let Dougie tell it and when nothing was said he would say more until something was said. That was the way.

'Seemingly she had this system. You know? Introductions. Right people. All of that. But different from the others. She'd get you to do things you'd never thought of. And then tell people you were doing it. And they'd never thought of it. So that made you special. You understanding me?'

Leonard sighed. Blinked. Dougie took a drink. Didn't move his head. Just the glass. Not a drop spilled. Not yet. His head went down and the eyes came almost up into the skull. Peering through bushy dark brows like some forbidding elder.

'She said she'd take me to premières, galleries, galas, recitals . . .'

He waved an arm at directors, painters, divas and cellists. Each beckoning him towards his new-found celebrity. The arm dropped. The glass came to his lips. Now the head back and the whisky drained. He refilled the tumbler. The bottle empty. He seemed not to notice. Focused on Leonard. He offered the glass. Leonard shook his head. Slowly. Keeping in focus.

'People get to know me. Think me. Think the whisky.'

He raised the glass to what might have been.

'And that was that, Inspector. That was, as you people say, jolly well that. But it wasn't, was it? Oh no, Dougie. It wasn't, was it?'

Dougie moved his head from side to side. Then up and down. Then side to side. Confused in his agreement. The head swung to the silent Leonard.

'And you know why, don't you? Mm? You know why, Inspector, don't you? You see, I know you do. It was her. Mm?'

The delayed sip was noisy. Dougie stared into his glass expecting to find a gremlin messing with his single malt.

'God, she was beautiful. You know that? Class. Legs right up to here.'

213

He raised his hand to his eye level. Moved back his head to focus.

'I couldna stop looking at her. I tell you, Inspector, if I'd seen her in the street, I wouldna dare look at her. You know? I wouldna dare look at her. So beautiful.'

Dougie's voice was slipping into his imagination.

'And the way she just sat there in that big sofa. That dress. You remember the one on the train, do you? You remember? It was like she had nothing on. I couldna look at her.'

The solemn shake of the head. Of times past.

'So beautiful. And she knew it. I tell you, she knew it. No hiding, that one. Och, no.'

Then silence. Leonard took off his spectacles. Polished while he waited. The words came slowly. The thin, blue, silk dress. Disappearing into the folds of the couch. The tanned hypnotist still working her magic.

'I couldna look. So beautiful. She knew it. I could see that. And I tried. I tried. I really did try, you know.'

The head now back. Who was he telling? Not Leonard. Someone.

'I made myself think of Jenny. You know that? Think. Think. Think. Jenny. Jenny. Sleeping in her room. My lovely Jenny. Think. But I couldna. You understand that? Do you?'

He looked across for understanding. Leonard blinked. Leonard wanted to hear the agony. Wanted the justification. Wanted the truth. Wanted to hear Dougie tell him what had happened.

'The more she talked the more I knew why I'd come. It was her, you know. You know that? It was her. Not all the things she said she could do. Oh, no.'

The head shook. Arguing. Dismissing the excuse.

'Oh, no. Not anything else. Just her. I wanted to look. Wanted to look at her. And listen. I wanted to touch her. Kiss her voice. Stroke her. Do things. You understand?'

Leonard did. Did not say so.

'Then she started talking about a place she stays on a moor. Where she can be alone. Freedom, she says. She keeps asking me if I understood freedom? Then she says that when she's at the place on the moor, she takes all her clothes off and wraps herself in this big duvet affair in front of the fire. And she wants to know if I can imagine it. And she's talking like I was there. I can see her. I tell you, I can.'

One large hand came over the cupped tumbler. The demon would not be allowed out. Another illusion. It was gone.

'I had to go out. I really did. I went to the bathroom. You know? Washed my hands and face. But when I came back she'd got this white wine and she said that I was to pour it for us and sit with her. With her. On that sofa of hers.'

The head was right forward. The arms came up like muscled derricks. The whisky slipped down. Leonard waited. Took a silent breath. He wanted to hear. Wanted Dougie to tell.

'And she keeps moving her legs and she knows I'm looking. Och, I have to look. I'm a man, you know. I'm shaking inside. And I'm telling you, Inspector, she knows it that one. Aye. She keeps moving about and she doesn't bother to hide anything. It's terrible, I tell you, terrible. And then she starts asking about my kilt.'

Leonard remembered. The hotel receptionist. Remembered the kilt on that Sunday morning.

'Wanted to know about it. Clan. Colours. And then . . .'

He sipped once more. Then deeply. As if for the final time. Looked long at Leonard. Still listening. Listening very carefully. Wanting to run ahead. But not wanting to miss the race.

'And then she starts feeling it. She's telling me the kilt fascinates her. It's a mystery, she says. She calls it a Celtic mystery. And all the time she's feeling it. Feeling it. Says it does things to her. Then rubbing my legs. And all the time she's looking in my eyes. I tell you, Inspector, I was scared. Scared. I just sat there. Scared. Letting her do it. I didna touch her. That was worse. And then she's standing in front of me. Right in front of me. And she's wearing nothing at all.'

The glass was empty. The bottle stood on the small table by his elbow. Empty. Dougie lay back in the firm-framed hotel

215

armchair. Drained. Confessed. Still guilty. But nothing more to tell.

They were walking back to Manvers Street. Most rode. Leonard walked or cycled. The cycle was invariably abandoned.

'Where's he now?'

'Asleep. Or he was when I left him. I've told them he's staying another night. Maybe two.'

'But you don't think he's our man?'

'No.'

'But?'

He looked at her. She was looking ahead. Watching where they were going. As usual.

'But what?'

'You're not sure. Are you, sir?'

The lanky one with the beard that never quite made it was outside Waterstones with his fist of *Big Issues*. He didn't look homeless. But then who'd have thought of having a magazine for the homeless? Leonard gave him a pound. Didn't look for change.

'How you doing?'

'Earning a crust.'

He smiled. He didn't spend his money on dentists.

'Hear anything about the girl on Sunday night?'

Half-beard danced from one foot to the other. Not his scene. Nothing to say. Leonard shrugged. It was worth a try.

'Take care.'

'You too.'

The news-stand on the corner of Quiet and Milsom Streets had the black-and-white bills on both sides. *Society Killing – Latest.* So now it was a society killing. They'd dragged that one up from the thirties. DS Jack bought a paper, but there was nothing new. Just an update from the Press Office. Police were continuing their inquiries. He stopped. Sighed.

'You know what? I fancy lobster under some awning on a hot beach with a cool breeze.'

Madelaine Jack laughed.

'Mauritius?'

'They have big lobsters there?'

'Must do.'

'Mauritius will be fine.'

'White wine or a Cuba libre?'

'You chose. Mm?'

# THURSDAY

## Twenty-Nine

John Smith stood on the main concourse at Paddington station. The departure board told him that he had five minutes. He took out his mobile, tapped a number. Listened. Answer service. He went to the news-stand, bought a couple of magazines he'd probably never read. Went back to the top of the platform. He redialled. Answer service. He flicked his mobile to off, slipped it into his inside pocket and boarded the first-class carriage with forty-five seconds to spare. But then he'd always had just enough to spare.

Dougie Gordon woke in a room very dark on the inside, too bright on the outside. Dougie Gordon felt very much the same. He remembered every word from the night before. He remembered the silence. Leonard. A ghost. Nothing. Listened. Got up and left. He knew. He must know the rest. Dougie Gordon was frightened of Leonard. Yes, Leonard must know the rest. He dialled her number. Out. Running some messages for her mother, didn't he know. He'd so wanted to tell her. Now he needed to. Now he knew he never would. He showered. Shaved. Brushed his wet black hair. Carefully knotted his naval tie. Brushed the lapels of his blazer. Did all buttons up. He looked at the hotel headed paper sticking from the folder on the dressing table. But not for long. He had nothing to say. He left the room, quietly closed the door and handed in his key.

Jane Boxer made three telephone calls. The first was her answering service. As she listened, her face hardened. Then with an expression that would have neither charmed Mr Firmani nor surprised Cynthia Rathbone, Jane Boxer stabbed with a long unbending finger at the telephone dial buttons. The second call was a London number. She slammed down the receiver before the recorded message could finish. The third was a mobile. Please try later.

## Thirty

She said nothing as she placed the carton of orange juice on the desk. He was drawing handguns on the blotter. He stared at the carton. Looked up.

'Different.'

'The canteen didn't have Cuba libre.'

He nodded slowly and solemnly.

'Oh. Fings ain't wot, are they?'

'No, sir.'

She leaned over the desk.

'Is that what we're looking for?'

'Could be. Tell me, where would Dougie Gordon get a gun?'

'I've just, um, I've just asked the Speyside police to check on his gun licence and also on any firearms certificate. Said they'd be back inside an hour.'

'Good.'

'Did you put it to him, sir?'

He thought about the formality of it all. I put it. You put it. He, she or it puts it. The conjugation of the investigative process while below it all a murderer wonders. A victim no longer wonders. He, she or it no longer wonders. He was tired. He shook his head.

'You know what he said? He said he loved her.'

'Well, sir, he wouldn't be the first lovelorn fool to blow away his lady.'

'Why would he do it?'

'Guilt? Blackmail?'

'Quick.'

'Disturbed. Could be quick.'

'But that would mean he was already carrying the gun. Why would Dougie Gordon, not very good salesman of very good single malt whisky, be carrying a gun on a Sunday night in Bath?'

'Someone gave it to him?'

Leonard narrowed his eyes. Thinking. Who?

'The brother? He's the only one he knows.'

'I'll check the firearms tickets.'

'What about the fat woman? He knew her.'

Madelaine Jack was perched on a pile of boxes. Dumped from the overflow in the Incident Room.

'Mrs Hanbury-Collings may be pretty gruesome, but I can't see that she would know where to get a gun any more than he would. No, sir, if he didn't bring one, then the brother's the best bet.'

'And that's what it is, isn't it? A bet. An outsider at that. My God, even I wouldn't know were to get a handgun in this town. Bristol? Ask DI Lane. He'd know where to get everything but the Absolution.'

She slipped off the boxes. And started to go. He was tapping the desk. That buzz again. She waited. Just in case.

'Tell me, what do you make of this son thing?'

'Depends what you make of Jane Boxer, sir. What did she say? Fantasy? Isn't that what you said she called it? Lot of people like that. And Cynthia Rathbone says there's no son. She should know. She practically brought her up.'

221

'Okay. Why should Mrs Hanbury-Collings say she didn't hear her talk about her son? Fantasy or not, that old bat doesn't miss a thing.'

'Always a first time.'

'No. Never for people like her. Nothing on the birth certificates?'

She shook her head.

'I got them to double-check. Nothing at all.'

'What about her doctor?'

'I'm sorry. No one's done that.'

He was angry. Should have done. Doctors. Priests. Bank managers. First ports of call. Could tell you almost everything you wanted to know. There was a floor squeak and laughter from the corridor. And then there he was. DS Somers-Barclay on hospital issue crutches, perfectly framed in the doorway.

'How you doing?'

'Fine, sir.'

The assegai was protruding from his back. The mamba coiled and gripped as its fangs pumped venom into his naked ankle. The crocodile closed its jaws over his thigh. His manservant stewed in a nearby cauldron. Through it all, a Somers-Barclay smiled and said it was fine.

'Absolutely fine, sir. Just on my way if that's all right, sir. Swelling a bit, you know.'

'Good. Take a couple of days.'

'Rather. Doc said I should get to bed. Get some rest, you know.'

'Do you good.'

'Rather. By the way, sir. No luck with Randy Bowen. Not answering his phone. I've asked the Met to take a look-see.'

He waved his hand. It was a near salute. The teeth glistened. The sun-blond mane flicked away to lie perfectly in a casual sweep across his head. The young North American lady who had driven down from Oxfordshire to make sure he 'got some rest' waited outside to help him down the few steps into her Mercedes convertible.

The young North American lady had a very full figure. She had, it was said, once appeared in the centre pages of a certain magazine. Now she waited in the police station lobby. Carefully she studied the poster. Ladies' self-defence course, it stated. The training to include use of voice, holds, locks, blocks and other techniques. Bath Sports & Leisure Centre 6.30 to 7.30. She wondered what could be learned in an hour. She kept on reading, feeling the open stare of the only other person in the lobby. When she'd come in he'd eyed her up and down like a strip show manager. His eyes had pierced the light linen jacket and lawn shirt. She was used to men looking. Didn't mind it. But this one was strange. Hungry. He looked the sort who didn't need to be. Good looking. Expensively dressed. But it was in the eyes. She didn't like those. She heard him move. She turned to the other wall. 1836–49 Rear Admiral William Farebrother Carroll. City Chief Constable. Come on, Nick darling. Come on. The man was quite close. She could smell – not aftershave. Something stronger. He was very close. Something animal. The inner door opened. The cavalry, fresh from scattering the monarch's enemies across the Kush, had arrived. He looked so handsome with his immaculate cuff-linked shirt, perfectly cut dark blue jacket, soft, loose cotton trousers over his plaster. And his crutches. So brave. So aware. He noticed her half-glance at the man. He sensed the man move away. Had his back to them.

'Are you being looked after?'

The man looked about. Surprised. Nervous? Somers-Barclay's memory bank clicked over.

'Eh, yes, thank you. Someone was trying to find someone for me.'

'Can I help?'

The man looked at the young North American lady, then at Somers-Barclay. A constable slid back the glass panel.

'Won't be long, sir. Just trying to find someone for you. Perhaps this officer could help?'

223

He nodded at Somers-Barclay. The man turned again. Full face. Of course! This officer most certainly could help.

Three minutes later, a hobbling and beaming Somers-Barclay had made it up the stairs with his centrefold nurse at his elbow. Through the swing doors and second on the left and he was back in Leonard's doorway. Leonard was reading a file. Jack was bent over his shoulder. Somers-Barclay, for the tiniest moment, wondered. But then didn't.

'Excuse me, sir, I think I've got something for you.'

The young North American lady half-smiled a hello.

'Thought you'd gone to bed.'

Somers-Barclay had hopes.

'Actually, it's not something, it's someone. Randy Bowen.'

Leonard's eyes flickered. Jack grinned.

'Nice one, Nick, nice one. Finally answered. Who's a cutie then?'

He wished she wouldn't say things like that to him. The others he didn't mind.

'Oh no, better than that. He's actually here.'

Leonard stabbed at his desk top with a bony finger.

'Bath?'

Somers-Barclay nodded.

'Right. Here in here. I've put him in the interview room.'

Leonard's chair scraped on the bare floor. Now the jigsaw was looking good.

'Brilliant.'

It wasn't a Leonard word. Somers-Barclay beamed.

'And just one thing, sir, his name's not Randy Bowen. Apparently that's his book name. He says, would you believe, his name's John Smith.'

224

# Thirty-One

Someone had left a copy of the mission statement in the interview room. We must be compassionate, courteous and patient, acting without fear and favour or prejudice to the rights of others. John Smith was alone. The door had been closed, but not locked. It wasn't what he was used to. Not first-class travel in this place. A narrow room. Cheap black plastic covered chairs down one side. Low enough for a primary school. A chromium hat-stand that looked as if it would topple at the sight of a cap. A chipboard desk against a bolted door. A clock showing the wrong time. Dog-eared posters in clip frames. Tiger cubs. Dolphins. He looked down from the window into the police yard. Clapped-out stolen vehicles. A 1962 convertible in the Chief Inspector's bay. The spire of the church next door above the bland three-storey wall of the rest of the police station. What the hell was he doing here? She was right. Should have stayed cool. No place for him. No need. They'd never have known. He felt the weight of his mobile phone. Wondered about trying once more. Not too late. A notice in the yard.

## DO NOT!!

Transmit on VHF
in this car park.

Nothing to do with him. But he left his telephone in his pocket. The man who opened the door could not be a policeman. Country lawyer? Doctor? The woman standing behind him was tall, dark haired. Athletic. Very pretty. He half-smiled at them. Looked back into the courtyard. Wondered who they were waiting for. It was getting crowded. He heard the door close.

'Mr Smith?'

He turned. Odd. He knew the man from somewhere. Not the woman.

'Yes?'

'Detective Inspector Leonard. This is Detective Sergeant Jack. Won't you please sit down?'

All the way from London, he'd been rehearsing what he would say. Now he forgot it all. He was sitting on one of the plastic chairs. The seat squeaked. He was uncomfortable. Leonard was at a high chair by the desk. Jack stood by the door. Out of his line of sight unless he turned his head. He felt uncomfortable.

'How may we help you?'

This wasn't right. They were supposed to be formal. Hard. Questioning. Interrogators. They weren't. This guy was soft-spoken. Nice. Glasses. She had nice ankles.

'It's about Sally.'

Leonard said nothing. Took off his spectacles and polished. Head bent. Always polishing. Always hiding. Peered short-sightedly at the clean lenses. Hurred. Polished again.

'Oh yes, Sally Keemer. You knew her, of course.'

'I, eh, well yes, I suppose I did.'

'Yes, we suppose that too.'

John Smith looked away. He could read the mission statement from where he sat. '. . . compassionate, courteous and patient, acting without fear and favour or prejudice . . .' What the hell did that mean? Now. What did it mean? The small pile of forms alongside were real. Form MG 11. Witness Statement. That was him. He'd walked into it. But where was the caution? The tape recorder? The notebook? He wanted to lick his dry lips. Wouldn't let himself. Whoa boy. Whoa. Going too fast. He'd walked in to help them. Shit. Help himself. And her. Get himself eliminated from their inquiries. That was it. That was the jargon. Everyone knew that. He looked back. Leonard was

226

smiling. Half a smile, really. A formality. Leonard would help him. Then ease him.

'You were at Paddington with her, weren't you?'

'How the hell did you know that?'

'We have witnesses, Mr Smith. You are, after all, well-known.'

To the headquarters constable and Somers-Barclay, anyway.

'I guess so.'

The accent was mid-Atlantic London.

'So?'

Leonard still looking helpful. It could have been a run-down building society office.

'Well, I wanted you to know something. I was, well, I was in Bath on Sunday night.'

Leonard's eyes flicked. Confession coming? He didn't think so. Something too clever about Mr Smith. Much too clever. Did he have anything to which he should confess? Maybe. Leonard went to work. Short questions. No time to think of answers.

'You met Miss Keemer?'

'Oh no.'

Too quick.

'See her?'

'No. Not at all.'

'Telephone?'

'No, I just . . .'

Leonard got up. Smiled.

'Well, thank you for coming in. I think we've a telephone number should we need you again.'

The other man started to his feet. Then sat. Then started up again. This wasn't it at all. No. He needed clearing. On his terms. In his way. He didn't want them coming back. This Inspector looked a gook. Was a gook. Had to be told.

'You don't understand.'

Leonard was by the door. Holding it open for him. Smiling.

'What don't I understand, sir?'

227

'I stopped by the apartment. Brock Street, you know?'

Leonard closed the door. Quietly. Returned to his seat. Indicated the nasty plastic chair. John Smith sat. His first interview. Edge of his chair. On the edge. Leonard smiled. It hadn't taken long.

Polite smile. Not a police smile. Still waiting.

'Well, I called and, um, well, she wasn't in.'

'Oh.'

'Yes. I rang the bell a couple of times, but she didn't answer.'

'What time was this, Mr Smith?'

'Let me see, ah . . . yes, well, it must have been about nine-fifteen, nine forty-five.'

'Only about?'

Leonard looked at the gold Rolex. Watches like that were never only about right.

'In fact I would say closer to nine forty-five. Maybe I got there about twenty-five to. Rang the bell a couple of times. Waited. You know? That sort of thing.'

'Then?'

'Got back in the car and, um, drove back to London.'

'You'd come down from London?'

'Yes, of course.'

'Why of course?'

John Smith tried a laugh. Wouldn't have got him into RADA.

'Well, Inspector, that's where I live.'

'Just to see Miss Keemer?'

'That's right.'

'But she was out?'

'Yes.'

'All the way from London?'

'Yes.'

'Was she expecting you?'

'No.'

'Long way to come on the off chance.'

228

'Maybe.'

'Why?'

'She had some idea that we could get back together. I needed to tell her that, well, we couldn't.'

'Back where?'

The cheeks swelled into a tight balloon. The bottom lip over the top. The balloon burst in a slow jet.

'I guess you could say that we had been very close.'

Leonard's eyes weren't smiling. Not unfriendly. But different eyes. Blank. Nothing.

'I'd prefer to hear what *you* would say.'

'Okay. We were very close. Or had been.'

'How close?'

'Well, let's see. We first met about six years ago. She was my publicist on a book thing. I'm a writer, you know.'

Leonard nodded.

'I don't pretend to be Proust . . .'

Now there was a mercy. John Smith seemed to have difficulty in deciding how to finish what he'd started to say.

'. . . but the sort of thing I write takes a lot of doing and, well, sells a hell of a lot more copies than he did. My publisher decided that we could get even more out of it if I had a publicist. He'd met Sally, introduced us and signed her up for six months. I suppose it went from there. We spent a lot of time together and, well, I guess you could say we became an item.'

There was no earthly chance Leonard would ever say such a thing. But he nodded. The nod of an understanding priest.

'An affair.'

John Smith shook his head.

'Oh, no. No way. No. It was far more than that.'

'But it ended. When?'

'Some time ago.'

The three words snapped out. Dismissed whatever had been between Sally Keemer and John Smith.

'And yet on Saturday evening, you seemed to be, um, on very close terms.'

'What's that mean?'

'You and Miss Keemer were observed at Paddington Station to embrace.'

'We weren't enemies.'

Leonard remembered the exhibition in the carriage just before the train left the station. Later. They'd talk that through later.

Leonard got up, looked out of the window. A constable was backing a patrol car into the only space. The garages were no good. Packed to the roof with bicycles, garden ornaments, televisions, golf clubs, lawn mowers, stripped down car parts. Not a boot sale. The garages had been taken over by the Detained Property Officer. Goods stolen. Goods evidence. Goods no good. The officer squeezed the car into the space and just about got out himself, banging the white easily-marked door in the process. Just another car. Not like it used to be. Something mysterious about the old black police Wolseleys with their chrome bells and bumpers. Fabian of the Yard. Long time ago. Today? All Fords. Any colour as long as it's white.

'What colour's your car?'

'White. Why?'

'Make?'

'BMW. Why?'

'Big one? Small one?'

'730.'

'And you're sure you drove down from London?'

''Course I'm damn sure. What is this? I came in here to help.'

'Sergeant?'

Leonard turned back to the view from the window. Jack turned the page in her pocketbook.

'A white 730 BMW saloon was seen in the vicinity of Simonsbath on Exmoor earlier in the day. We have reason to

230

believe that it was your vehicle, sir, and that you were driving it.'

'That's crap.'

Leonard liked that. Control going. Jack liked it. The next bit would be easy.

'We have a witness, sir.'

'Crap.'

Even better. She switched to monotone.

'Your vehicle was seen at Barledge Cottage late on Saturday night, Sunday morning and it was seen departing Barledge Cottage on Sunday evening. Time . . .'

Elaborate pause as page turned.

'. . . 18.00 hours, that is, six o'clock.'

He took out a packet of cigarettes. Raised an eyebrow at Jack. Oh no. No comforts at this point.

'This is a no smoking area, sir.'

The packet went back in the pocket. He crossed his legs, tapped at his knee. Took two or three deep breaths. Symptoms as expected. Leonard was back at the desk. Not sitting. Leaning. Long legs crossed at the ankles. Boots dull brown. Taller than John Smith had thought. And the eyes. Magnified. Not sinister, but . . . yes, sinister.

'Look, Mr Smith, you did not drive down from London. You were at Barledge Cottage. It doesn't take three and three-quarter hours to drive from Barledge Cottage to Brock Street. Certainly not in a BMW 730. You want to start again?'

It took an hour and a half. He'd gone to Brock Street to tell Sally Keemer that it was all over. There was someone else. That was it. Eight o'clock. She wasn't in. He'd waited. Driven around for an hour. Come back. Still no answer. Came back later.

'How much later?'

'About ten-thirty.'

'How long did you wait this time?'

'Half an hour.'

'You didn't have a key?'

'No.'

'But you had one for Barledge Cottage.'

'That was ours. Brock Street was strictly hers.'

'Anyone see you?'

John Smith had this rehearsed. The helpful, appealing look. The eyes widening. Leaning forward.

'I don't know. That's partly why I'm here. I went in all innocence. Someone may have seen me, taken the number of my car. So I thought it best to come and tell you.'

Leonard sat down and rocked his chair back against the wall. Hands clasped behind his back. Took a chance. Everyone's allowed one lie.

'What if I told you you were seen. And you were seen to go in. Wouldn't you like to flex your memory, sir. Before it's too late?'

John Smith tried to look into Leonard. Bespectacled façade. Still a policeman. John Smith was on the defensive. Hadn't told the truth. It was getting closer. She'd been right. He should have listened. But now this? It wouldn't have mattered. He leaned forward. Elbows on knees. Head in hands.

'Okay. She was there. We talked. I said it was all over. She got stressed. Real stressed. She said she didn't believe me. She wanted to know why. They always do.'

Jack closed her eyes. Soft lashes. But her voice firm.

'Did you tell her?'

Long pause. Long regret.

'No.'

'Why not?'

'Bottled out, I suppose. But that was it. I swear.'

'And then?'

He looked at Madelaine Jack. What the hell did she know about it? How the hell could she know what he'd gone through? The pleading. The threatening. Then the pleading again. He believed it. Why shouldn't she?

'Did you know she was pregnant?'

John Smith smirked.

232

'Bullshit. That what she reckoned?'

'No, Mr Smith, the coroner did.'

Not remembering. Not caring. He took out a cigarette and lit it with a green lighter. Disposable.

'Really.'

Her problem. Not his. He wouldn't look at Jack. She stared into him.

'Yes, Mr Smith, really.'

Then he did look. The smirk was now defiance. One ankle across his knee. The foot waggling. Impatient? About to boil? No one said anything. Leonard was back at the window. The uniformed Chief Inspector was examining the front bumper of the convertible. God help anyone in the station if they got within fifty feet of it. Leonard coughed. Quietly. Now was the time.

'Mr Smith, I'd like you to have a DNA test.'

The waggling stopped. The ankle came down. The foot ground the cigarette into the clean flooring. She'd been right. He couldn't handle something as big as this. John Smith snapped.

'What the fuck is this? I come in here to help. Fucking volunteer, you know, and the next thing I'm being treated like some fucking rapist! Some fucking criminal. Fuck your DNA test! You're not pinning some fucking kid on me. Okay, I was giving her one. Put me hand up to that, okay. But wasn't just me. Oh no fucking way. I mean she was putting it about, she was. Not just me. Oh fucking no, mate, not just me. Me? I was just one of her fucking scalps. She'd had more cocks than you've had hot dinners.'

John Smith was running. The mid-Atlantic accent had gone. The gold neck-chain triumphed. Leonard guessed south London. But that didn't matter. The law did. The law was with Smith. They couldn't forcibly test him unless they arrested him. Even making an attempt to DNA test him would be a common assault. Leonard needed that test.

Jack's voice was softer. Smoother. Friendlier. She sat beside him. The black plastic seat was low. He looked at her legs.

'D'you mind if I ask you a very personal question, Mr Smith?'

'Mm?'

'When you went to see Sally, did you, well, to be very blunt, did you and she go to bed?'

His head was juddering. His eyes were burning. What in hell was this woman saying?

"Course we didn't. For fuck's sake. It wasn't like that at all. Let me . . .'

She put her hand up to quiet him. He spluttered, then relaxed.

'Okay, fine. I believe you.'

He was slipping back to his Armani style. The hands not yet still. The mind becoming so.

'Thanks a bundle.'

'Let me explain why I had to ask you. We have reason to believe that a sex act took place in Sally's bedroom on the day she was murdered.'

'You not been listening? A fucking sex act, as you call it, took place every fucking day in her fucking bedroom. I tell you, she was a right goer.'

'Which, Mr Smith, is why I believe, quite sincerely believe, that for you personally, especially as you are famous, a celebrity, there is every advantage in taking a simple DNA test. It'll clear you from this investigation. You want that and, personally, I want that.'

He looked into her eyes. Deep eyes. Kind eyes. He looked away, but very slowly. His eyes travelling along her neck line, her throat, her softly moving breasts, her thighs. He sighed. She could be right. This could be the way out.

'I never touched her, you know.'

'But we need to show other people that. I'll make sure that it is done very discreetly.'

He looked at Leonard. No interest. Gazing from the window. She looked all right.

'What happens?'

234

'Well, we have two sorts of test. One we call "not intimate". The other's called "intimate form".'

She could have been selling bridal suites.

'We can simply take something called a Buccal Swab. A quick rub on the inside of the cheek. Then if we need to do anything more, we'll get the police surgeon to take an ordinary blood sample.'

'Do I have to?'

She smiled. Counting to ten. Counting to ten again.

'Of course not. We're not arresting you. Of course then you would. But no, it's entirely up to you. But just think, this is the way of putting the record straight.'

He'd come this far. They weren't looking for him. Looking for whoever else had been there. This could work out nicely, thank you. He nodded. Smacked his knee with the flat of his palm.

'Let's do it.'

He stood up.

'Only you got to be there. Maybe even do it, okay?'

She said nothing, but she didn't look put off. Perhaps he might even enjoy this. Could get to know her. Always useful. And you never knew what might happen. But Leonard wasn't finished. Still looking out of the window. His voice tight.

'What did you do when you left the flat?'

'Split. Started back for London. Then felt bad about it and went back.'

'To the flat?'

'Right. Rang the dinger. No reply.'

'What time was this?'

'Ten forty-five. But she wasn't there.'

'You're sure?'

John Smith was playing with his cigarette packet. Marlboro. He would have looked silly in a Stetson. He looked into her eyes. Easier than Leonard's. Big eyes. Warm. Maybe she did know. When he spoke, the voice was tired. The heart was gone. This time he might have got into RADA.

'Yes, I'm sure.'

There was one thing he'd forgotten. Now was the time. John Smith snapped his fingers with all the guile of a Latin American band leader.

'Of course. Look, if you don't believe me ask that strange-looking guy. The one on the train. The guy with the skirt. You must know who he is by now.'

Leonard's arms were folded. He dug his fingertips into his biceps. He'd known there had to be something else. But this? Dougie? Where did he fit?

'And if we had, how would that gentleman have known?'

'Just as I was leaving, he was walking along Brock Street.'

'He saw you?'

John Smith shook his head.

'No. No. I'm pretty sure he didn't. I was just driving into The Circus when he came round the corner into Brock Street. The fact that I saw him and he didn't see me proves I was going, doesn't it? Must prove something.'

Leonard thought it might well. But not what John Smith thought. Leonard shifted. Jack closed her notebook. Then Leonard had something that had bothered him.

'Why Rick?'

'Why what?'

'Why did she call you Rick?'

The other man thought it funny. In a quiet way.

'Rick. Richard. It's my middle name. When your name's John Smith you've got to have something to put in the hotel register, haven't you now?'

# Thirty-Two

The hotel said he'd gone out. Where? He hadn't said. Which direction? It wasn't that sort of hotel. Once out of the door? Any direction. But he'd been wearing his naval blazer and flannels and naval tie. You couldn't miss him. If he recognized him what difference would the tie make? But Leonard hadn't bothered to ask. He'd wondered about Brock Street. But he wasn't there. Went back to the hotel. Nothing. Key still there. McKittrick took him to the room. Room cleaned. Luggage where he'd left it. Razor in the bathroom. They forgot their toothbrushes, never their razors. The receptionist promised to call the moment Gordon came back.

Leonard thought of waiting, instead walked through the city towards the station.

If she'd stayed on the train to Bristol then she didn't have a car. She'd have come back on the train. Someone must have seen her. Late cabbies on a Saturday night. Was she alone? Should have thought of it before. Should have done a lot of things. He forgot Dougie for the moment and set off for Bath Spa station. He didn't get far.

Today was a purple leather day. Mustard silk shirt. Lime green headband. Shoes the same but suede. When she saw him, she ducked her head and would have gone the other way if she could. But she couldn't. The alley into Shire's Yard was too narrow.

'Mrs Rathbone, just the person.'

The head came up. The eyes bulged. He guided her to one of the outside tables, ordered hot chocolate. Double espresso for her. The day was warm but there was a draught through the Yard and the chocolate was too sweet.

'Tell me about John Smith.'

She sucked hard on a cigarette until the end glowed like a welder's rod.

'Sodding prick.'

'Trouble?'

'No. Good as gold. Paid on the nail, or his publisher did. But still a sodding prick.'

'Why?'

She sucked more smoke through thin lips. Gagged the grey fumes into her wretched lungs. Her knees threatened to poke through the black tangled fishnet as her scaly body shuddered. When she spoke, commas and colons of smoke punctuated each rasped phrase.

'She couldn't leave him alone. He was bad for her. Real bad. Called all the time. Just played with her. She'd cancel appointments just to see him. Bad for business. We lost clients because of him.'

'That all?'

She picked up the small white cup. Looked with one eye at the coffee. Put it down. He wasn't sure if she shook her head or her head shook.

'Well? Was it?'

'No. She was crazy about him. The only one she ever was. And he played her along. Took her months to get over him. Bastard. Sodding prick.'

Her lips formed into a grotesque straw as she sucked the coffee into her skinny mouth. Leonard was puzzled.

'When did they break up?'

She didn't look up.

'Year or so ago. Why?'

'You're sure?'

''Course I'm sodding sure. She only tells me she's doing a Clifton Bridge on us.'

'Mm?'

'Jump. Suicide. She meant it as well.'

238

'What stopped her?'

'Did what I'd done since she was a baby. Took her home with me. Cuddled her. Stroked her. Loved her. Put her to bed. Tucked her up with her teddy. Made her boiled eggs and soldiers for breakfast. You understand all that stuff?'

Didn't. But wanted to. He nodded.

'And that was that. She didn't see him again?'

'I used to think she did. Said she didn't.'

'She lied? To you?'

'She didn't lie. She believed her lies. Fantasies, not lies.'

'So you think she might have seen him?'

Cynthia Rathbone tore at her arm. Long nails. White powdery lines instead of red human scratches.

'Listen, last week I'd have said she wasn't seeing him. This week? Who sodding knows? I don't.'

Leonard stirred his chocolate.

'What about business?'

'Madam took him over.'

'Jane Boxer?'

'You bet.'

'They got on well?'

'Probably. But to her he was just bunce. She took twenty per cent. Different now, of course. Or she thinks it is.'

She was messing about with the cigarette in the ashtray. The end had burned too quickly. It broke away.

'Sod it. Sod. Sod it. Sod it.'

She was arguing with herself about something. Looked up at him.

'He kill her?'

'Would he?'

'Hasn't got the balls. Mind you, he might hire someone to do it.'

'She was pregnant.'

The fumbling with the packet. The lighter that wouldn't work. The two hands together trying to steady themselves enough to strike a flame. The cigarette wagging up and down as she muttered to herself. He'd seen it before. In the open it was macabre.

'Poor baby. Stupid sodding bitch. Poor baby. Stupid sodding . . .'

The lighter caught. The smoke went down and she spluttered across the table.

'She would, you know. But only for him.'

'Would what?'

'Come off the sodding pill. She'd been on it since she was about thirteen. She had. I tell you. She'd come off it to get him.'

'Smith.'

'Darling sodding Rick.'

'She must have loved him.'

'Obsessed. But he didn't want her. Oh no. He knew what she did.'

'He says she'd been unfaithful.'

The laugh was a cutting croak.

'Unfaithful. Sodding unfaithful. How sodding typical. Coming from him that's rich. Just like her father. That's the irony of it.'

'You said her mother wasn't married.'

'Yes, she was. Just about.'

'But not to Sally's father.'

'You don't listen, do you?'

What hadn't he heard? She was staring at him, willing him to remember. She wasn't going to say it again. Then it came. He remembered the bitterness. The slag, she'd said. The wedding. Sally's mother still in her wedding dress making love to her husband's best man. To Sally's father? What a history.

'Just that once?'

'It was enough. He could've sired the whole of sodding China in a morning without taking his socks off.'

'What happened to him?'

240

'Sodded off to London. Then Australia or somewhere. He didn't even know he had a daughter. Who sodding cares? I sodding don't.'

'You knew him well?'

She snapped. Ignored the people at the other tables. Each word came out like the closing chords of a venomous symphony.

''Course I sodding knew him well. I was sodding married to him, wasn't I?'

He left her sitting there. Muttering to herself. No collection of torn supermarket bags, hopeful cider bottles and string-tied discarded trainers. But no different.

He might have got to the station in time but Selsey was standing by the abbey. The recorder player, still baking in white wig and Hanoverian costume, thought he had an audience. He hadn't. Selsey was staring at his feet trying to make up his mind. Back to the restaurant or a late shop? Leonard stopped in front of him. For a moment nothing. Then Selsey's round, red face came up with all the speed of a wino summoned by hallucinations. The smile was pleasure, maybe, at seeing Leonard. But more pleasure that the decision had been delayed.

'Ah, Jim lad. The very man.'

He dug his hands deeper into his pockets, half-crouched and rocked back and forth on his heels. Whatever it was, it was important. Selsey was in that same stance Leonard had noticed when his friend was tossing up between a day's cooking or a day's racing. To Leonard, a photo-finish for Selsey's decision was never an outside chance. Selsey was as likely to pass up a day at a good farmers' track like Wincanton as say no to a white burgundy.

'And why would that be?'

'Step this way, sir. Step this way.'

There was a small public house in one of the lanes. Selsey and Leonard liked it because the beer still came from wood.

241

Neither of them ever drank beer, but they liked the idea. A bottle of cold Guinness and a glass of wine so cold its origins didn't matter.

'You see, Jim lad, I have a little problem. I need a tie. You know about these things. Bit of a dresser. So what sort of tie should I get?'

Now he thought about it, Leonard had never seen Selsey in a tie. Maybe that's why he'd never bought a racehorse.

'What for?'

'Tomorrow morning. Funeral.'

'Oh.'

'Respect, you know. He was a customer.'

'Oh dear.'

'Oh no. Not like that. Nothing he ate. But his widow said seeing as he spent more on me than he did on her, she assumes he would have wanted me at the, at the thing . . .'

'The funeral.'

'That's right. So as the old one has a few marks down it, well . . .'

'A few marks?'

'Someone was, well, ill.'

If that someone hadn't been Selsey, it must have been a horrendous spectacle. Leonard pressed on before he heard the full story.

'Something dark with small dots. Use it for anything. Tell me, when his widow says he spent more on you than on her, what does she mean?'

Selsey sipped. Thought about it. Looked at Leonard out of the corner of one eye.

'He, well, he used to bring a friend in for dinner.'

'Often?'

The black hair flopped back and forth.

'Oh my, yes. Very close, they were.'

'Female?'

'Yes, I suppose she was.'

'And his wife knew.'

242

'In Bath? They quite often do. So do the husbands.'

'You mean there's a lot of it about.'

'Quite a lot.'

Leonard contemplated the cream foam of his half-drunk stout.

'Was Sally Keemer part of that quite a lot?'

When they'd first spoken about Sally Keemer, Selsey had been reluctant to talk much. Nothing to hide, just nothing he wanted to say. Now? Someone had killed her. Now that was more obvious. Leonard understood this. Time transfers they called it. That certain period after a major crime when people with something to say begin to abandon the notion that it's nothing to do with them. Unease. Someone did it. Someone still out there. Not knowing where out there makes it worse. No one knows for sure.

'Sometimes she was. There were one or two regulars.'

'Not clients?'

'That, Jim lad, I don't know. Maybe at one point, yes. But who knows? Let's put it this way, consecutive, not concurrent.'

In Selsey's equation of social algebra, consecutive equalled boyfriend; concurrent equalled client.

'You remember who they were?'

'One or two.'

'Faces?'

Selsey nodded. Selsey had spent a lifetime memorizing runners at every major track in the South and Midlands and a few on his one visit to Longchamps. Not every nag had flared nostrils and teeth you could count. After that, humans were easy. Leonard wondered about pictures matching the client list.

'How far back?'

'Not sure. But a good way. Why?'

'Might want you to look at pictures.'

Selsey felt uneasy. Leonard sensed it. Enough for now. He picked up his glass and his voice was muffled as he tipped the dregs down his grateful throat. 'Come on, drink up. You're lucky. The shops are all closed.'

★

243

When he got back, DS Jack was looking more than concerned.

'Tried to get you, sir. Your mobile wasn't switched on.'

He walked by, heading for his office. Hated mobile telephones. Hated more being told he needed one. She was right behind him.

'It's Dougie Gordon, sir.'

He was slipping out of his jacket. Looked round at her.

'He's back? Good.'

'No, sir. About three-quarters of an hour ago, he threw himself in front of the InterCity.'

Leonard's head went back. Eyes closed. Mouth open. A long slow hiss of frustration escaped.

'Dead?'

'Right across the line, sir. Yes. Very dead.'

## Thirty-Three

It was late. Superintendent Marsh was bleak. His black tiny pupils freshly polished in their Nonconformist white balls. Marsh had never been known to take a drink. Now he faced the Major Incident Room with the look of what he was, the lay preacher come among those who did indeed take a drink. But this day, their sin was losing a vital witness, perhaps the murderer himself.

'No indication?'

'He'd been drinking.'

Marsh looked at Leonard. Long look.

'He was a drinker?'

'He sold whisky for a living.'

Another look. The corners of the eyes drooped. The soul plundered for pleasure.

'He'd confessed that he'd been intimate with Keemer?'

'Yes, sir. What he didn't admit was that he'd gone back there later that night.'

An ambitious constable handed Marsh his coffee. She smiled her thanks to him for accepting it. Leonard was looking tired. Face was deep with vertical lines. Eyes weary. Sad. So unnecessary. He thought of Cynthia Rathbone. Sodding sad she'd have said. Sodding right she'd have been. Ray Lane was leaning against the wall by the door. He looked along to the blackboard. The sightings of Gordon were scribbled in the right-hand corner. Underlined. Ruled off.

'We've only the boyfriend's word. He says he saw him at about ten-thirty.'

Marsh caught his line of sight. Turned to the blackboard behind him. When he spoke, the words came slowly as if he were unscrambling a complicated anagram from the chalk figures and letters.

'And Gordon says that he saw Mrs Hanbury-Collings at nine-thirty.'

Leonard coughed.

'Maybe later than that. He wasn't sure. And she denies it and her son says it's impossible.'

Marsh rubbed his hands. The crack of his knuckles made the cuddly constable from headquarters cringe.

'Which means that Gordon not only saw her, she saw him. So that would be two sightings. What about the girlfriend?'

'Sally Keemer, sir?'

Marsh's eyes bored into Leonard's.

'No, sir. Not Sally Keemer, sir. Miss Wilson, sir. Has no body thought to interview the young lady? Has no body thought to ask her what time she thinks they saw Mrs Hanbury-Collings? What she thinks her fiancé was doing at ten-thirty or whenever this Smith fellow says he saw him entering Brock Street?'

There was silence. A couple of the headquarters officers produced not very good stage sighs. Marsh looked about him.

245

'Well?'

Detective Sergeant Jack was across the room from Leonard. Didn't look at him when she spoke. Looked straight into Marsh's eyes.

'Sir? DI Leonard asked me to do that. I'm afraid she's not responding to my calls. However, I have asked the Speyside police to knock her up.'

Marsh opened his thin mouth to throw another question at her. She was too quick.

'I've also spoken to Speyside about gun and firearms tickets. Gordon has a shotgun licence. But he hasn't a firearms licence and, as far as they know, doesn't own a handgun.'

Leonard didn't look at Jack. Marsh nodded.

'Good. Good. Very clean. Now just as we still need to know what Sally Keemer did between the time DI Leonard left her and the time she died, we now need to know what Gordon did between the time that DI Leonard left him and when he died. We must explore the Bermuda Triangle of DI Leonard's interview room. Some body must have seen him. Check the telephone records of the hotel. Who did he speak to? When? What about? Who saw him at the station? Was he with anyone? Why did he go to the station? Did he buy a ticket? If so, where is it? Don't assume he went there to throw himself under the engine. Okay? Now let's get on.'

They were on the stairway going down to his office before Leonard spoke.

'Thanks. I owe you a drink.'

'White wine or Cuba libre, sir?'

'May have to be, Sergeant. May have to be.'

# FRIDAY

## Thirty-Four

Madelaine Jack had left her home number with Speyside. The toast was burning and the juicer had just fused when Jenny Wilson called at seven in the morning. She was flying down to Bristol that day with Dougie Gordon's parents. Jack said she was sorry and that they still had no idea how it had happened. She was careful. Officially, Gordon's death was still an accident. Jenny Wilson was talking about him slipping. Wanted to know if the platform was wet. What was he doing on the platform anyway? Jack fended off the questions.

'We'll have someone meet you at the airport. Before you go, are you up to answering a couple of small questions?'

There was a pause. A big breath. The voice sounded very small.

'Go on.'

'Did you see Mrs Hanbury-Collings on Sunday night?'

'She the old lady on the train?'

'Right.'

'Aye. In that Crescent place.'

'Can you remember what time?'

'Somewhere between half past nine and about a quarter to ten, why?'

'You're sure?'

'Aye. Perfectly. It was ten o'clock exactly when we walked back into the hotel.'

247

'Then what did you do?'

'I went to my bed. I'd not been feeling myself that day.'

Jack remembered the stories of the night before.

'And what did, what did Dougie do?'

The breath was quiet, but it was there. The voice even smaller.

'I don't know. He said he would be having a nightcap, then bed himself.'

'D'you know if he did?'

'Can this wait?'

'I'm sorry, Jenny, it's very important.'

Another breath. Tearful.

'I don't know. I rang his room, but he was no there.'

'You happen to remember what time?'

'Eleven twenty-five exactly.'

When she arrived at Manvers Street, Leonard was head down, coffee mug in hand and heading for the corner office. Nash wanted to know what was going on. It wasn't strictly his business even though he was also the District Commander. But Marsh and Nash had joined the force on the same day twenty-seven years earlier. No problems between them.

'Anything?'

She told him about the early morning call as they walked along.

'And we should have a DNA match from the cottage and Smith by lunchtime.'

'What about the flat?'

'I've asked them to match the sheets we took from there with Gordon. But it'll take another day. Oh, and just one more thing, sir, I bought that perfume you asked about.'

'And?'

'Chepstow promised me something by first thing this morning. Tennish?'

He could have kissed her. But officers didn't do that. Leonard

248

and Jack most certainly didn't. Instead she took the coffee mug from him as he knocked and went in.

Marsh was sitting in Nash's office. Nash cool behind his L-shaped desk in white open-necked shirt. Silver shoulder-crowns gleaming. Teeth in a sparkling smile of welcome as Leonard dropped into one of the blue chairs beneath the Rambo caricature. Marsh cool in dark blue three-piece suit. Silver cuff-links gleaming. Teeth dull, yellowed as his jaundiced view of society. No Marsh caricature had ever been sympathetic enough to be framed. Daubed. Not framed.

'What do we have?'

Leonard wished that he'd hung on to the coffee. Wondered if she were drinking it. She knew where he kept his gingerbread man.

'Six in the frame. Jane Boxer, Cynthia Rathbone, Melissa Hanbury-Collings, Ashley Hanbury-Collings her son, John Smith – yes sir, that really is his name – and Dougie Gordon.'

Marsh had scribbled their names. He looked up from his pad.

'Why not his fiancée?'

'She wasn't in Bath at the time. Scotland, I believe, sir.'

'We're sure?'

Leonard wasn't. Should have been.

'I'll double-check.'

Marsh sucked his mouthwash-stained teeth.

'Go from the top. The Boxer woman. Motive?'

'None obvious. Didn't much get on with Sally Keemer, but they'd just become partners. I think she was having an affair with Keemer's ex-boyfriend. Slight problem, Keemer didn't know he was ex.'

'Opportunity?'

'Not known to have a weapon. Said she was tucked up with her teddy bear and fast asleep at time of murder. No witnesses. Not even the boyfriend.'

'Ten Rating?'

'Five, consider six.'

Nash scribbled.

'You know she's a mate of Dover's?'

Leonard didn't. Wasn't surprised.

'And the son?'

'Which one?'

'Ashley Hanbury-Collings. I think I met them at some do earlier this year.'

Leonard certainly hadn't known that. Marsh peered at his watch. A budget meeting at Portishead. Not to be missed. Had to get on.

'What about the Rathbone woman?'

'Sally Keemer's aunt. Surrogate mother in more ways than one. Sad case. Her then husband whom she hasn't seen for twenty-odd years was Sally Keemer's father. He was the best man at Sally's mother's wedding. Apparently Sally was conceived in the powder room during the reception. She didn't even bother to take off her wedding dress.'

Nash looked away. Marsh, stony-faced, willing the judgement of wrath.

'What about her?'

'The mother? Disappeared to Italy with her latest stud. Hasn't returned. As far as we can make out doesn't even know her daughter's dead. Cynthia Rathbone's a mess. But no motive. No opportunity.'

'Sure?'

'Never sure, sir. But yes.'

'Mother and son?'

'The widow Hanbury-Collings? Something here I don't understand. She met Keemer for the first time on the train—'

'Apparently for the first time.'

'Okay, sir. Apparently. But pretty certain. What is certain to my mind is that she lied about something quite innocuous. Keemer said she was staying on the train to see her son in Bristol. Now, we've since found that she didn't have a son. Never had a son. But why should Mrs Hanbury-C lie?'

'But no motive?'

'None that we can find. However, she was out earlier in the evening. But so what? So was fifteen per cent of Bath. At first she denied it. Then said maybe, but not at the time she was seen.'

'By?'

'By Gordon and his fiancée, Jenny Wilson. We've checked with her this morning. Definitely saw her in Royal Crescent about three-quarters of an hour before the murder. But her son says no, mummy was at home with him. They didn't actually play Scrabble, but as good as.'

Marsh got up. Walked over to the glass display case on the back wall. Old ceremonial swords. Sniffed. Now officers had ASPs, nine-inch long telescopic truncheons. No bigger than their mobile phones. Sniffed again. He'd had the best years of the force.

'Do we trust the son? Lawyer, isn't he?'

'Corporate.'

Another sniff. First kill all the corporate lawyers. He didn't mind which ones went.

'Frankly, sir, he seems no more than mummy's boy. Goes to lunch every Sunday. Takes Richard, that's his son, takes him back to school, goes back, sits with the old lady, goes home to bed and lies to the police for her.'

'Why?'

'Frankly, sir, I can't figure it out. My Sergeant says that Mrs Hanbury-C is a ruffled, maybe frightened, elderly woman. Simply doesn't want to be mixed up in anything but bridge parties. Comes up with a porkie and Ashley does the honours for her.'

'No motive?'

'Neither of them. For Mrs Hanbury-C it's bad for her social position to be mixed up with anything like this. For young Ashley, it's bad for business. Which leaves us with John Smith alias Randy Bowen.'

'The novelist?'

Leonard looked up. Sharply. Nash might have heard of him.

But Marsh? Was Randy Bowen required reading for an elder of the church?

'Yes, sir. You know his work?'

'Of course, Inspector. Of course. Don't you? An example of bad influence. You should acquaint yourself with these matters.'

'Yes, sir.'

Leonard hurried on.

'Smith says he went to the flat, talked to her, left her alive, didn't see her again. They had a row. He told her he was leaving her. Said he went back about ten-thirtyish, she wasn't there and he saw Gordon approaching the flat as he drove away.'

'Motive?'

'She was pregnant. We're running a DNA. Apparently determined to hang on to him. Maybe had something on him. We don't know. Yet.'

Nash was looking from his window. The real world going by. Bargain toasters in the height of summer. Saloons and estates in the car park below stuffed with booty from the first of the summer sales. You kill someone for that?

'All that enough to kill her? Anyway, where would he get a gun?'

'Until he'd got one, we probably wouldn't know, sir. He's more likely to know where than, say, Mrs Hanbury-Collings, who wouldn't even know a safety catch from a hammer.'

Marsh was about to sit. Didn't. Really had to go to meetings. That's where the real business of policing was these days. Budgetary control.

'Gordon? It looks more and more like him. But why?'

Leonard took another breath. The buzzing was coming from below his collar stud. The spectacles were off. The polishing on. The neck sticking out.

'Shame?'

'He'd had his way with this woman and regretted it? Commendable, but hardly likely.'

'No, sir. She'd had her way with him.'

'A Jezebel.'

'A very over-sexy lady, sir, who apparently could not resist Gordon in his kilt. Gordon gets remorse. His bride-to-be is tucked up in her innocence. Gordon takes a drink. Strides across the banks and braes of Bath to take what he saw as revenge.'

'Where would he get a gun to do that?'

Leonard nodded. That's what bothered him. Still nothing on the brother. Didn't say so. They'd missed too much in front of Marsh. Marsh looked at his watch. Turned to the door.

'I must away. I leave you with one thought. Gordon in remorse may have confessed.'

'A priest, sir?'

'Wrong foot, Inspector. Wrong foot. No. To Miss Wilson.'

'Tells her then kills?'

Marsh bored into him.

'Revenge. If anyone would seek revenge, might it not be Miss Wilson?'

# Thirty-Five

As Ed Firmani of PanAmerican IT crossed The Circus beneath the great tree in the centre garden, Detective Inspector Leonard of Bath police finished browsing among the pavement trays of books in Margaret Buildings. The two met in Brock Street outside the green door. Firmani had gone to the address out of curiosity. Leonard because he was on his way to the offices of Sally Keemer Publicity.

'I heard about the Scotchman. I'm sorry. Nice guy.'

'You knew him?'

'I recommended he called Sally here.'

'Of course, the night of the famous party.'

Firmani looked down. Embarrassed.

'Coincidence, I guess. He taking the same railroad as she did. Then his brother's girlfriend, wife, or whatever she is, knowing the girl I was with.'

'Yes, I wonder—'

'Hey, you know that was all fine and dandy, don't you? Nothing to do with . . .'

'With what?'

'Well . . .'

He looked at the green door. Shut tight. No one at home.

'Well, what I mean is, well, you know what I mean.'

They started to walk back the way Ed Firmani had come. Slowly. Two old friends passing the time of a hot day in Bath.

'When d'you go home?'

'Tonight. I've given my big speech. You know what I called it? The Truth, The Whole Truth And Nothing But The Sales Pitch. You like that?'

'Did they?'

'Sure did. Thanks to Jane. You know, that girl is something else. Wrote every damn word. She's as good as Sally Keemer. Eh . . . I'm sorry, that sounds bad.'

It did. Everything was sounding bad this week.

'What would happen if I said you couldn't go?'

Firmani stopped.

'What in hell's that mean?'

'Material witness is what NYPD calls it.'

'You can't do that.'

'You a betting man, Mr Firmani? Is PanAmerican IT? Having a Senior Vice-President held in connection with a murder would undo a lot of the Sally Keemer Publicity good works, would it not?'

'Listen, Lieutenant, I only met the lady once, maybe twice. Okay? I have nothing to tell you that would be of any interest. Okay? Okay? You hear me?'

'Apart from write your speeches and fix VIP appearances, what extras did she provide?'

An estate agent with a friar's gait crossed the road in front of them. He nodded to Leonard. He'd sold him the best value for money apartment in the city. He should have known. It was his own and he'd regretted it ever since. Firmani looked after the man as he disappeared into his comfortable office. No distraction. No help.

'This official?'

'Yes.'

'Does it have to be?'

Leonard flicked his eyes. It meant nothing. But Firmani was looking for a way out.

'Okay. Let me tell you something hypothetical. Okay? Purely hypothetical. If a visiting fireman is a long way from home, well, sometimes he may want to have a little fun. You understand me?'

Leonard blinked. Firmani took a short deep breath.

'Okay. Let's say Jane Boxer is pretty good at fixing everything. All very discreet. Appears on the account as new contact arrangements or something. No one says anything. Corporation picks up the tab. Hey, it's even tax deductible. Everyone gets a slice. Okay?'

'You sleep with her?'

Another deep breath.

'With Nikki Dunn?'

'We had a few drinks and maybe a little fun. Okay. But in no way does that line this little chicken up for a homicide rap. Okay?'

'I need to know for sure where Jane Boxer was on Sunday night between say ten and eleven-thirty.'

Firmani stubbed at the black base of the red letter box with his shoe. Across the road, the estate agent glanced from his window. Thought they looked serious, even at that distance. Ed Firmani had plenty of deep breaths to go.

'She was with me.'

'Sure?'

Firmani's mouth hung open like someone who has forgotten what he is about to say. The eyes picked out the intelligence in Leonard's. The persistence.

'Spending quality time with Jane Boxer, my friend, is not something you're not sure about. You want I should have Polaroids or something?'

'I'll be in touch.'

Hands deep in pockets. Buzzing more atonal than ever. Head forward and down. Staring at the ground three feet in front of him. Leonard loped across The Circus looking neither to the right, nor to the left, nor right again. The answer he wanted, he was sure, lay not a hundred yards from where Sally Keemer had been shot to death.


The Saville Row door was open. A faint smell of freesia on the narrow stairway. He started to climb the stairs. Looked at his watch. Tenish she'd said. It was gone tenish. Changed his mind. He crossed Albert Street. Looked across at the restaurant. No sign of Selsey. Friday. The funeral. He wondered if he'd found a tie. The phone box on George Street was free. He was glad. Another excuse to avoid the mobile. They spoke for twenty seconds. He was puffing when he reached the top of the slope and the sweet-smelling office stairway.

Cynthia Rathbone was not at her desk. Jane Boxer was. Running through the answermachine messages. Yet another outfit for the Farewell and Come Back Soon session of the conference. Fully dressed. Revealing. He could see what Firmani had meant. But then he'd always felt that. It was the dress. A special dress. Scary.

'Mrs Rathbone out?'

'Permanently.'

'Why?'

'Sacked her. Is that police business, Inspector?'

'Could be.'

'She's a headcase and a very nasty one at that. Look at this.'

She swung the computer screen towards him. Blank.

256

'She's wiped it?'

'Every sodding, as she would say, file. Every record, every invoice, every letter, every back-up disk. All gone, Nanny. All gone.'

'I still need to see her.'

She laughed. No humour. Contempt.

'You don't really think she'd make a reliable witness? That old soak wouldn't make it further than the oath and then she'd have a crisis of conscience.'

'Witness to what?'

That didn't put her off.

'I'm sure you'd think of something. You people usually do. Now, what can I do for you? As you see, I'm short-handed.'

'Do you mind telling me where you were on Saturday night and Sunday evening?'

'You already know. I've told you. Went to meet Ed Firmani on Saturday. Introduced him to Nikki Dunn then . . .'

'By the way, do you know that's procurement?'

'What?'

'Procurement. Prostitution.'

'What in hell are you inferring Inspector?'

She was sitting up straight. Eyes blazing. The pose would have thrilled any stills photographer.

'I'm not inferring anything, Miss Boxer. I have a statement from Mr Firmani. That's worth a couple of years at least. But let's press on. Tell me, what did you do after you left Mr Firmani?'

For a moment, nothing. Calculating. Thinking it through. Getting her breath without disturbing the thin silk of her dress.

'I was in bed early. I've told you.'

'Where?'

'Where what?'

'Where were you in bed?'

'What's that got to do with you?'

'Okay. Your way, Miss Boxer. You were in bed at Barledge Cottage. You arrived sometime during Saturday night. After

257

dark, so well after ten or thereabouts. You left the following afternoon. You slept that night in Sally Keemer's bed and you slept with the man whom she thought was still her, um, boyfriend.'

'And I suppose you have a statement about that as well.'

'From Mr Smith? As a matter of fact, we don't. But we do have traces from the sheet and duvet that suggest you shared the bed. I have to tell you that these include DNA and matching traces from your scent. Your perfume. Oh, and for good measure, we have tyre treads.'

Jane Boxer leaned back in Cynthia's seat. Ran long fingers through her short soft hair. One long leg resting on a tall wastepaper bin. She wasn't trying to be provocative. Not much point in that now.

'What are you suggesting? I don't actually hear the tinkling of broken laws. Or do you now decide moral standards as well as parking regulations?'

'I'm suggesting—'

She was looking at the ceiling.

'You're a prude, aren't you, Inspector? You're a neuter. You look but you're frightened to touch. You show the emotion of an ice lolly. Take you out of your official freezer, unwrap you and when you've finally melted, all that would be left is a thin, straight stick which would taste of nothing.'

The sigh was short and sharp. She swung her head towards him. No reaction. She hadn't expected any.

'Fine, Inspector, fine. Okay, so I was fucking him in her bed. Make you feel better? And it was very good, Inspector. Very good. She was finished. She was finished with him. She was finished with the business. And we, Inspector, had finished with her. None of your laws broken. None of mine.'

'But she wouldn't go.'

'Right. But I didn't help her on her way, if that's what you're suggesting. By the way, what was it that you were suggesting?'

'But your boyfriend might have.'

258

'Rick? Why should he?'

'She was carrying his child.'

The leg came down. The back straightened. The fury there but no longer the beauty.

'You're a liar.'

'One a week I allow myself. And I've had that. She was carrying his child. His child. DNA. QED. When you see him, tell him I want him.'

He got as far as the door. Turned. Not too theatrically because he really had forgotten to tell her.

'Something I forgot. I know you couldn't have killed her.'

One thin eyebrow asked the question. In a thin voice he answered. But a voice everyone could hear.

'At the time someone shot Sally Keemer across the road from here, you were, to use your language, being fucked by Ed Firmani. He's made a statement about that, too. Including how much you charge. Don't forget to tell Mr Smith I want him.'

She was still staring at the softly closed door when the one behind her opened. For a second or two he stood over her. For a second or two. Then he drew back his hand and hit her as hard as he had ever hit anything or anyone across the face. The edge of his gold krugerrand ring tore into her cheek. She fell screaming to the floor clutching her face. He then kicked her as hard as he had kicked anything or anyone.

Leonard trod quietly down the expensively plum-carpeted stairs. Glum. Fed up with the world and his part in it. Wondered if the blood had stained the silkiest, skimpiest dark blue shift.

# Thirty-Six

She was waiting outside. She was clean. Normal. Oh to be normal.

'Any joy, sir?'

He stood polishing his spectacles. Perhaps listening for sounds of breaking people. None came.

'Joy? Depends on your definition. No. Nothing.'

They walked. A normal couple. He perhaps too tweedy in the June sun. But apparently uncomplicated. She nearly as tall. Cool in still uncreased linen. Both knowing they were close.

'Do we rule out Cynthia?'

'That's what Jane Boxer's done. Kicked her out.'

'Unwise.'

'Could be. Depends how much revenge she wants.'

'I'd have thought a lot.'

'Maybe she's taken it. She's wiped all their computer files.'

'That, sir, is bad. I've been through the ones I had from her. Nothing at all. They don't go back much beyond the Inland Revenue and Customs and Excise returns. Six years.'

'They don't go back at all now.'

He stopped. Bath suddenly noisy with George Street traffic. Across the way, the colourful, utterly odourless hanging baskets of Milsom Street. Shops where the assistants were as well dressed as their windows. Here no one called a customer My Dear, or My Luv. No West Country brogue asked Where's That To? Here Bath was gift-wrapped. A hundred and fifty yards away a beautiful woman bled into her expensive carpet. A hundred fifty yards away, her school friend had been murdered.

'Why would she do that? Destroy the recent stuff, yes. That's revenge. Vengeance. Throws the business in a heap. But why the old files? As you said, even the taxman isn't likely to cometh after that lot. They're history. That's all.'

'Unless . . .'

'Unless there was something in them that incriminated Sally Keemer. It wouldn't have bothered the person she really hated, Jane Boxer. She wasn't around then.'

The light changed, they crossed with a column of small capped-and-stripe-tied schoolboys, led by a fat and jolly teacher. Each boy with a clipboard, a felt-tip and a chattering friend. Bath was the subject of another classroom project. As the last boy in the crocodile disappeared around the corner, Leonard wagged a forefinger after him.

'Of course, of course, of course. What a dunderhead. The kid. The Hanbury-Collings kid.'

'Sir?'

'The one person who can tell us when he went back to school and what time his father left him.'

'Ashley Hanbury-Collings isn't in this is he, sir? An alibi for his mum, but that's about it.'

Leonard shook his head from side to side. Determined. Something here. Not quite sure. But something.

'No, it's not about it. I'm damn sure she lied about what time she was out. Why?'

'Didn't want to get mixed up. Flustered. Getting on. I can hear her lawyer at it now.'

'I don't believe it. It was too close to the murder. Gordon said she made some excuse about going the wrong way. Mrs Hanbury-Collings owns Bath, or thinks she does. She knows every inch of that area. When someone walks about in the evening, it's either for a stroll, or she's going somewhere, or she's looking for something. Mrs Hanbury-C does not stroll. She was heading in the direction of Sally Keemer's flat.'

'Coincidence?'

'Okay. Perhaps. But what if she were looking for someone in that direction?'

'Sally Keemer?'

261

'No. Suppose she was looking for her darling son? Suppose this alibi thing is not to protect her at all. It's to protect Ashley.'

Jack moved her head slowly up and down. Dawning. Bit at the corner of her lip.

'Motive?'

He shrugged.

'Dunno. Let's find one. But first let's check out his story. We need to get at the kid. Richard?'

'Yes, sir. We can't. We're not allowed to. Certainly not without his father being there, and then, well, it's impossible.'

'What about his housemaster or whatever they have up there? Gentle inquiry? Give him a big smile?'

'From memory, I imagine he'd prefer one of yours.'

The prep school boys on their way from The House to the cricket field loved the scarlet Alfa Romeo when it snarled into the drive. A few of the more mature boys preferred the driver. The senior games-master caught his breath when she climbed out. Richard Hanbury-Collings' housemaster saw none of this, but greeted DS Jack with considerable courtesy and she thanked him for seeing her so quickly. It was, she said, a mere formality, and explained what she wanted. Mr Snow had once been an army officer. In Ashley Hanbury-Collings' time at the school, the master's predecessor would have probably called himself Major Snow. Nowadays these matters, like army officers of that rank, were inevitably passed over. But this Major Snow still looked more Education Corps than minor prep school and his staff work was exacting. The In & Out Book was brought to his study where he was pouring freshly made lemonade for his guest. The boy who brought it mentally stripped her and scurried off to tell the rest of the games malingerers that Old Snowy had pulled. The boy was not yet sensitive to the truth that DS Jack was perfectly safe in Old Snowy's company.

'As you see, Sarn't, the In & Out's all shipshape and Bristol fashion. Each boy signs out with name, time and reason. Signs in with name, time and whereabouts. So, let's see . . .'

He ran a long, now soft, finger down the Sunday names.

'Ah, here we are. Hanbury-Collings Four Alpha. Out at zero nine-thirty – that would be after chapel, of course. Reason: lunch father.'

She leaned over to read for herself. His aftershave was sweet-smelling. Lily of the valley.

'And that's him back?'

'Right. Eighteen hundred. Excused chapel. Prep room. That means he was off to the library to do his prep for Monday morning.'

He left the book open. Smiled. Sipped at his lemonade and removed the muslin cloth from the glass jug.

'May I?'

She offered her glass and a smile.

'There's no doubt about that? I mean, if a boy were to be late?'

'Could he fix it? No. Trust, first and foremost. And, of course, there are boys above and below his signature. So no. Young Richard was back when he said he was. He's a fine chap. Had a little problem the night before, but it was soon sorted. All hunky dory '

'Saturday?'

'Yes. Nothing at all. Boys have to be in by eighteen hundred. Visitors gone by eighteen-thirty. Just a mix-up.'

'What happened?'

'Nothing really. Occasionally in the summer a boy can have a family visit after that time if there are exceptional circum-stances. But only in the sitting room and only up to twenty-thirty – um, eight-thirty. And strictly family or Rels, as the boys call them. Relatives, you know?'

She'd guessed. But smiled her thanks anyway.

'Richard got into trouble?'

'No, no, not at all. Grand little chap.'

Jack sipped. Smiled.

'It would be very helpful, Mr Snow, if you could just tell me.'

'Well, I'm afraid he had a very late visitor. Permish had, um, that's what the boys call permission, anyway apparently he'd got permish, but his guest was delayed.'

Jack could feel the tingles in her tummy.

'May I see the In & Out?'

Snow gave a slight spring on the balls of his feet. Wished he hadn't started this. Couldn't really stop now.

'Of course, Sarn't. 'Course.'

He flipped the page back to Saturday. Hanbury-Collings was the only boy with a visitor. The expected arrival time was 20.15. Fifteen minutes permish had been granted. The expected visitor's name was spelled, firmly, in black felt-tip capitals: **S. KEEMER (Rel).**

## *Thirty-Seven*

Madelaine Jack cursed the Bristol traffic. It took nearly an hour before she was back at Manvers Street Police Station. By that time, what Nash called the do-doos had hit the fan. Major Snow had felt it his duty to inform the headmaster of the police visit and questions. The headmaster had immediately spoken to the school solicitor and then to the boy's father. Ashley Hanbury-Collings had called a very senior officer who was a member of his Lodge, who had called an even more senior officer, who had called Marsh, who was between conferences and not to be found. The even more senior officer had then called Nash. Nash had called Leonard, who was to be found. He was eating a left-over head of a gingerbread man with a warm cup of tea. As he sat once more in Nash's office, Leonard was ignorant of what had happened at the school. So was Nash. Before them was a boiling complaint which had, through the tunnels of personal telephone conversations, built into the story that Jack had been to the school, unannounced, and had attempted to interrogate a ten-year-old boy. What in hell's teeth was going on?

Leonard looked bewildered. Might have stayed that way if Jack hadn't tapped on Nash's door with a huge smile and the truth. When she finished, Leonard, who had sat throughout with his glasses off and eyes closed, rocked forward on the blue seat of the visitor's chair.

'So there was a son, but not hers?'

'According to the housemaster, sir, she'd been visiting since last October. He got the impression that she and Ashley Hanbury-Collings were going to marry. These visits were part of the getting-to-know-Richard thing.'

Nash, as ever, was making notes in his battered black official Police Pocket Book.

'Then why didn't she go to Mrs Hanbury-Collings' on Sundays? Surely that was the ideal way of getting to know your future stepson?'

Leonard looked surprised at the question.

'Because the old girl didn't know about it. I mean, when she met her on the train, she didn't even know who she was. And, come to think of it, Sally Keemer didn't recognize her. They'd obviously never met.'

'And don't forget, sir, Ashley told you that he'd never met Sally.'

Leonard pushed back the chair. Stretched. Energy. That's what he needed. Energy.

'I think I'll take a walk over to Queen Square.'

Nash looked at the clock. Two o'clock.

'What happens there?'

'There, sir, Ashley Hanbury-Collings, barrister-at-law practices deceit. Thought I'd go and find out why. That all right?'

Nash sifted the confetti of telephone call notes. Nodded. Looked up at Leonard.

'Tread softly, James, for you tread on my promotion.'

He was smiling when he said it. Leonard didn't know that. He was polishing those perfectly clean spectacles.

The receptionist did not smile. Probably never had. She was young. Not at all pretty. One day she would look hideous. The eyes, the teeth, the nose, the flabby-lobed ears had been stuck on by an angry sculptor who had then turned to something else. Sour. Resentful. Why not? Nature's evil humour was sure of its victims. She asked him to take a seat and made no attempt to tell Ashley Hanbury-Collings that he had a visitor. Leonard gave her one hundred and twenty seconds.

'Would you mind telling him Detective Inspector Leonard is here?'

She looked through him so thoroughly that Leonard wondered for a moment if a door were opening behind him.

'Mr Hanbury-Collings is in a meeting and does not wish to be disturbed. When that is no longer the case, he will let me understand that.'

The head went down. Leonard got up.

'If I don't see your master inside sixty seconds, I shall arrange for a warrant to be up here before closing time. Understand?'

They were both saved from any further foolish positions by Hanbury-Collings himself. He came into the reception area, started to say something to the woman, caught sight of Leonard, turned and strutted back to his room leaving the door open behind him. Leonard followed. Closed the door. Quietly.

Hanbury-Collings was in white shirtsleeves. Starched collar. Knotted gold cuff-links. Wide dark blue braces pulling his fine suiting half-way up his rib cage. Didn't look at Leonard. Instead he stood, hands on hips, at the window, glaring at the summer traffic in the square below. Leonard waited. Hanbury-Collings half-turned. A long look. A summer tan drained to a long winter pallor.

'Satisfied?'

'You lied. You said you didn't know her.'

'You don't understand.'

266

'I understand you denied knowing a woman who, according to your own son's housemaster, you had introduced as the woman you were to marry. A woman who, presumably with your consent, regularly visited your son. A woman who was shot four times until she was dead. What more do you want me to understand, sir?'

Hanbury-Collings rubbed at his face. He flopped into the green leather chair, propped his clean elbows on the large mahogany table and held his face in his hands. Eyes shut. Shut tight.

'My mother would never have approved of Miss Keemer. We, that is Miss Keemer and I, agreed that by getting to know Richard, by easing our relationship into all three lives, then we would eventually bring her round.'

'Why would she have disapproved?'

'My mother is a devout Catholic. A convert. After my father died. I am divorced. My mother does not recognize that divorce.'

Leonard did not believe him. Did not believe anything anyone had told him during the past week.

'Do you mind answering a very personal question, sir?'

Hanbury-Collings said nothing.

'Were you sleeping with Miss Keemer?'

Hanbury-Collings moved his head. Stared with eyes that now seemed gouged from his well-nourished skull. Lips thick with salt.

'That, Inspector, is a despicable question. I will . . .'

'Miss Keemer, you see, sir, was pregnant when she was murdered. She also had a regular boyfriend with whom, sir, she was sleeping. That doesn't seem to tie in with your claim that you were to be married.'

'Get out.'

'Perhaps sir, you found out about all this. Perhaps, sir, you decided it was time to do something about it. Perhaps, sir, the alibi you've lied to protect was not your mother's. Perhaps, sir, it was yours.'

267

'Get out.'

The two words were two seconds apart. The head was buried deeper into the hands.

'Do you own or have you ever owned a handgun, sir?'

'I said . . .'

'A small calibre handgun sir. A point two two.'

The calibre, the size, the type of gun had never been mentioned by the police. Nothing in the papers. Leonard watched. The slightest hesitation. Hard to spot in the head-hugging figure before him. But it was there. Yes, it was.

'Inspector, at the time Miss Keemer was murdered, I was with my mother. There is nothing that you know, can ever know, or think you know that will change that.'

Now the head came up. The grand statement brought bravado. He stood behind the table, fingertips splayed to support him. He could have been addressing a successful meeting of shareholders.

'I have one aim in my life. It is to protect my son from all this. If you so much as go within a hundred yards of him, I will have you strung from the highest disciplinary committee in the land.'

The right hand came up in an arc. The finger pointed to where Leonard sat blinking.

'If you do not get out, I will have you thrown out.'

Leonard did not move.

'The school tells us that Miss Keemer visited your son on Saturday night. We have witnesses to say that your mother was out when you say you were both in. Shortly before Sally Keemer was murdered. Close by where Sally Keemer was murdered. We have witnesses who say your mother made an excuse that she was going in the wrong direction and turned away. She was looking for you, wasn't she? She was looking for her son. Because your mother did know. Your mother had found out what you intended to do. She tried to stop you, didn't she? But she was too late, wasn't she?'

Ashley Hanbury-Collings mouthed the words once more.

'Get out. Get out.'

But no sound came. Just mouthed words.

And then a soft tap at the door. But it was not her master she wanted.

'Inspector, would you please telephone a Detective Sergeant Jack immediately. It is, or so she says, of enormous consequence that you should do so.'

It took him ten minutes to get back to Manvers Street. Somewhere he must have crossed with the officer sent to keep an eye on Hanbury-Collings' movements, but he didn't see him. Maybe because he did see Selsey emerging into the bright sunlight from the gloom of his bank. Selsey was having a glum day. His understanding bank manager had been moved on. So had his old friend and customer. He'd come from the funeral. He'd eventually found a tie to wear. Blue and yellow polka dots. The colours of an owner Selsey followed with interest. The widow had shed more tears over his neckwear than over her unlamented late husband. Leonard only half-listened. He was breaking away when Selsey tugged at his sleeve.

'By the way, Jim lad, I remember who the boyfriend was.'

'Sally Keemer's?'

A bit late. Leonard now knew. Didn't say so. Wanted to get on. Waited.

'Can't remember his name, of course, it was a long time ago. But I believe he's no longer with us.'

Leonard was confused.

'Moved?'

'No need to be delicate. Snuffed it.'

'Don't think so.'

Selsey shrugged. Didn't matter. He was used to getting things wrong.

'So I heard anyway.'

'Tall man. Lawyer. Early forties.'

'Oh no. Nothing like that, Jim lad. Tall, yes. Bit flash for a lawyer. Wild Colonial Boy, you know the sort?'

269

'But in his forties.'

'If he was, then he'd led a terrible life, that I can tell you. I'd have put him at sixty-three, sixty-five.'

'You're sure?'

'No.'

'Okay, how sure?'

'How sure can you be after ten years? It may even have been eleven.'

He grinned. His brown eyes sad. Losing two friends in one day was bad. Having a tie no one liked and for which he had no further use didn't help. He waved a hand. Stuck the other in his pocket over the crumpled Order of Service and trudged up Milsom Street.

Selsey must have made a mistake. Selsey never made mistakes, except about horses. But ten, eleven years ago? Colonial. Wrong man. Same woman. Same style.

He was still grumbling with his confusion when he got back to Manvers Street. It had taken Leonard longer than he thought. It made no difference. She was still there in his office. Her hand still shaking. Still trying not to spill coffee and at the same time drag on a furiously burning cigarette. Still sodding at the world.

At his desk, almost hidden behind two thick piles of crisp paper, sat Madelaine Jack. She gave half a sorry half a smile as he came in.

'Cynthia thought we might like to see these sir. Every single record since the company started. She, well, she took the precaution of making hard copies before the little accident with the computer.'

Cynthia was nodding. Nerves or agreement, he couldn't make out.

'Sodding, sodding, sodding bitch. Sod her.'

Today was a red leather day.


It took two hours. Leonard and Jack began to build a picture of the early days of Sally Keemer Publicity. Cynthia got to know the ladies' washroom. The first eighteen months were hard going. The invoices overtook the expenditure columns. Creative accounting, perhaps. But the figures weren't impressive. Then for nearly a year, nothing at all. Income: nil. Expenditure: office expenses.

'What's the gap?'

'Oh that? That's when it became all too much for the little darling. Chickened out. All very nice to start with. But when the taxman started knocking and the bank raised its charges, well . . .'

'It was left to you.'

'Sodding right it was, while madam swanned off to God knows where. Not even a postcard.'

Jack was going through the old and new client lists.

'But she managed to hang on to a couple of her old clients.'

'Just.'

'A. J. Benson. Who was he?'

'She. Some sodding dyke. Fabric designer. So she said. But we got her into a couple of magazines. Something in the *Express* as well, as far as I remember. Last time I heard she was big and farty in New York.'

Leonard was looking at the accounts. They were simple. In the early days they wouldn't have cheered many bank managers. Big payments. Then nothing for weeks. Jack had moved on to the next column.

'What was HHC Packaging? Doesn't sound her style at all.'

'Paid the gas bill.'

'Stuck with her after the gap year, though.'

Leonard was following the accounting column for the same period.

'Ten thousand a year. Quite a lot.'

Cynthia was spluttering on a fresh cigarette she was trying to light from the stub of the last one. Jack had opened the window. Didn't help.

'Oh, we were sodding grand in those days. A retainer, she called it. Thought we were the bees knees.'

271

Leonard was staring at the wall. Nagging at his lower lip. Not listening to Jack and Cynthia's question and answer session. What had he missed? Benson. Benson. Designer. New York. Gap year. HHC. Retainers. Bees knees. Packaging. Gas bills. Jack's deep voice was a murmur in the background. Cynthia's a rasping hiss. Just like that train ride when he should have stayed awake. Snatches overheard then filed then forgotten. He juggled them once more. Benson. Gas. Packaging. Bills. Bank managers. New York. Designer. York. Retainers. Gap year. Year. HHC. Bees. Nothing. Nothing. But there was something. Had to be. He got up. Said nothing. Walked out. At the end of the corridor, Nash was talking to Marsh. Marsh said something. Leonard didn't hear. Walked on. Into the conference room, the Manvers Street Museum. Wandered about the room looking at the pictures, trophies, artefacts of policemanship someone called them. HHC. Hanna. Elsie Hanna. Who was she? Walked out again. Nash was still there. Marsh had gone.

'Who was Elsie Hanna?'

Nash looked surprised.

'Mayor of Bath, wasn't she? Didn't she open this place?'

Leonard didn't answer. Walked on. Yes, she was. Seen the words on some wall: 3 May 1966. Councillor Elsie Hanna. Not important. More juggling. Split the words. Get rid of HHC. Too confusing. Bees. Year gap. Gap bees. Bill gap. Bees year. Year. York. New designer. Packaging. Bank. Packaging. Manager. Bees. Packaging. Bees knees. Knees. Legs. Legs. Beautiful legs. Long legs. Long legs scarcely beneath the silkiest, skimpiest dark blue shift. The train. That Saturday night. Beautiful long warm legs. Dozing in the train. People still talking . . . Widowed for ten years last February . . . Of course we were in Rhodesia for most of our lives. Grand days those, didn't they know. Wouldn't have tolerated this sort of affair. Taken a whip to them or better still . . . In packaging, didn't they know . . . The train trundling then speeding in his dozing head. In packaging, didn't they know . . . The train picking up more speed. Packaging. Packaging. Packaging. Packaging.

272

He stood in the doorway looking hard at Jack.

'That packaging company. Who authorized their payment?'

Cynthia's nose was deep in the coffee mug. She wanted a drink. Not this one. But it would have to do. Jack was running her finger down the payments list. Cross reference. Flicked the invoice file. Finger down to the bottom. A squiggled, illegible signature. The name typed beneath it.

'Someone called Roger A. Mount. He appears to have been the Contracts Manager.'

'No one else?'

She turned through all the invoices. Shook her head.

'No, sir. Why?'

'What about the original contract?'

The voice stuttered from deep inside the coffee mug.

'Weren't no sodding contracts.'

She looked up. Coffee from thin lips dripping stains on her soft leather skirt. Eyes popping. Rum yellowed. Criss-crossed by an Ordnance Survey of minor blood vessels.

'Someone must have agreed to hire her. She didn't simply present herself and the bill.'

'Oh, that was Flash Harry. Reckoned his hand was his contract and all that sodding stuff. More likely his sodding dick, if you ask me.'

Leonard closed his eyes. They were getting there. Must be. Surely. Take it slowly. Don't set her off.

'Cynthia, who is Flash Harry?'

'Was. Dead. And hip hip sodding hooray as well. That's why the contract didn't last no more than a year after we started up again. He clogged it.'

'Okay then, not is but who *was* Flash Harry?'

'Guy that owned the company. Harry Hanbury-Collings.'

Leonard and Jack became quite still. The straight. They were in the straight. Jack's voice was gentle. Coaxing.

'Not Ashley Hanbury-Collings?'

Shook her head. Ash spilled down her skinny front.

'No. Harry. Flash Harry. Never heard of an Ashley.'

273

'How old was he when he died?'

'Sixties? About that.'

Jack dropped back in her chair. Tossed her pencil on the files. Leonard leaned against the door jamb. Eyes closed. Head back. Exhausted. Almost. Remembered the train journey. '. . . Widowed for ten years last February . . .'

'Got it. Got it. Got it.'


# Thirty-Eight


Nash was back at his desk. Marsh in the blue chair. Leonard against the window wall leading to Nash's private bathroom. A warrant was a formality.

'It seems that Ashley met Sally Keemer when she was working for his father. They kept in touch. Met up again and he wanted to marry her. But the big problem was his mother. She is a Roman Catholic convert. Apparently quite devout.'

Marsh, the most devout of Nonconformists, nodded.

'Converts do have that habit. Go on.'

'As far as she is concerned, her son is not divorced. That's that. So he's easing himself into a position where he can tell her. Using his son in some way to smooth granny. And then he runs out of time, because Sally Keemer runs to form. She's still having an affair with her old boyfriend, the eponymous Smith.'

Nash made a tiny note.

'He finds out.'

'And kills her.'

Marsh was looking at his immaculately shined shoes.

'Really?'

'So it seems, sir.'

'He'd kill her because of that?'

'A very strange man, sir. Don't forget—'

Marsh coughed his interruption.

274

'If she was backing out, why would she go to see the son on Saturday night?'

Leonard had not stopped to think about it. Nash looked down at his notebook. He had.

'Maybe she thought the son should hear it from her. After all, she did make a big effort to get there. It was well after hours. It must have been very important to her. Not just topping-up the tuck box.'

Marsh continued to look doubtful.

'But kill her? You've made him sound a weak character. Doesn't he just sulk? Threaten in his bedroom mirror to do all sorts of terrible things, but that's it? That's the normal behavioural pattern.'

Leonard knew deep down that the loose ends needed gathering and knotting later. Not now. But Marsh needed something. Something reassuring.

'Don't forget, sir, that this isn't a normal relationship. He is a cardboard cut-out of someone who has been given everything he wanted all his life and Sally Keemer is no ordinary girlfriend. She is totally bewitching. Beautiful. Sexy. Passionate. I know, I saw her when she was alive. And Hanbury-Collings is obsessed. According to the school, he's already told them that an engagement is on. The son is learning to call her Mummy. Somehow he finds out that she's two-timing. He's humiliated. This is the biggest middle-aged mummy's boy you'll ever meet. If he's not going to have Sally Keemer, no one is.'

The tap at the door was Jack.

''Scuse, sir. DC Rogers—'

'Who?'

'He's marking Ashley, sir.'

'Right.'

'Says he's on the move. He's left his office and he's gone to an address in Landsdown. It's his mother's, sir.'

Leonard nodded at the two senior officers. It was time to close it down. Jack held the door open for him. Marsh's voice stopped them both.

'James. Where did he get the gun?'

Leonard looked back. Marsh wasn't buying this.

'I don't know, sir. But I will.'

'Second question: where is it now?'

Leonard said nothing. Blinked. Marsh did not blink. Marsh had never blinked at anything in his professional or pastoral life.

'Think on, James, think on. So take care.'


# Thirty-Nine


This was not the moment for leaping out into Manvers Street with flashing lights, loud-hailers and crowd scenes. An Armed Response Team was in the yard. The whole crew was briefed in the Incident Room by Detective Superintendent Marsh and DS Jack. It took time. Marsh didn't mind that. The tighter and graver the situation, the more time he believed should be taken. It was possible that Ashley Hanbury-Collings was armed. Nothing should be left to chance. Was the property a flat conversion? Private house? How many people lived there? Was there a back way in – and out? What was either side? Back? Front? What time was it? Time meant traffic conditions. Numbers of people. Was there a school nearby? What was pick-up time? Was the medical team on standby? Where was Leonard?

Leonard had gone.

The afternoon had pressed on. The hanging basket at the front door waited on Mrs Hanbury-Collings and her small green watering can. DC Rogers nodded towards the front door.

'Went in about half an hour ago. Still in there I think, sir.'

'Back way?'

DC Rogers looked horrified.

'Think he might have legged it, sir?'

Leonard's mouth turned down in a silent shrug. He didn't really think so. Ashley Hanbury-Collings had done what Leonard believed he had done all his life. Run home to mummy.

'One way to find out.'

Leonard crossed the road and rang the bell. He rang three times before the door was opened. Not Mrs Much. Not Mrs Hanbury-Collings, but her son.

Ashley Hanbury-Collings stood looking at Leonard but hardly seeing him. In his right hand he held a pistol. Leonard knew almost nothing of guns. He'd fired standard weapons and could just about recognize the square-shaped 9mm Browning semi-automatic because that was the weapon the range master had handed him. He didn't like guns. He particularly didn't like guns when one was held by a murderer. That Ashley Hanbury-Collings held it loosely and pointing at the gound hardly mattered. It was a gun. Always be polite to armed suspects, the instructor had said. He could think of only one thing to say.

'You'd better give me that, sir.'

Ashley Hanbury-Collings said nothing and walked along the hall, still holding the gun and leaving, once again, Leonard standing alone. For the second time that day, Leonard followed him.

The living room was as white and as spotless as it had been on Leonard's last visit. This time, instead of Mrs Hanbury-Collings posed in blue pleats against the fireplace beneath the portrait of her husband, her son in wide blue braces and grey silk tie stood, as ever, with his father looking down on him. He seemed to gather some hopeless strength. Haughtiness. Arrogance. Misunderstood breeding. But the eyes. So pitifully weak.

'Presumably you know everything now, or think you do.'

'I think we do, sir. Do you mind?'

He held out his hand and looked at the gun and then at Hanbury-Collings' face. Hanbury-Collings ignored him.

'It took you some time.'

277

'We like to be sure, sir. Now . . .'

Once more he held out his hand for the gun. Once more Hanbury-Collings ignored him.

'You are, I suppose, a persistent little man, Inspector. Presumably you take pleasure in your work. There must be some reason. Status? Is that it? It gives you status. And rank. Yes. You get a rank. A modicum of brightness will get you some promotion, although the rank of Inspector at your age is hardly an achievement. Mm?'

Leonard let him go on. He wanted Hanbury-Collings to talk himself out. A man with such weak eyes should not have a gun. Yes, best let him talk.

'And you think you've been rather clever. In fact, Inspector – you like the sound of your rank? – in fact, you have been nothing but tiresome. You may now know why she had to die . . . mm?'

Leonard said nothing. Looked. Waited. Did not look at the gun.

'But if you think you have solved the great conundrum of Miss Sally Keemer then you are wrong. No one will ever do so. Do you know why? Do you? Do you?'

The last question was shouted. The eyes changed. Wilder. Frustration.

'No, sir.'

Hanbury-Collings sneered.

'No, sir. No, sir. Three bags full, sir. Of course you don't. You don't even know why, do you?'

Leonard gave the slightest shake of his head.

'You don't know why, Inspector, because Miss Sally Keemer didn't know. She spent her whole life searching. Searching for something she wanted to be. Wanting to be part of everything. Wanting to be accepted and, more than that, she wanted to feel that she had the right to be accepted. But she hadn't, had she? Did you know she was a bastard? Did you?'

'Yes, sir.'

278

'Oh you did, did you? Well at least you know something. And do you know what that means?'

Leonard blinked. All those years ago. Huddled in that room. Then another. Then another. Not even his own name. All the years of never knowing. Yes, he knew.

'No, sir.'

'Of course you don't. How could you? My point, Inspector, is that Miss Sally Keemer spent her life in the company, the society, in which she wanted to be, but deep down felt a fraud. Felt all the insecurities of someone who believes they should have at least the social credentials. Miss Keemer had no past, Inspector, and therefore was totally insecure about the present and the future. And therefore, Inspector, she wanted to touch everything and everyone she came across.'

Hanbury-Collings sagged. Not to the ground. To the base of his flimsy courage. But he did not put down the gun. Muttered again to himself.

'Wanted to touch everything and everyone she came across.'

'Including your father.'

Hanbury-Collings' head came up very slowly. So did the gun. Leonard did not blink.

'Tell me, sir, is that where you first met her? We know she worked for your father's company. We know he employed her when she came back from Italy. Is that how you met her?'

Hanbury-Collings did not understand what Leonard was talking about. His face said that. He lowered the gun. It was irrelevant.

'Italy? What are you talking about?'

'Miss Keemer worked for your father when she started the company and then again after she came back from Italy.'

'Italy?'

'Yes, sir. Her aunt has told us about the business being on hard times. Your father stood by her when she went to stay with her mother in Italy and when she came back.'

Hanbury-Collings' head rocked back. His mouth opened

279

wide. He gave a great roar that became a laugh that became a guffaw.

'Italy? Is that what you really think?'

'We have evidence, sir.'

Hanbury-Collings' mouth fell open in amazement. He was half-laughing, half-shaking.

'You don't know, do you? I thought you knew.'

'I think you'll find we know the whole story. We have all the company files. We've talked, as you know, to the school. We also have evidence from Miss Keemer's boyfriend which shows you were being thrown over for—'

Hanbury-Collings held up his hand. The amazement on his face had to be genuine.

'Please, my dear little Inspector, let's not go through all this again. It's absolute poppycock.'

'And, sir, we also believe the reason Miss Keemer went to the school on Saturday night was that she wanted to tell your son herself that it was over.'

'My son?'

'Yes, sir, Richard.'

'But I thought you knew.'

'I think we do, sir. Now if you'll just give me that weapon.'

Hanbury-Collings hardly heard him. He was still taking in what Leonard had just told him.

'Richard's not *my* son, Inspector.'

Leonard blinked. Waited.

'You silly little man. You're even more stupid than I thought you were. I thought you'd figured it out for yourself. I thought you got your little policeman's building blocks out and put it all together. I thought that was why you're here. You really think Richard's my son?'

'Of course, sir.'

'Of course, sir! Richard, you silly little man, is my brother.'

Leonard blinked. Dawned. He looked, very slowly, from Ashley Hanbury-Collings to the portrait above him.

'Right, Inspector. It's his son. His. His. His bastard son. A bastard sleeps with a bastard and they have a bastard. Go on, you silly little man. Go on. Laugh. It's funny, Ha. Ha.'

Leonard wanted to sit down. So Sally Keemer had been telling the truth all the time. She really was going to see her son.

Hanbury-Collings slumped into the fireside armchair. Leonard was no hero. He sat at one end of the sofa. At least the angle would be difficult.

'You want to tell me, sir?'

Hanbury-Collings' squashed, fleshy chin was on his chest. His head turned. His voice sounded as slurred as a late party-goer's. His mood changes were frightening Leonard as much as the gun, or maybe because of the gun. He waved a hand in Leonard's direction. He might have had a paper hat and a whisky glass. Instead he had a gun.

'Why not? Why not? He hired her for the same reason he hired everyone. To use her. Most people took their wages and went on their way. Not her. Silly little cow got herself pregnant. Mm. That's it. Pregnant. What d'you think he did. Mm? Go on. Tell me. Guess.'

'Paid her to go away.'

It might have been a laugh. It sounded like one. It held no humour.

'He wasn't that daft. I was in Zimbabwe. Born there. Learning the business. My darling wife was, was, was, having an affair with some, some dago bastard. She was leaving me. She did. Mm. You know what the bastard said? Mm? "Great opportunity."'

Hanbury-Collings shook his head. Some Indian Army colonel remembering an audacious cavalry charge.

'He packed Sally off to France. Italy? Nonsense. France. She had the baby and left him with the blessed nuns. Six weeks later he was delivered like a food parcel to me in Harare. He'd arranged some elaborate story about my wife giving birth and not wanting to keep him. So there I was, as far as most people were concerned, with a son. A few thought it strange. But not many. Got quite a lot of sympathy, actually. You know

281

something, Inspector? He even decided on what to call him. Richard, he said. Richard the Lionheart. I came back eighteen months later with him as my son. You savvy, Inspector? Savvy?'

'And he had her retained as a payoff.'

'Mm mm.'

'She wasn't allowed to see him?'

'She didn't know. I never saw her, not until last October.'

'Why October?'

Hanbury-Collings laid the gun on the arm of his chair. It was now pointing directly at Leonard's stomach.

'Pure chance. One of her clients had known me in Harare. Mentioned my name. Asked how Richard was. Said something about it all being rather strange. Well, Inspector, she was bright all right. And so we met.'

'And you offered to marry her.'

He nodded. Slowly.

'At least you got that bit right. At first it might have worked. But not really. She became obsessed with Richard. Even gave him her damned mobile phone so he could call her at night.'

Leonard ticked it off.

'Then last week she flipped. She said she wanted Richard. He was her son and she wanted him as her son.'

'And you said no.'

'And I said no.'

Hanbury-Collings pulled himself up from the chair. He seemed to have aged a half-lifetime. Leonard glanced from son to father. Suddenly the resemblance was uncanny. He moved slowly to the lacquered cabinet. Opened one door and poured a large whisky. The gin was there. The Italian vermouth was there. He looked at the glass. Looked at the far door. Turned. Didn't offer Leonard a drink.

'She said she would create a stink. She said she knew how. I suppose she did. After all, it was her business, wasn't it?'

With aging had come maturity. The step now had the shuffle of a stage don. Hanbury-Collings paused at the fireplace.

282

Leaned against the mantelpiece. Matched his father sneer for sneer.

'Yes?'

'When did you see her?'

'On the Sunday morning.'

'What time?'

'Does that matter?'

'Yes.'

'Lunchtime.'

Leonard nodded. He remembered Gordon saying she had a meeting. Bundled out of her bed in time for Hanbury-Collings.

'Go on.'

'I tried to persuade her to forget the whole thing. Offered her money. Thousands. Offered again to marry her.'

'What she say?'

'Laughed. Said I was a joke.'

'So you decided to kill her.'

'So I decided to kill her.'

Leonard could see the lovely creature on the train. Full of life. The still body on the slab. Full of the Screaming Skull's cigar ends.

'As simple as that.'

'No, Inspector. Not as simple as that.'

He leaned over and did what Leonard had dreaded. He picked up the gun. Walked over to stand in front of the policeman. Pointed it at him.

'I could no more have killed Sally than fly. Know why? Do you? I hadn't the guts. As simple as that.'

He took a deep breath and then came a long sigh and, as if losing interest, let the pistol hang on his index finger by the trigger guard. Leonard stretched out a barely steady hand and very gently, every so gently, took the gun. Hanbury-Collings shook his head. A dawning, slow, sad shake. Looked up to the sneering portrait.

'Simply hadn't the guts.'

283

Hanbury-Collings turned and went back to the fireplace.

'I had to tell her. You see, she'd never known. My father had protected her. She didn't know about father. Had maybe met Sally years ago at a reception. But had no idea of what had gone on. She played bridge and shopped and spent his money on labels. Nothing else. To her, Richard was her grandson. Then I told her when I came back after school that he wasn't. He was her stepson. Her husband's son by another woman. And now that woman wanted to take him and would tell the world. She couldn't allow that. She simply couldn't.'

Leonard's eyes were closed. He was dozing on the train. He could hear her voice still. '. . . Of course, we were in Rhodesia for most of our lives. Grand days those, didn't they know. Wouldn't have tolerated this sort of affair. Taken a whip to them or better still . . .'

'Your mother.'

'Yes, Inspector. My mother.'

'But how?'

'That.'

He pointed to the gun in Leonard's hand.

'My God, man, this family had never been without them. Mother still called the place Rhodesia. Northern Rhodesia. Southern Rhodesia. The lot. She learned to shoot before she went to school. In those days we had more guns than clocks. That one's a tiddler. There're a couple more around somewhere.'

'So she simply went out and shot her? It's too easy, sir. Too easy.'

Hanbury-Collings hadn't heard.

'Worse than that. I told her where she would be. Didn't realize it at the time. But I told her about the phone-box calls from Richard on Sunday evenings. Not to the flat because the number would show up on her bill. So she knew, didn't she? She knew. And you know something else? I didn't know until you mentioned the gun this afternoon. Then it started to make sense.'

Leonard got up. Went to the window. Half the police strength was outside. No noise. No flashing lights. But there. He let them see him.

'Where's she now?'

For the third time that day, Leonard followed Hanbury-Collings. Through the corner doorway. Along the passage to the back of the house. The door was open. A large white room with a royal blue canopy over a queen-sized bed. Mrs Hanbury-Collings lay across the bed, her head hanging over the edge. A single hole through her forehead.

Leonard walked over. Knelt by the bed. Went through the motions. Put a finger to her neck. He heard voices in the other room. Looked back. Hanbury-Collings was gone. Leonard didn't mind. Hadn't closed the front door behind him. Not the sort of thing you do when a man's got a gun. Even Johnson knew that.

He went back to the living room. He looked about him. Then at the portrait. Tired. Very tired. He took off his glasses and rubbed at his temples. He turned at a noise behind him. Jack was in the doorway.

'You all right, sir?'

'Mm. Think so.'

'Sure?'

He allowed himself a half-smile.

'For the moment. Drink?'

'White wine or a Cuba libre?'

'You chose. Mm?'

# EPILOGUE

The taxi dropped Leonard at the large double gates hanging from granite pillars. The white gravel drive wound through high laurels and great rhododendrons that wouldn't bloom again until the next spring. The House needed the paint that had been promised in the summer holiday, but had never happened. Always a priority somewhere else in the bursar's budget. At the top of the stone steps, he shook hands with Major Snow and then solemnly with the boy. For the next hour, they walked the already soft turf of Big Field and watched the Extra As practising line-outs in the weakening autumn sunlight. They talked of this and that, both careful of each other. At Chapel Bell, they shook hands and the boy stood on the steps and watched him walk down the drive. At the bend in the laurels he turned. They waved and then the boy went in and carefully signed the In & Out book. He was quiet with his own thoughts. But believed the promise that he would come again.